SIOUX FALL

Bruce Drake

authorHOUSE®

AuthorHouse™
1663 Liberty Drive
Bloomington, IN 47403
www.authorhouse.com
Phone: 1 (800) 839-8640

Published by AuthorHouse 10/18/2016

ISBN: 978-1-5246-4471-0 (sc)
ISBN: 978-1-5246-4470-3 (e)

Library of Congress Control Number: 2016916935

Print information available on the last page.

THE DANCE

The force of the unseen punch had me staggering backwards and off balance. My foot caught on something and down I went, landing flat on my back in the loose straw. My eyes wanted to close while I was struggling to stay alert. From the barn floor looking up I saw lanterns giving off a warm yellow glow and folks staring down at me.

From the straw covered barn floor where I'd ended up, this Michigan farm boy watched Greg Howard circle with both his hands made into large ham like fists. His handsome face showed anger as he glared down at me. From that look on his face I knew I was in for it.

The crowd at the local barn dance was silent as they watched two friends fighting over Michele; Michele Stevens that lovely flower, so beautiful, shapely and so wonderful. This young lady, with her sweet smell of perfume was often on my mind. Oh how pleasing she was to my senses. She was a warm wonderful woman that I desired and wanted. Let me tell you about her long lovely curls cascading down over her shoulders in waves of glossy brown hair. A charming desirable young woman and was she ever a pleasing sight to behold.

This awesome lady had asked me to dance and I'd accepted knowing it would make Greg unhappy. Gregory was my best friend since the third grade and I liked him a lot. But Michele was something else, she was a mighty fine looking lady and the temptation was too much for me to resist. That is if I had wanted to.

What I really wanted was to dance with her and hold her in my arms. I'd spent many a marvelous moments thinking about her. I often dreamed about her walking with me hand in hand through green meadows of grass and flowers. I always hoped, maybe, someday it would happen for us, but Gregory had asked her to the dance first. I was way too shy to invite her to go with me. I thought about it a lot but never did ask her. I hated being so backwards around women.

Greg had brought her to the Grange Hall Dance and I guess I was way out of line while not enough to end up down here. A slow anger burned within me at first. He had sucker punched me; hitting me without any warning and now he stood over me and with a gruff voice he said, "Ron Holden, you stay away from my girl! You hear me?" His tone held no sympathy in it at all. I guess you could say he was more than upset with my actions in the last few moments.

But sucker punching was way out of line between friends. As I started up a stabbing pain exploded in my left side as his big shoe made contact with my ribs and the stabbing, throbbing pain blotted out all else. Now that red-hot temper of mine started to flare up and all I could think about was Greg Howard that was way too much among friends like we were. It doesn't feel all that good when ya make me hurt like this.

Pushing hard on the floor I ended upright, on my feet. My legs did a shaky little dance as I wobbled around a bit. Forcing a weak smile onto my face, while glancing at Michele, she looked concerned, but for who? Gregory seemed so cocksure of himself and was now closing the gap between the two of us. I knew in my heart he would finish me off quickly if I didn't move out of his way.

Circling to my right to stay away from him and his big right fist, the excruciating pain in my ribs got my immediate attention. I was moving to protect my right side and my head. His next shot was a haymaker designed to put me down for the count, like a sharp scythe cutting through tall grass it came my way. I felt that haymaker, as it touched the hair on the top of my head and sailed on by. That my friend was way to close!

With a short shot I hit pay dirt. My target was his small stomach. It was hard, although I heard a breath of air escape his lungs; otherwise it didn't look like it made any difference. His facial expression didn't change that much. With lots of confidence he was strutting like a Banty Rooster, as he stalked me.

The barn dance crowd was gathering around standing in near silence. As I back peddled I noticed Michele in the crowd with her left hand covering her mouth and fear showing in her baby blue eyes. Those pretty eyes that captivated me so. She was so breathtaking it's no wonder Gregory didn't want me near her. I guess I didn't blame him for that.

Gregory's big right hand tried to catch up to me as I danced to my right. There was no sting left in his punch as my left forearm blocked it. While he was recovering from his wild punch, I bounced a right fist off his suddenly flattened nose and blood sprayed all over his clothes and the straw on the barn floor. While he was thinking about that I stung him three more times. First to the side of his face and as he covered up then twice more on his upper arm and shoulder with two good solid shots that I knew had hurt. Then one more for good measure to the stomach as his elbows came up to high. It was a bad mistake at this stage of the game. Thinking to myself, Greg my boy, you better start thinking or I'm going to lay it on you hard and fast. My side still hurt as he gave ground. Putting a big smile on his face Greg said to me, "Is that all you got? It looks to me like you're in a heap of trouble, Ronald." I'd heard him use that kind of psychology on other people; it meant the opposite, it had hurt him.

Stepping in I pressed him, faked a left and my right uppercut found its mark, then this ole hayseed followed that up with a hard left to his eye and a right to his upper left arm. A hard mad look came to his face. Then like a windmill in a wind storm he threw wild punch after punch as he pressed me. Back peddling to stay away from those big fists I covered up and caught several shots on my arms and they hurt. I could feel it down to my fingertips.

He slowed a bit and as I uncovered to retaliate I took a hard punch on the forehead. A red flash went off in my brain and I fell into Mr. Brown's arms and he held me up off the floor and shoved me toward Gregory who tried another roundhouse to my head.

I somehow blocked that hay maker with my left arm and that even hurt. If that punch had connected with its intended target that would have ended this little go round, here and now.

Recovering first I used my hand speed. With my right fist I hit him flush on his left ear. I moved to my right away from that huge right hand. I then pressed him again and I followed that with a long looping left to his right eye and then nailed him square on his left cheek.

Greg could really take a punch, although he was now back peddling and I was closing in. I faked two short lefts then a well-aimed right connected to his head, just back of his temple and I felt it to my spine. While he was still on his feet his eyes closed and he was out cold. When he hit the floor on his back, his head took another jolt, bouncing off the hardwood floor and he lay dead still. This worried me some for we were friends. I didn't like the way it sounded. Gregory could be hurt bad, really bad. "Lord, please watch over him."

As I stood watching, Michele slipped in beside him and cradled his head in her lap. Mr. Stevens, Michele's father brought her a cool wet rag and she washed his face and neck, wiping the blood away. To me it looked like Greg Howard was hurt really bad from that hard whack with the barn floor. A long ten minutes went by and he hadn't moved.

I began to get nervous. Greg's mother had taken Michele's place, on the barn floor, holding his head, and Mrs. Howard began to cry. This was her youngest boy. The favorite of both his ma and pa and you could see her loving touch as she worked on him.

Gregory Howard had other family members here also. He had three older brothers to home and their large family was really close. Their long hard stares sent my way made me feel mighty uncomfortable. At this very moment I felt out of place with so many eyes on me. I noticed that Michele Stevens' beautiful blue eyes were filled with tears. While watching her, the dam broke and tears came streaming down her pretty face and landed on her dress. My heart went out to her as she stood there alone. She caught my eye and came over and stood by me. In a whisper she said, "You had better slip on out of here Ronnie, Greg's three older brothers are here a watching you."

Moving closer to Greg I asked Mrs. Howard, "Can I help in some way?"

Anger came onto her face and harsh words exploded from her mouth, "You young Holden, you get yourself away from me. You did this to my Greg, now get away, you hear me!"

"Ma Howard, I'm sorry. I didn't want to…."

"You get before I horsewhip ya!"

Glancing at Greg's three older brothers, a dark storm cloud hung around them. Michele was right it was time for me to leave. Turning I walked by her and said, "Good night Michele." Man-oh-man was she ever a lovely young woman, a real treasure that I wished was mine.

She smiled a slight shy smile and said, "Good night, Ronnie."

It looked to me like the Saturday night barn dance was all over anyway. A couple of church friends said, "Good night, Ronald, see ya tomorrow." I slid through the opening in the barn door and disappeared into the cool spring night air. This hurting kid mounted the pretty gray mare and eased her on out of the yard pushing her toward home. It was a long dark six-mile ride to our home place.

Around midnight I entered our dooryard. Ma had left a coal oil lamp burning in the front window. That mom of mine was a sweet wonderful lady. A little old fashioned, but she had a real love for people. She loved everyone and people that knew her loved her. I was one lucky son-of-a-gun to have the family I had and I knew it. This bushed kid put Molly in the barn, then headed for the house. I must get to bed for tomorrow is Sunday and chores came early. We would rise up early to milk the cows long before the sun peeked over the horizon. We must feed the pigs, horses, calves and chickens, clean the barn, then wash and dress for church. By nine o'clock we were in our light wagon heading for the little church in Sumner, Michigan.

As a town Sumner wasn't much of a much, just another Podunk place in the middle of Michigan, about five miles from our home. Pa had purchased a hundred and sixty acres, in Montcalm County, five years ago, when I was thirteen years old. The home place had good soil, a sandy loam and would it ever grow great crops.

Most of the roads in this area were little more than straight paths through the woods where the surveyors had cut down trees and brush to get a line of sight to survey the land into six hundred forty acre sections. (One square mile) In the wooded areas where they cut down the trees there were still some large stumps in the roadway. In those places we would just drive around them. People were burning the pine stumps to clear the way for wagon traffic.

In the spring of the year the roads were often a quagmire, with mud hub deep in wet places. In Michigan, March is a cool muddy month too early to work the soil and maple syrup season was just about over for this year.

Going to church was a fun time for our family, every Sunday as we moved along the muddy tracks heading for church, our friend and neighbor Mr. Pugsley would wait for us at the Klees School House. Pa and Bill had this little thing they did as they rode east toward Sumner. It was a horse race. Pa used to win it until Mr. Pugsley purchased a good buggy horse last winter. Then the tide had changed. Now Bill had the best of it. His big bay gelding was a runner. He was bigger than Pa's little gray mare, the bay had longer legs and was a really nice looking horse.

Today Pa said, "Let's race all the way to the county line. It was a long mile away and off we went with both wagons bumping and splashing eastward. This was great fun for the whole family and we made it a family affair. Everyone, even my younger brothers, sisters, my mom and dad we all got involved in watching those two runners work. Pa loved to see fine horses run and we had a gay ole time as we rumbled along the road. Those fine horses were neck and neck at the three quarter mile mark. Then Mr. Pugsley slowly pulled away. Dad slapped the reins on Molly's rump and said, "Come on girl."

She worked even harder pulling us and slowly closed the gap. But in the end Bill's big bay held her off. It was close and we talked about how close it was. Our gray mare had real heart and she would kill herself if paw asked it of her. That gray lady just wouldn't call it quits unless dad asked her to. She just didn't know what quit meant. She was a good ole gal and Dad loved her and that gray lady loved him. After the race pa stopped and hugged and petted her, running his hands all over her body. You could see the horse flesh quiver under his strong hands.

In the church yard folks asked, "Well, who won today?" They all knew Sunday morning was a time of enjoyment for us, on our way to church. Mr. Pugsley would say, "Ask Mr. Holden who won and if he won't tell you the truth, I'll tell you it wasn't him." Everyone that stood in the church yard would get a good chuckle. It was a ritual right down to the kidding around, in the church front yard.

Our pastor, Reverend Underwood, was a fine man and the love of God shone on his face as he preached the truth of God's word, every Sunday. God was really blessing our church. This good man came from Eastern Canada to teach us about Jesus and His great love.

Someone said, "Greg Howard hadn't regained consciousness." I wanted to see him but, I knew I should stay away until he woke up. I was still nursing some sore spots of my own which I didn't tell anyone of. Not telling my folks about the fight last night wasn't a good idea as others told and retold about the fight over Michele Stevens. As the story was told, dad kept glancing my way. They told it a wee bit different than I would have. Well, it's too late he'd heard it all by now, anyway.

Sumner was a small settlement on the Pine River. It had a general store, livery stables, hardware store, blacksmith shop and about fifteen houses; it was a small town that serviced this local farming community. Everything was on Main Street. It would one day grow with the lumber business, in Michigan, and then return to a farming community as the trees were harvested and floated down the pine river to the saw mills.

On Sunday the church brought seventy or eighty people into town and many a Sunday we had potluck dinners on the church grounds or in the park. Later we boys would go fishing on the Pine River. Today the suckers bit really well. This was my lucky day. Fifteen large fish were hooked onto my stringer. Except for the forked bones, suckers were good eating. After the four o'clock service we headed for home and the evening chores that awaited us.

Molly was a bit frisky and Dad let her have her head. She knew the way home by heart. Anyone could see that pa loved this gray lady. Dad was a born farmer, a good man with livestock, and a hard worker. It was his life and he loved it.

Tuesday in the evening, I went to visit with Greg. His mother allowed me to see him. He had regained consciousness and was sliding in and out of consciousness. He looked so white it worried me. I stayed for a short time, while receiving the silent treatment from his mother.

A short time after the three older brothers went out to do the chores, I left for home. The cool night air blew a damp mist and it was a miserable night. I slipped through the split rail fence. The rails were newly split and a sliver buried itself into my left hand and it stung like blazes. I tried to extract it in the dark without much success.

I took my folding knife from my pocket, flipped it open and, dug deep with the blade point and finally snaked it out of my palm. Man-oh-man did that ever hurt. I carefully replaced the rails in the fence not allowing them to slide in my hand this time. I didn't need any more slivers stuck in my hands tonight. Through Ted Johnson's pasture was a short cut home. Greg Howard and what happened was on my mind and I prayed again for him. Michele, that sweet little lady, jumped into my mind and stayed for a while.

As the last rail was set in place a bullet hit the top rail and then came the report of a rifle from a good ways off. The split rail had stopped the slug. Hustling to my horse I grabbed leather and quickly made tracks away from there. No need of staying here and let them reload and try it again. Who could have done this? Gregory's brothers came to mind instantly. Those three boys never liked me much and I don't know why.

They now have a reason to not want me around. But killing, I don't understand that at all. The fight, the other night was of Greg's making, not mine. He threw the first punch, not me. I didn't even see the sucker punch coming while thinking on that this nervous kid skidded the gray to a stop by the other fence across the pasture. I then opened it up and left it down, as I hurried through. Later I would return and fix it, when I could see better and not be surprised by a shooter. I didn't care for that kind of a surprise.

The very next day I took to carrying my squirrel gun even around home. That shot was no mistake. Someone had it in for me and I needed to be cautious in whatever I did. Two days later Dad and I were cutting trees in the pasture fencerow for winter firewood, when a slug hit the crosscut saw, just missing my right hip. The slug caromed along the saw blade, just missing dad's hand and we dropped to the ground. My squirrel gun was at hand and I got to it quickly. Whoever shot at me needed to reload his weapon.

From down behind a huge chunk of wood, we hid from the shooter or shooters, whoever they might be. The distance was great and they were shooting a long ways uphill from the creek bank. With my rifle resting on the log, I waited. Soon

I saw the sunshine glint on brown steel. Then I fired a slug down there as another bullet hit the log where we lay on our stomach concealed.

I could make out a yell of pain and saw someone high tailing it out of there in a mighty big hurry. He was running through the thicket on foot. Standing up, our clothes were wet from the cold soggy ground. The horseman, whoever he was, vanished into the pucker brush down there and headed west away from us. This is the second time I'd been shot at in the last two days.

Our big team of horses were harnessed and hooked to the log skidder ready for a load of wood to take to the house, so there was no pursuit from us. Although I was sure who the shooters were, Dad had his suspicions also.

My dad and I paid a visit to the Howard's place that afternoon. Mr. Howard denied that anyone had left the place or had any reason to hurt anyone. His brown spaced teeth showed through his slightly twisted smile and tobacco juice slipped from the corners of his mouth as he conversed with us.

I was not at ease listening to his explanation. He said, "Why would my boys want to do such a thing? No sir, it wasn't any of my boys." I thought to myself if it wasn't the Howard's then who could it be and why had they singled me out to shoot at? No, it had to be one of the Howard boys. He can say whatever he wants to, but that dog just won't hunt. Why would it start just after my fight with Greg? It didn't make a lick of sense to me. No one had a reason at all, except maybe the Howard boys and that seemed rather weak to me.

With a loud cough he brought up a gob of green gunk and spit it and some tobacco juice onto the ground at his feet. With a scuffed boot toe he covered it with dirt then said, "No Mr. Holden, you're barking up the wrong tree. These boys have been here all day long."

Greg had regained full consciousness and I was glad about that. Peeking in on him I said, "Hi Greg. Glad to see ya up and around. Hope you get to feeling better. Man you hit that floor hard, and your head sounded like a ripe watermelon." He smiled and we talked for a while then Greg said, "Come over when you can, Ronald." As we left for home my prayer was for him to get well soon. I wanted him well, up and around and living life again.

The stiff March breeze whipped wildly as we hit a leisurely pace for home. Molly's mane and tail blew every which a way, pushed by the cool spring breeze. Over head I saw three long V's of geese heading toward the Canadian north woods to build their nests on some pond or lake to raise a few goslings.

Dad had said nothing since leaving for home. My paw was a hard thinking man and he would work this whole thing out, he always did. All my life my dad was a quiet influence for good and people that knew him looked up to him and listened to his wise council.

My hope is that someday I would be just like him; an honest hard working man of God, at peace with the world and with a big family that loved me. Yes, my pa was in his element here on this farm in Montcalm County.

The next morning after chores, as we sat drinking coffee, dad said, "You must stay close to the buildings until Greg is up and around however long it takes. Son, keep the Hawkins fifty caliber close. Exercise lots of care when you're out and about. Be real careful when you leave the house. Take the rifle even when you go to the outhouse."

"Dad, "I wish I hadn't gone to the dance last week."

"Well son, last week is gone; it's like water under the bridge and we can't bring it back. It's gone and done with. Son, there's no sense fretting about it now."

In the next few days my dad didn't want me to do anything the way I did it yesterday. He didn't want me to help whoever was out there looking to get a shot at me. This was an uncomfortable situation to be in. This whole thing could be a matter of life and death to me.

After morning church on Sunday we didn't stay for the afternoon service, which we usually did for the fellowship and good fun. This long lean kid spent Monday cleaning the guns and pulling the slugs and powder from the Hawkins and with boiling water cleaned the locks, barrels and oiled the stock then swabbed the hot metal parts with a fine coat of oil.

Then I pulled the lead from dad's revolver by firing it at some tin cans on the rail fence. Pa had an extra cylinder for his Colt revolver which gave him more firepower. You can bet I loved sending them on their merry way. With all the weapons reloaded I poured a cup of coffee and sat in a chair on the porch, enjoying the warm spring day.

THE SHOT

The warm March sun was really quite nice today. Pa and ma came out on the porch with hot coffee in their cups. The talk was about the farming to be done and how they would soon be knee deep in field work. Field work on the farm was hard work but we loved it for we were farmers at heart. I just loved to see the green grass turned over by the mo-board on the plow.

Usually I carried a tin can fastened to the plow handle and I would often stop and pick up night crawlers and worms and put them in the tin can when I rested the horses at the end of the field. The worms would be used later when we went fishing at the Pine River or at one of the small lakes in the area. This family just loved fish.

As we sat there talking on the porch, suddenly without any warning a shot rang out from the south and my chair leg broke and dumped me on the porch floor. As I climbed to my feet pa handed me the big rifle that I had just cleaned and reloaded.

Whoever it was that fired at me jumped up and raced for a patch of brush down by the woods, just beyond the ambush spot.

Whoever it was he never made it. (My skill as a rifleman was not well known by many.) When I fired both his arms flung out wide as he slammed face first into the water and soggy soil and he didn't move. Death came home to stay for that bushwhacker, whoever he was.

As I got ready to mosey on down there, Dad stopped me. "Wait Son, there may be more of them." Ma and the kids had made a bee line for the front door and dad and I followed them inside where it was quite a bit darker; we waited and reloaded. We stood inside the house and way back away from the windows and doors, keeping low as I reloaded the weapon and studied the wooded area off to the south. The whole family watched for a good half hour and saw nothing move. A red rooster, near the barn, strutted his stuff and crowed for all he was worth.

Pa picked up the revolver and handed it to me. I slipped it into my belt and with the shotgun under his arm we slowly and carefully made our way to the spot where old man Howard lay face down in the new spring grass, a bullet hole between his shoulder blades. He was dead as a mackerel and sprawled out in the mud and water of this marshy area. Why in the world did he do this to us? What was his reason for shooting at me? This was just too crazy for words.

I knew the questions that would come our way from his family and others. Why was he shot in the back? Did you murder him in cold blood while he wasn't looking? Were you afraid to face up to him, so you had to shoot him in the back? As pa and I sat on a big pine stump he said, "Son, this is going to look bad for us. I'm sorry that I handed you the rifle. Because of that shot we must be ready for the Howard family and whatever they decide to do about this.

Old man Howard has four brothers, and they are a lot like him. They live over west of here by the settlement of Fred. (Later to be called Stanton after Sec. Stanton.) No one in this area is going to like what happened here today. Son, I'll take the body home and you pack your things, take the gray and the light wagon and hide out at Henelmire Lake over by Mr. Pugsley's place. I'll come and get you when things cool off a bit."

We loaded Mr. Howard's body on the big hay wagon so pa could take him home. Ma was crying as I packed my things, a tent, food, blankets, pots and pans, fishing equipment, plus a few odds and ends. I took with me a lot more than I really needed for such a short stay at the lake. I took all of it to satisfy my mom.

That sweet lady was helping me pack this stuff. Moms are wonderful sometimes. After saying my goodbyes and getting hugs and kisses all around, I took my handkerchief and wiped mama's eyes. Ma this little vacation is only for a few days and I love fish and fishing. I'll bring some fish home for you, Laurie, Lindy, Marky and Brian when I return."

"Land da Goshen Ronald, I'm really going to miss you, will you be alright?"

"Ma, it's a dirty rotten shame I've got to miss all this hard farm work and have to go fishing from morning until night and lay around and soak up the sun. It is terrible ma; I'm going to miss all the fun around here. Holy cow, what will I do besides fish and sleep? It worries me to no end. But somehow I'll make out."

"Goodness gracious, sakes-a-live, life can sure be rough on a poor country boy like you just eating, sleeping and fishing. It could be really tough on ya. Well son, you can even get a few baths while you're there. Heaven knows you need them."

"I don't know about that ma, you know what they say, 'too much bathing can weaken ya real bad,' and I need all my strength to haul in all those big fish."

"Poor, poor boy, life can be really rough."

"Yes, yes, you can say that again."

"Okay! You poor fellow, life is sure rough and mighty tough on young men around here. Ha! Ha! Ha! Ronald if worse comes to worse and you have no idea what to do or where to go, you always have a home here with us, if you're good and bring home a big mess of fish when you come."

"Ma, I love you."

"I know my son. Take all my love with you everywhere you go. Now get along with you, you ole scaly-wag you, and stop doodling like an old hen. Now get out of here you hear me, before we change our minds and get you on that plow."

I was anxious to get started. I said my "goodbyes" to all the kids and kissed them on the head. Within the hour I was moving away from the house thinking about the big bass I would have for breakfast tomorrow morning. Dad would get things settled down and in a couple of days and I would be back home helping them plant the corn and oats.

I hoped my son, Ronald, would lay low until things cooled down a bit. The Howard clans were an unpredictable bunch. Like old Dan out there trying to bushwhack my son for no apparent reason. It just didn't make a lick of sense at all. Was it because Ron whipped Gregory in a fistfight at the barn dance? Was it because Greg had ended up in a coma from striking his head on the board floor?

Who knows what old man Howard was thinking when he fired a shot off at Ronald this morning. I think the old man had a couple of screws loose if you ask me. That whole clan always acted kind of peculiar if you ask me. Ya my boy, Ronald, is a tough capable young man. I wanted to see him married and on his own land someday.

I liked Michele Stevens and I'm a thinking maybe she likes Ron. She really is a nice girl. Oh how proud I am of Ronald. He is a great kid, a hard worker and has a good head on his shoulders.

This ole man really loved this boy of mine. Ronald is a good kid and he loves people. His sisters and brothers maul him all the time when they play together. You can bet I'm proud of all my family. Not one is hard to get along with and love abounds here in our house.

Up the road a ways stood the Howard place. I hoped the family would listen to reason. Who can tell about those folks? This whole thing didn't make a lick of sense to me no matter how I looked at it. Why would old man Howard do what he did?

As the big team plodded into the yard the three older brothers came from the barn and Gregory left the privy and headed for the house.

"Hello Mr. Holden, how are you?"

"Hello Greg. I'm doing fine, how ya feeling today, is everything okay?" He still looked quite pale yet and a little bedraggled.

"I'm feeling much better. Tell Ron to come by and see me."

"I will, Greg. I think Ronald would like that." The sun was red in the west and the red sky says Ron will have a good day tomorrow, at the lake. A stiff breeze swept across the yard pushing old leaves ahead of it. As it came near I turned my back, closed my eyes and let them sail on by. The top of the ground was nearly dry already. This has been a funny spring. I stopped my big wagon in the dooryard near the barn as the three older boys came closer.

"Howdy boys." Jim Howard, the oldest, came along side as I dismounted the wagon.

"Hello Mr. Holden, how's your family? If we get a couple more days like this it won't be long and we will be in the field working.

"The family is doing fine Jim. Son, we need to talk a bit, first off, I don't know how to say this, but your paw was over to our place and tried to shoot my boy and ended up dead for his trouble." Ouch, that didn't come out just liked I'd hoped it would.

The Howard boys had a stunned look on their faces. While answering Jim's questions, Jerry started to cry and carry on. "You Holden's think you can do whatever you please riding roughshod over anyone that gets in your way!"

"Jerry we're sorry. I…"

Jerry interrupted, "But not this time, you won't get away with it. You and your whole family will pay for what you've done to paw and Greg."

"Listen son, your pa came to our house trying to kill my son and the other day down by the woods someone took a shot at us. It wasn't us that came over here." In a voice so soft and pleasant I said, "Jerry we like you boys. Gregory and Ron are the best of comrades. We would like to have your ma and you boys over for dinner some Sunday. Son, we are so sorry that this all happened. But it wasn't of our making; your father came to our place with a rifle and shot at my boy."

As I turned back to talk with Jim, I heard Jerry cock his shotgun and he fired it. The whole charge hit me in the back. In no time flat the red hot pain in my back turned to a throbbing pain that consumed me. The shotgun blast hurt something awful as it slammed me against the big wagon. The force of the blast hit me hard and I reached up to grab the sideboard. I held on for all I was worth. My weight became too much to hold up and I started to slip down the side. Then everything began to fade.

"Oh dear Jesus watch over my fam…." Off in the distance I could see an angel beckoning to me and everything around me went dark.

Jim Howard jerked the double barrel shotgun away from Jerry as Jerry yelled out, "I got him dead center Jimmy! I fixed him good this time, for what they done to our paw. I got him Jim. I got him Don. Ha, Ha, Ha! He's deader than a doornail and he won't mess with us Howard's anymore. He's dead meat now Jimmie! Ha, Ha, Ha!"

The fish were biting really well here at the lake, although I've been here at Henelmire Lake for a week now and I haven't seen hide nor hair anyone. Surely it would be okay by now. I had a big mess of fish all cleaned for Mom and the family. I was running a little short on flour so tonight after dark I will leave the buggy here, ride home and pick up some food and see how things are working out with the Howards. My dad would have it worked out by now, that's for sure. Dad knew how to reason with people.

When I left that night I took a big mess of fish with me and approached the house cautiously. The dark shadows made it look black. The smell of creosol (wood tar) from the chimney was strong as I rode near the home place. There were no lights on in the house whatsoever, something was wrong. This cautious kid pulled his rifle from its scabbard, dismounted and moved silently through the big pine trees and approached the house from the backside. The roof seemed to have caved in. Were my eyes playing tricks on me, in the dark, or had the house burned?

The moon peeked through the clouds for just a moment and showed a littered dooryard and a burned out house. The roof of the house was sagging in the middle. What happened here? Had someone done this? Did the folks have a fire? Did the Howards do this? Where was my family? I had a sinking feeling as I quickly surveyed the dooryard.

The horses and wagon were gone so they might be staying with someone close by like, maybe the Pugsley's. Pa and ma liked Mr. and Mrs. Pugsley a lot. I will stay close by tonight and find them in the morning.

Moving away from the house I slept on some leaves, with two blankets over top of me. What really was nagging at me was no one was working the fields. The fields hadn't been worked up yet, oats hadn't been planted either. Why? Something was wrong here and I was a bit on edge because of it!

The night was a long one for me and a little bit cold. As false dawn made the sky a light gray, I was up and moving toward our family home. As Molly entered the dooryard I could see that things were not quite right here. I saw that there were household articles scattered across the dooryard and way down toward the barn. It looked like someone had ransacked the house and then fired it. Why?

The barn was still intact and so was the buggy shed. I could hear chickens in the hen house, so I unlocked the door and swung it wide open; they would need water and time to catch a few bugs to eat. At the well I opened the wind mill and pumped some water into long trough.

They would need water later on in the afternoon. The livestock were out in the pasture and they could get to water at the pond. The cows were hurting, although it looked like someone had been milking them. Paw must be coming back during the day to milk them.

Our big wagon and team were missing so probably dad had the family living somewhere else for now. But why was everything scattered across the dooryard and why hadn't they come for me? That nagging feeling was back. "Lord, please make them be safe."

Where would they go? Mr. Pugsley's place came to mind first as I climbed into the saddle and eased Molly out of the dooryard and it wasn't long and this ole kid was raisin' dust toward the Pugsley place. I urged the gray into an easy lope. She felt good between my legs as she ate up the distance to their home place.

Although the sun hadn't peeked over the horizon yet it was getting lighter by the minute. The sky was clear this morning. But nagging doubts about my family kept weighing me down. Where are you dad and why aren't you tending the home place? Fields needed plowing and oats planted. Where-oh-where was my family?

SIX DAYS EARLIER

At the house, I heard someone coming into the dooryard. I thought to myself it's about time you got home Lyman. How long did it take to go to the Howards' place and back? The kids were sound asleep and I'd put a lamp in the window earlier to say all is well here at home.

With a lamp in hand I stepped outside onto the porch just as our hay wagon reached the porch steps. I realized right away that it wasn't Lyman Holden. Jim Howard was driving our team; Don and Jerry were on horseback following along behind. I asked, "Where's Mr. Holden Jimmy?"

"Mrs. Holden, we found your husband's body out on the roadway dead. Shot in the back. We loaded him up and brought him on home to you. We're so sorry, ma'am but we have no idea what happened to him. He was by our place earlier and told us about our paw."

"Oh no not Lyman!" a scream escaped my mouth and I ran to the back of the wagon. Oh dear God, no! Tears started flooding my eyes, my stomach was churning, my hands were shaking like an aspen leaf in a wind storm and I almost dropped the lamp right there in the yard. Oh God what is happening to us? Sobs wracked my body and all I could say was, "oh no Lyman, not you." I gagged and almost lost my supper in the dooryard.

Someone had shot gunned him in the back. Why would anyone in his right mind do that? Things were getting crazy around here. I sat down on the steps for a moment, my knees were weak and wobbly and I couldn't stand without shaking. I knew that life without Lyman would be a rocky road for this family.

"Jim, do you have any idea?" A sob caught me in mid-sentence, "Jim, who could have done this dreadful thing? Do you have any idea who could have done this?"

"No Mrs. Holden. Who would want too, Mr. Holden was a well-liked man. He was a really good man in our community. Mrs. Holden, I can't think of anyone, can you? This whole thing doesn't make a lick of sense to me."

"Jimmy you know your paw tried to kill my Ronald earlier today. Are you, sob, are you sure you boys didn't have a hand in this?"

"Mrs. Holden, that's a terrible thing to say, we found him on the road and we took the time to bring your husband's body home to you."

"I'm sorry Jimmy, I'm just all worked up with this and worried half sick."

"That's okay, we understand. Here let us help you take him into the house; is that okay with you ma'am?"

My crying continued as they unloaded poor Lyman. I hurt all over. I didn't know what else to do and I did need the help to move him. I sure didn't want his body left in the wagon until we could get Ronald home.

As they moved him into the house I put a clean white sheet on the kitchen table and we laid him out there. I placed two candles on candlesticks beside his head and got some warm water from the stove to wash him up before the children saw him. He had such a pleasant peaceful look on his face. He must have had a visit from God before, sob, he died.

The coffee I made for Lyman was hot so I gave the three Howard boys a cup each. I asked Jimmy again, "Jimmie, who could have killed my man? Mr. Holden didn't have a mean bone in his whole body. Mr. Holden was a mighty good man. What are we going to do without him? Who could have killed him?"

"Mrs. Holden, I don't really know. We saw no one in the area around his body. You lost your husband and we lost our dad today. Everything seems to be going haywire lately and I can't make heads nor tails out of it."

"Jim were there tracks on the road, around his body? Were there any signs of what could have happened out there on the road? Jimmy can you think of anyone that might have done this? It seems like I just keep repeating myself, I'm sorry."

"Ma'am, it was dark and all we saw was his body there on the road. The horses and wagon were a short ways off." We need to get the sheriff in the morning and have him come and check the crime scene."

"I believe you Jim; I just wondered who would do such a terrible, terrible thing. Lyman really was a good man. Oh what are we going to do without him?"

Jerry who hadn't said anything stood up and addressed me. "Ma'am, we killed your old man and I'm happy about it." Then he grabbed me and started dragging me toward the bedroom. I went kicking, screaming, scratching, hitting and biting all the way.

I heard little Linda, from the loft, say, "Ma, what's the matter?" Mark and Brian joined in and I screamed again just before something hit me on the side of the head and volumes of pain exploded in my brain and down my spine. The pain overwhelmed me and I felt nothing more as consciousness slipped away and blackness overtook me.

While traveling toward the Pugsleys' farm I was sure Mr. Pugsleys would be anxious to be in the field turning the green down and fitting his fields for his oats. It was going to be a nice warm sunny day, here in Mid-Michigan. As I rode into the yard I hailed the house. "Hello the house." Mr. Pugsley stepped out onto the porch, milk pail in hand. He looked like he was about ready to head for the barn to milk his cows. This was planting season and Mr. Bill was a worker.

"Land-a-Goshen Ronald, where you been? We all thought you were kilt somewhere. Where you been, Boy? Mabel! Mabel! Come see who's out here."

Mrs. Pugsley stepped to the door and looked out. "Where you been son? People have been a looking for you near a week now. We thought you was lying dead somewhere out in the brush. Where ya been hiding yourself?"

"You should have asked my folks they knew where I was. I was camped out down on Henelmire Lake. Dad said he would come and get me and he didn't come. I went home and it's burned to the ground. I was a hoping they'd be here. Have ya seen them? Do you know where they are Mister Pugsley?"

"Ron, have you had your breakfast?"

"No Ma'am, I was looking for my ma and dad."

"Well you come on in here and we'll talk and you can get your chops around some warm chow. The food is still good and hot."

I thought to myself, what's to say that can't be said out here? Tying the gray to the hitching post I ascended the steps and went on inside. The house had some mighty good smells in here. She had something baking already. Hot cookies were cooling on the breakfast table. Nervously I waited for hot coffee to be poured and soon, crispy bacon, eggs and warm bread were placed before me.

With impatience I waited for them to tell me where my folks were. All the while there was this uneasy feeling that my family was dead. No, it couldn't be. No it just didn't seem possible. They must be visiting someone. While thoughts of that yard, the mess and no activity around the place left me uneasy inside. "Lord, please make them be safe." Tears were a messing up my eyes and Mrs. Puglsey shed some tears with me.

She came and put her arms around me like ma does when I need comforting. Now I was sure how bad it really was. It was worse than my worst fears, no, no not the whole family. The tips of her short fingers had a good hold of my hand and she held it to her stomach and said, "Ronald, we're sorry! We're so sorry!"

Mr. Pugsley said, "Ron, your family is gone, someone killed them all. Son, they are all dead, murdered in their own home, whoever it was set fire to the place. It looks like drifters might have done it. We figured maybe some vicious killers, the scum of the earth, some low down no good trash. I'm sorry Ronald. Oh this is hard for me; son and I know it's a whole lot rougher on you.

This same thing happened down in Ingham County about ten years back. They never found out who did it back then and I'm not sure we will either. They will probably go off somewhere and sell the things they took. Truly I'm sorry about the whole rotten mess Ronald. Your folks were wonderful people and a credit to our community and wonderful friends. Ronald, what are you a figuring on doing now?"

As they talked my mind drifted off somewhere else, my ma was a good woman full of love for her family, and Jesus. I remember my last hug and how she held me close and said, "She loved me," and she really did. I knew now that everything worthwhile is gone in my life and I was all alone. Oh how that hurts me. My paw was a mighty good man, a real man who did his best to provide for his family and do right by everyone he knew. A man who knew you couldn't make it without God in your life.

I'm a wishing I had spent more time with my little sisters and brothers. I guess I was thinking more about myself. "Oh Lord, I'm sorry. These kids never did anything really wrong, not to anyone. Lord as a family we tried to live like you wanted us to, and now this. Who would do such a terrible thing? All men don't love you, Lord, and they'll do whatever they want with no consideration for anyone else. Oh Lord, what will I do now?"

As I came up from my thoughts they were both looking at me. "I'm sorry I was lost in my own thoughts and didn't hear what you said, forgive me."

"Ronald, are you going to stay at your place? You may stay here if you want to. We have no idea who did this dastardly deed so you must be extra careful. Ronald, take some time and think it over, you take all the time you need. Just remember we love you and want you"

"Right now Mr. Pugsley, I'm at the end of my rope and don't know what to do, let go or hang on. But thank you for all you've done, Sir. My family loved you folks. You're good people. Can you tell me where my folks were buried?"

"We put them there in the dooryard under the big Maple tree. We made a crude marker for them. You'll find them there by that tree." With coffee cup in hand I took a long drink and set it on the table, stood for a moment, then ambled slowly toward the door, straw hat in hand. In a semi-daze, not sure of what to do next and with the door latch in hand I turned and said, "I want to thank you folks for everything you've done and how you've been such a great friend to my family. Thank you."

I paused for a moment, then lifted the latch, stopped and asked "will you look after our livestock for a couple of days Mr. Pugsley I have a lot of thinking to do? I've always had my folks to sound my ideas off."

He nodded yes and I slipped outside and closed the door behind me. My sobs were heard inside as I descended the porch steps and moved toward my horse. Wasting no time I mounted Molly and turned her toward the road. I grieved so bad that I was sick to my stomach.

As Molly moved out of the dooryard I let her have her head, touched her with my heels and cried as she moved out at a frantic gallop. I just went where she went. My mind was lost in thoughts of my family. After a bit Molly slowed to a walk. I soon found myself at my campsite on Henelmire Lake. I crawled into my tent and lay there thinking about how my life had crumbled to ashes and now it lay in ruin.

Those unwanted friends, death and poverty, often walked hand in hand across the frontier. I didn't think either were a dogging our heels that close. Somehow they snuck up on us and did their dirty work and we didn't even know they were waging war on us. Well what is done is done and that's the it of it.

THE DECISION

I stayed at the lake for a couple of days and thought it through. The second night at Henelmire Lake I finally made up my mind and wrote a long, long letter to my Uncle Leroy Gross, in Matherton telling them of the catastrophe that had befallen us, and asked him to come and stay on at the homestead until I finally decided what I would do with the home place. For right now I had no idea how long I would be gone, but I must head on out of here.

I couldn't live here, not now. Bad and good memories were getting me down. Most everything I loved was either dead or gone. I felt empty and rougher than a corncob on the inside. Early the third day I broke camp and moved on home with Molly harnessed to the light wagon and with the tent, saddle and supplies all loaded and ready to go.

This half sick nitwit spent the morning cleaning up the dooryard; storing things in the wagon shed, tack room, and was vigilant every moment. I visited the six lonely gravesites in the side yard and fixed it up some, hauling split rails from the barnyard. Then I fenced in the little gravesites. It took some time to carve a headboard from an old wooden bed stored in the shed.

I dug up some roses from ma's flower garden, along the house, planted them next to the fence and sat there by the gravesite; I worked until way after dark.

The next day I loaded my small wagon with anything that was of use to me, things that belonged to the family and tools that I might need and things that meant something to me. No way could I haul the big stuff in this little wagon. There were many things I wanted and lots of things I needed, but they were too heavy to transport.

At the little graveyard I said goodbye to ma and the family. I love you guys and I couldn't say more as I got choked up. Yes, I loved Laurie, Brian, Mark and little Linda too, we were a great family and we loved each other a lot.

I'd found some hard cash in one of dad's old tobacco cans in the buggy barn. (Seventy-three dollars) Ma had nine dollars and thirty-five cents in coin in a jar under a floorboard in a metal box. A little over eighty-two dollars, was not much to work a miracle in starting a new life, but this was all they had saved in cash their whole life and the farm of course, plus three cows, ten pigs and a bunch of chickens. Paw had a fine team of horses (if they could be found) and some fine farm tools and equipment.

Mr. Pugsley came over and said, "He would continue to take care of the livestock and watch the place, for a couple more weeks, until my Uncle Leroy and Aunt Norma arrived." My Uncle Leroy always liked dad's place and said, "If you ever want to sell it let us know." So I knew they would come as soon as they could.

For me there is just too much heartache with the death of my family. This place stirs up too many memories and that caused me way too much pain inside. No way can I stay here any longer. Maybe after a while but now my grief hurts like billy blazes. Every time I turned around I wanted to cry for my family that I'd lost. Many a time my Adam's apple would get stuck in my throat. All my sad moments left me unsure about everything. At the gravesite, in the dooryard, memories danced in and out of my head bringing more sadness.

I'm sorry dad, mom that I wasn't here to help out. I know you're in a much better place, but I still miss you so very much. Here it is planting season and I never dreamed it would be my family that I was laying out in God's good earth.

With all my heartache I was going to leave, right away, even before Uncle Leroy and Aunt Norma arrived. Danny and his sister, Susan, must be teens by now. I sure would like to see them, but no way could I stay around here any longer. There were just too many ghosts here on the home place and many sad thoughts, cold hard memories and they chilled me to the bone.

It was near noon when I left the dooryard. The Pugsley's already knew my plans about leaving. My plan was to visit Michele and tell her of my idea and what I intended to do with my life. Say my good-byes and leave. Michele was my special friend. She was a warm, loving individual and now the only person I would really miss here in Michigan. Once she started blossoming, into a woman, I was always shy around her and I can't explain why. This I know she had a warm place in my heart.

I guess I fell in love with her, way back, in our last year at Klees School. We were in our eighth year. Her sweet loving soul captured my heart. If I wasn't leaving this place, I would pull my courage together, pursue her and maybe win her heart. I liked that thought. This sweet little lady was always great to be around.

That night back at the barn dance, it was Greg's head she cradled in her lap but I would have taken a beating to put my head in her lap. It was Greg Howard that brought her, so that was okay. I could see her lovely face as Molly plodded along. At that thought I had to smile.

I was remembering her light hearted laughter and her incredible smile that thrilled me down deep in my soul. Her fantastic smile was always close to her lips; in seconds it would light up her face and change her whole countenance to something that warmed my heart.

Yes, I loved her. It was no secret to me. In fact I wished she was mine. Today I will stop and spend the rest of the afternoon with her and her family and then in the morning move on to a new life out West. Way up ahead I could see the Stevens' house about a half a mile away. It was a two story dwelling and set on the other side of a small patch of woods.

Ouch! Something hit me hard. The red-hot pain felt like a sledgehammer blow to my body. It flung me forward with a great force. My head smashed against the iron on the dashboard of the small wagon and everything went black.

"Jim! Jim! I saw him. I saw that Holden kid a coming this way in his wagon. He's got it all loaded up. It looks like he's a leaving for someplace. He's headed west on the road going toward the settlement of Fred. What's he up to you think? Is he after us you think? Where's he been a hiding' at? What do you think, huh? Jimmy, you think he knows about us? What are we going to do, Jimmy? Are we going to get rid of him like we did his paw?

Jim, you know maw's been a praying for him most ever day. What we going to do, Jimmy? Are we going to do to him like he done to our paw? Huh? Are we going to get him for that?"

"Pipe down Jerry, before the whole world hears you. Jerry, listen now. Go to the barn. Saddle three horses. Jerry, saddle them and bring them up to the house. You got that? Jerry, then wait for us. Do you understand me? Do you understand Jerry?"

Ya, I'll go get the horses and bring them up here to the house and wait for ya.

Okay Jimmy, I'll do it, I will, I'll hurry. I'll be back in two shakes of a lamb's tail. You go get Donnie, okay."

"I intend to. Jerry, we must keep it quiet now. We don't want to let ma and Greg know what we're up too. Ma won't like it very much."

"OK Jimmy. OK, I'll be quiet." And off he ran toward the barn. Man-oh-man, this kid was just too flaky for me. His mind was never right and now he has dragged me into something I didn't want to be wrapped up in; killing off a good family. Pa and Jerry were a lot alike. What was pa doing out there shooting at the Holden's and scaring the oldest boy? Well what's done is done. We can't change things that have already happened.

We called the tune so now we must dance to it. I didn't ever want to dance to this kind of music. Well today it will be finished once and for all. In the house I stood waiting for Don to finish his meal. We heard Jerry yelling from outside and it made me nervous.

"Let's go Jimmy, let's go get him." Then he repeated it again.

Don got up quickly and we headed outside. Climbed into leather and shortly we were on the move out of the door yard and down the roadway in a flat out run, racing our horses to a point well ahead of Ronald Holden and his wagon. As we drew near a patch of trees we slowed to a walk then dismounted. I had Jerry take the horses away and tie them out of sight.

Jerry was the one that shot Mr. Holden in the back killing him. That incident made me sick and then I made a mistake and took him over to the Holden's place and we told Mrs. Holden we found him already dead on the road. She believed the story we invented and everything seemed to be all right until Jerry grabbed her, shot his mouth off and started dragging her into the bedroom. That's when all hell broke loose and we ended up killing the whole family to keep a lid on it. Damn, I just stood there and let it happen. I must be nuts! Crazier than a squirrel in nutting season and now here I was about to kill another innocent victim.

Don and I made a bad mistake, back then; we should have turned Jerry over to the law when he killed Mr. Holden instead of trying to cover it up. Now it's gone way too far. Well one more death and that would end it. I'm a damn fool for what I've done. Just one more loose end and no one would be able to point a finger at the Howard family.

Ma leans on me way too much, always has. Paw was warned; he just went off and did what he wanted to, good or bad. He would give me that twisted toothless smile and ride off. Well, that Monday he died in that little game he played.

I had nothing against the Holden's. They were a decent honest family and paw had no business shooting at them. What was he thinking of anyway? Sometimes he acted crazier than a coot and loonier than a loon. Off in the distance I could see Ron was a coming up the road toward us. It did look like he was loaded and leaving for parts unknown. Maybe we should just let him go. What did he really know anyway? He was hid out somewhere and probably knew nothing. If he is leaving we'll let him go. If worst comes to worst we can do this later. He is a good kid. Yes, we'll let him leave.

Turning to Don and Jerry I told them of my decision to wait and just watch him and see if he was leaving. If not we can get him anytime. If he suspects us we can take care of it later. It won't be all that hard to get rid of him, if we need to.

As we laid in wait we watched him draw even with us, in that track like road, the gray mare came with an eagerness to be on her way. It did look like Ron was packed to travel. Good! I wasn't in the mood for anymore killing anyway. I've had enough and I'm glad it's over.

The boy wasn't a bad kid and this thing with his family hurts. Our treacherous actions made me feel like the pits. Then KA-BOOM I jumped and I saw Ronald pitched forward in his wagon.

"Damn you Jerry! You shot him! Man-oh-man this kid was nuttier than a fruit cake!" As I stared at him he looked excited and a big smile lit up his face. It was dad's twisted smile looking back at me. The numskull was happy and glad at what he did, what an idiot!

He said with excitement, "I got him Jim! I got him Don! I hit him dead center! He's dead that's for sure. That boy ain't going anywhere. He ain't going to mess with us no more. Ha! Ha! Ha! He's dead ain't he Jimmy? He ain't dangerous anymore. He's done for, this time for good!"

That ole gray mare of the Holden's was a carrying him farther and farther away from us. Right now I wish we could get our hands on his body. Well it looks like the Stevens will have to bury him now. I guess it'll work out all right after all. This isn't the way I wanted it. But, oh well. "Come on let's get out of here and get back to the horses. We don't want to be anywhere around if Mister Stevens comes out here looking around"

Mr. Stevens heard the rifle shot and thought to himself someone was getting some venison to eat. Looking down that way he thought to himself, what is Ronald shooting at anyway? His wagon was loaded down without a man in the driver seat.

I saw no one and chuckled. He shot and his horse ran off. He's without a wagon to haul the deer meat home.

The boy got careless down there. My smile got bigger as I thought on the situation. That'll teach him to hold onto his horse when he's a shooting a gun nearby. The pretty gray cut across the front yard bouncing the wagon as it came, heading for the barn. As I thought about this incident it confused me somewhat. People said the Holden's were all dead. If that is true, who is using their wagon? Mmmm!

Someone is using their gray horse. Was it the killers? Whoever it is will need the wagon to haul the meat in. I will cautiously check this out and find out what's going on. I'll get my gun and return the wagon and I'll help dress out the deer, if everything down there looks okay to me.

What's that on the floor in front of the seat? A body, who was it? My first words were, "Abigail, Michele, help! Abigail, Michele come here and help me, quickly. Ransom, Ransom where are you?" I saw lots of blood from a wound and worry overflowed into the peace of my mind. It was Ronald Holden in that wagon and he was shot pretty bad.

Abigail poked her head out of the kitchen door and said, "What is it Dear, what do you want? Is that the Holden's horse and wagon? I thought they were dead somewhere."

"So did I, Come quickly, Honey, Ronald Holden has been shot and he's bleeding badly. Hurry Abigail! He looks real bad!"

"Land-da-Goshen Brad, what's with that family? If it isn't one thing it's another. Brad will you move the wagon up closer to the back porch"

"Abigail, you get the kitchen table ready! Michele you go find Ransom and get him out here quick. We need his help. We've got to get Ron into the house and stop the blood flow somehow."

Instantly Michele was headed for the barn calling, "Ransom," as she went.

Before she got there Ransom poked his head out the sliding door and said, "What do you want, Michele? I'm busy. I've got work to do."

I heard her say, "Hurry, Daddy wants your help. Ronnie Holden has been shot and dad says it looks mighty bad." Ransom glanced toward the wagon then took off running and that daughter of mine hustled her bustle toward the porch in hot pursuit.

The ladies helped as Ransom and I lifted Ronald from his rig, then up the steps onto the porch and on into the house. Gently we laid him on the blanket on the kitchen table. "Honey, you and Michele get washed up quickly." Abigail was holding a clean rag tight to the exit wound while I pressed a rag to the entrance wound in his back.

The boy had taken a slug in his back and was bleeding badly. Someone had bushwhacked him and was trying to put this boy six feet under the sod and make him a resident of marble city. Michele was washing her hands with a cake of homemade lye soap when she finished she took Abigail's compress and let Abigail wash up.

Michele had retrieved some clean white rags for Ronald's wound and kept up the pressure, holding them tight to the wounds. Ransom and I washed up and we all took turns holding rags tight to his wounds, when it slowed a bit Abby took tweezers and pulled cloth from the entrance wound in his back. The poor kid was in really bad shape.

After a bit the entrance wound was down to a watery bloody seepage. The exit wound was a different story. Taking a dull kitchen knife, we heated it on the cook stove to a dull red glow and slapped it onto that nasty hole. This was hard on me but harder on poor Ronald. I wasn't use to doing this kind of work on human flesh. Even though Ronald was unconscious his body arched in pain. A loud yell exploded from his teeth. The word that came out was, "Ma." The knife seared the wound well and soon Abbey and Michele were swabbing salve on both wounds and then bandaged up the wounds real tight.

Cauterizing the wounds caused the blood flow to nearly stop. Abigail had placed clean bandages over the wounds and was binding the pads real tight with strips of clean white cloth. The boy's face was a grayish white; he had lost way too much blood and that was real serious.

Ronald was lucky that they missed his lungs. The real worry was we didn't know what else was torn up on the inside. We really didn't know what had happened on the inside of him. It was a mystery to us. I wished we had a doctor here to look at him and fix anything that might be messed up on the inside, but we didn't.

The large bump on his forehead was black and blue from striking the cast iron rail on the front of his rig. Cold packs were applied for about an hour. We saw little change in him over all. His whole family was a disaster and death was chasing this last survivor and had him running hard. Who would do this to them? I wish I knew.

Thank God, no blood came from the entrance wound now. The exit wound was a different story the blood still flowed a smidgen; it was just a piddling amount. Somehow we must get it all stopped or he would run out of the red stuff long before morning. His heart was pumping much too fast and Ronald couldn't afford to lose much more blood or he would be a goner for sure. Man-oh-man sometimes just living was hard out here on the frontier of Michigan.

At dark Ron was still alive. "Abbey, this boy is a fighter. I hope he makes it. He's a good kid." We dared not change his bandages. It looked like the red flow had stopped for now.

Thank God for that much. Was he bleeding inside? No way could we know for sure.

Moving him was out of the question. We might start the blood flowing again. Without seeing the slow rise and fall of his muscular chest, you would think he was dead. His heart was pumping fast and furious; almost out of control. At least he isn't pushing up daises yet. This kid was really a fighter and I liked that about him.

Who could have done this dastardly deed? His family was thought to be killed by bushwhackers and drifters, a predatory bunch of cutthroat thieves passing through. This attack put a whole different slant on this whole mess. I was thinking differently now on what had happened. Someone that knew the family did this or how else would they know Ronald was a part of the Holden Family as he came down the trail?

There was a skunk in the woodpile somewhere and we needed to find out who it was. Someone was laying in wait for him. It put a worry in my mind for this incident took place far too close to our home; right in my backyard so to speak. Are they still out there and why did they do it? Somehow they knew Ronald was still alive, and a part of the Holden family, when all the rest of us thought he was dead out there in the brush somewhere. This could put my family in danger if they knew Ronald was in our house. Whoever they were, killing came easy to them, way too easy to my way of thinking. We placed a grave marker out under the maple tree to fool whoever did this to him.

At any moment Ronald's life could be gone. Gone like a drop of water on a hot stove, becoming just a vapor. His life at this moment was hanging by a thread and all he is and all he ever would be would be lost. Lost like sad tears in a summer rainstorm. I hoped that didn't happen, for this young man had potential. I must admit it I liked him.

Michele insisted she watch over him tonight. Abbey said, "Honey, you go up to bed and get some rest. Get some sleep tonight honey and you can watch him tomorrow. He isn't going anywhere."

Michele wasn't satisfied with Abigail's answer, "Ma, I'm troubled by this, I really like Ronnie."

"Off to bed with you. Don't go bending my ear about this boy. Honey, before you go to sleep, give all your troubles to Jesus. He'll be up all night anyway."

"But mom, I…"

"Good night Michele. See you tomorrow. Honey, don't forget to pray for Ron."

"Oh Ma," at this point Abigail knew the best chance of Ronald dying would be tonight. So Michele was sent off to bed among lots of protests. But in the end she obeyed her mother and headed up the stairs.

I was really surprised at what I'd heard as I got ready to make some coffee for the long night ahead. Out of the clear blue Abbey said, "Ronald, this is your mother and I want you to know I love you. Ron you must fight this. Son, you will not give up. Do you hear me? You will fight this thing." I heard him moan softly in his sleep. He didn't say anything, in words, although he did respond. As he laid there he often groaned in pain, but this was different. It is good that he was unconscious, if he wasn't the pain would be far too much for him to bear.

I marveled at the wisdom of this wife of mine. She was a wise woman, that's for sure. She knew the power of a positive attitude. She said to me, "No negative talk what-so-ever in front of Ron." If you did you would get chewed out good. Each and every hour we put cold packs on his bruised forehead.

At the very first rays of the early morning sun, that daughter of ours came down the stairs from her room and asked, "How is he Ma?"

Out of ear shot of Ronald, Abigail said, "Well Honey, he doesn't look very good to me but he is holding his own. I felt he should be dead by now, that's one nasty wound. I don't know how, but somehow he's still alive. You can be sure that boy is a fighter.

"That's a good sign, don't you think?"

"Talk to him Michele, about anything you did with him. Honey, only let him hear positive things that you did in school or whatever. Say nothing negative; keep it light and positive for his sake."

"Honey, your mother talked to him like her own son and it seemed to help. Let us know if anything changes. Good night Michele. I mean good morning."

Man oh man did this girl ever want to be with Ronnie last night but ma and dad just wouldn't let me stay up with him. I thank the Lord that he is still alive this morning. I headed for the dining room table to take a good look at him.

MICHELE

"Well, well, well, so you've been up all night with mom and daddy. Why is that? You know, they made me go to bed early last night. Looks to me like you're their favorite. You got to be up all night long and I didn't. Just who do I complain to when my folks play favorites and let you stay up and not me?

Do you remember when you took all my marbles from me back at Klees School? Do you remember that? Well my family is remembering and saying to me, 'have you lost your marbles'? Well Ronnie, that's okay, if I lost them to you. Remember all the good times we had together up at that old school house? Those were good times, Ronnie, do you remember those days? I do.

Ronnie, dad said 'I can say anything I want, so Ronnie here's my first question, are you going to marry me or shall I become an old maid? Ronnie, you know I love you a whole lot more than burnt toast. Look at me, here I am throwing modesty out the window and you don't seem to care one way or the other.

This is the only way I can ever speak out. Goodness gracious sakes alive, how I carry on. I have liked you for a good long while now and it's about time you recognized it. If you don't marry me I think it would break my heart. Listen here Ronnie; you know frogs are a lot smarter than we are. Really did you know that? You see they eat what bugs them. Ha! Ha! Ha!

Our house was so much cleaner last week. I'm so sorry you weren't here to see it. Ronnie, I'll be glad when you're up and around again. I need you to keep up your end of the conversation. Ronnie, tell me about yourself. That is if you're not a fraidy cat. So you won't talk, huh? Come on speak up or do you want me to tell daddy. Hey daddy, Ronnie won't talk to me. You know I wanted you to ask me to the barn dance. You, Ronnie, are so darn slow. A girl could die of old age waiting for you. I could be old and gray and you would still be thinking about it. No way would you ask me to dance that night so I took the initiative and asked you. I know I shouldn't have, that's a man's job, but Ronnie, I'm weary of waiting for you to pursue me. Now let that be our little secret.

I know I'm not perfect. My Lord is still working on this ole gal. No way is He finished with me yet. Look at that barn dance; I connived to spend some time with you. You know the saying, 'the best laid plans of mice or man often go astray.' Look at the aftermath of our small amount of time with each other, first the fight, then death and destruction for your family. I'm really sorry about that Ronnie. What am I doing this for? Ma said, 'to make it light.' If you let me do that again I'm going to wallop ya good, do you hear me.

Supposing ma would have heard me acting like that. She would have put the whammy on me good and I have a hunch you'd just lie there and snicker to yourself. It just seems to me you will go a long ways to get a little attention directed your way. Don't you think getting shot is a little extreme? The way you went about it is a little on the outrageous side, seems to me. OOPS, I've got to keep it light, like ma said."

This was kind of ridiculous, this one-sided conversation went on for most of the day and I was running out of things to say. This was a one-sided exchange with no real depth to it; it seems like I was just talking to hear myself talk. Mostly just nonsensical stuff well at least you didn't get up and walk away or tell me to quit.

Ransom relieved me about four o'clock until eight when mom took over. Mama kept the dressing on until late in the afternoon. With great care we soaked the bandage off with lukewarm water. The salve we used protected the ugly wound where it was red and tender. The bandage didn't stick to the injured area at all. The salve had done its job.

Hokey Pete was that wound ever ugly! The minor operation was successful in that we didn't start it bleeding again. The medicated salve was a lifesaver being applied onto the open wound. A low-grade fever had developed so ma bathed his injury and then washed his body with cool water from the well every other hour or so and put a cold wet rag on his forehead and neck."

I thank you Jesus for what you are is doing in Ronnie's life. What a great and wonderful God you are.

With my teeth clenched I felt the hard pain hit me. It racked my frame and I was fighting the punishment my body was dishing out on me. My eyes fluttered a couple of times and then popped open. Man-oh-man I hurt bad! OHOOO! I sucked air back and forth through my clenched teeth. What happened to me? It feels like I've been shot, OHOOO, in the back. OHOOOOOOO! I hurt really badly all over! What's a matter with me anyway? It seemed like death was stalking me too? It got my family and now it seemed like it was after me.

Where am I? It was hot and my mouth was dry as cotton and I don't recognize this room. The sunspot on the floor was long so it was either early morning or late afternoon. I don't know and right now I don't care. OHOOO, Lord! I think it's Mrs. Stevens at the big cook stove doing something or other.

Ever so slowly I tried to sit up. Moving was a bad idea, as a red-hot poker of pain slammed into my chest. I was exhausted so I settled back into my pillow as that red hot fire burned deep in my chest.

OHOOOO, Lordie what happened to me? Steeling myself against the burning hot pain, I fought it with clenched teeth and with fingers digging into my palms and still the flames of pain exploded in my head and overwhelmed me. Then God gave me blessed relief in the spinning darkness that overwhelmed me right there on that table.

As my eyes opened again, Ransom was staring at me with a big ole smile. The throbbing pain held me like a vice and I remained still. Movement was something I didn't want to try again. All I could think about was that excruciating pain that I battled when I had moved earlier. I could hear myself moaning. Oh how I hurt. Wave after wave of pain rolled over me. You know sometimes living is hard when there's no one to lean on along the way.

This sick-a-bed dude closed his eyes and fought back the agonizing pain with all he could muster. Then sweet blessed relief came as I fought the pain and drifted into that foggy dark haze that swept me away from all that pain and finally a black relief swallowed me up. It was deep and it was dark and I hurt until I remembered nothing more.

A lighted hole of consciousness opened up above me. I lay still and Michele was there. I laid there listening to her talking, it sounded so good to me. The pain had eased a smidgen, though it was barely manageable. Through this hard struggle I heard her say, "You've been here almost a week now, just lying there with your eyes closed." Oh how nice her voice sounded. I didn't dare move for fear of the pain that would quickly gobble me up and spit me out again, the pain was bad enough just laying here without any movement.

"Ronnie, my good man, you've been here a week now and still you won't talk to me. Why are you dishing out the silent treatment to me? Come on Ronnie, speak up."

So with all my effort I mustered up a, "Hi Michele," and fought hard and lost, slowly slipping away from her as pain overpowered me and held me in that dark hole. Her sweet voice sounded so far away. Oh how I wanted to talk to her. When consciousness came again they were laying cold cloths on me and it felt good as it cooled my hot body. I could barely handle all the hurting that wound was piling on me. With my eyes closed I said, "Hi, again" and hung onto consciousness with all my might.

"Well, well, well, ma, he's back from la, la land again. I think this young man is trying to sleep his life away. He must love slumber land very much, he stays there enough. He must think its home or something."

"Michele honey, find out if he wants something to eat."

I felt my face twist into a smile, they sounded like my ma and our family. After thinking for a bit I settled down. In my mixed up mind I said, "I'm sorry ma, I didn't protect you."

In my state of confusion I heard ma's voice so soft and gentle, filled with lots of sympathy say, "I do, Ronald, I do forgive you." The tormenting pain began to melt away. Oh what a soothing relief it was.

"Dad."

"Ya, Ronald."

"Look after mom will you?"

"Yes my son, I will take good care of the whole family, Ronnie you just rest now and get well, we want you up and around."

I lifted my hand ever so slowly and gently. Ma held it and kissed it and held her face against it. I broke into tears and a sob came forth. Oh so softly she said, "We love you, Ronnie so very much." She touched my face with her finger tips and I felt it throughout my body.

Right then something caught in my throat, "Oh Lord help me, I'm so sorry" I, I tried to say, I love you too. Right then a whirling, swirling sound came to my ears and blackness overpowered me and whipped me far away from all other sound.

It was early and the morning sun was low in the eastern sky shining through the kitchen window and dust danced suspended in mid-air. Someone was at the stove putting wood in it. The stove lid clanked on the stovetop and wood was dropped onto red-hot coals. I didn't turn my head as I heard Michele humming a church song. It sounded like Rock of Ages.

Then a cast iron skillet clanked on the stovetop and the skillet was moved back into place. Soon there was the sound of bacon as it snapped and popped in the hot frying pan. The smell made my mouth get all juicy like. Then the egg shells cracked, on the pan edge, and the contents dropped into hot bacon grease. I swallowed to get rid of the saliva that gathered in my mouth. My mouth wanted some of that delicious tasting food.

Slowly this fool kid opened his eyelids and followed Michele movements with my eyes. As she turned she focused those baby blue eyes on me, those eyes that could look right through ya. A face so sweet, and beautiful, yes; she was very pleasant to look at. I could fault nothing from head to her toes. This sweet wonderful lady was all women. Her lovely dark brown hair lay draped down around her shoulders.

This morning she wore a white dress with a pink rose pattern and a pink ribbon in her hair. She looked really nice and I hoped it was for me. They had put me in a narrow bed along the dining room wall. At sometime or other they'd moved me off the old oak table.

She was toasting homemade bread on a stovetop toaster. The table was already set for a good breakfast. While I was watching all this, Mrs. Stevens came into the room and said, "How's our sleepy head today, it looks like he's back amongst the living?"

Without turning, Michele said, "He's resting much better, mom."

Mom Stevens looked at me saying, "How do you feel, Ronald?"

"I'll not do any plowing today I'm pretty sure of that." I liked her smile; it reminded me of Michele's smile. It was big and showed lots of white even teeth; it was oh so pleasant.

"Are you hungry?"

"Yes ma'am." She had some hot soup cooking on the stove. While she was getting it for me, I dosed off. Fighting my way back up out of the fog, Michele sat by the bed holding my hand and talking to me.

"You know you were meant for me. Ronnie, you were leaving weren't you? What would I do if you did leave? Your wagon was packed and you were on your way to who knows where. What I want to know is, were you coming to see me first or were you just heading out to only God knows where, without me? I thought someday maybe you and I would marry. I know you like me. You're so shy. Do I have to propose to you? It's beginning to look like it, if anything's going to happen here."

Faking a wake up I moved the hand she held with a short quick jerk. She asked, "How do you feel today, Ronnie?"

"Somewhat better Michele, I have pain that feels like someone knocked my block off and I'll not take it lying down anymore. Ah, ouch! Well maybe I will. I guess I couldn't whip a mouse today, unless he was mighty small."

"Ronnie, you need to eat something so stay awake, will ya? You need nourishment to keep up your strength, what little you have left."

"Michele, I'll take anything you've got for me. Michele."

"Yes?"

"Thanks for being a friend."

"Ronnie, that's okay. I like being your friend."

The food they gave me was a soup with some substance to it, like bits of meat, carrots, potatoes, onions, and milk gravy. She would only let me have a small bowl full saying, "Later."

When she looked at me I winked at her. She stopped dead still and that pretty mouth dropped open and those piercing blue eyes fixed on me and didn't move for a long moment.

I found my tongue and said, "Michele, I've wanted to know you better, but I have trouble talking to you about what's on my heart. Will you help me? We need to talk about you and me. I've always liked being near you and, and having you as a friend."

She recovered, came near and sat next to me on the bed saying, "I've often wondered about that Ronnie. You've been in a coma for over a week and I liked being near you. I wished you had come a courting, although you never did. Why, Ronnie?"

"Michele, I've thought of you oh, so many times. I guess, I guess I'm just a shy backwards country boy. Listen honey, now that I know you're interested I need you to be prepared. Ah, I'm going to ask you, to marry me, real soon. Not today, not now, but real soon. I want you to think on it and check me out. Watch me in good times and bad. Watch me up close.

Talk it over with your folks. I've known your heart from the fifth grade and how you love people. I've watched you girl and down deep inside I've wanted you for quite a spell. I've desired your loving heart to love me and be a lot more than just good friends. I've seen your love at work Michele and I like it. It's like the heat from a heating stove, it radiates out to everyone around you. That night of the dance, you held Greg's head. I believe a blind person could see it and a deaf man could hear your love. I find myself thinking of you with most every breath I take. I want you to know I'll be leaving and if you want me I must know before I leave."

"Ronnie, where are you thinking about going?"

"Away from here, my uncle Leroy is on the homestead and I'm going out West somewhere. I've thought about raising cows and maybe start a ranch. I've heard tell there's lots of good grass out West." While looking at her I had a sinking feeling when she didn't respond.

Possibly she didn't want to leave her family or didn't really love me. Man-oh-man is this talking ever hard work but I needed to get it said. I closed my eyes and relaxed for a long moment. This woman is a living dream and I love her. Why would she want to marry me anyway? This lovely woman could get any man she wanted. All she had to do was say so.

Maybe I've over stepped my bounds. Maybe she's not ready for marriage. Ronnie my boy who do you think you are anyway? I guess maybe I'd better forget it. But then what did she mean, you're meant for me. This is way too confusing for my mixed up mind. Ma often told me, "Nothing ventured, nothing gained. I wanted her so badly. "Oh ouch, oh Lord do I ever hurt," The edges started to crumble and dark shadows from that black hole began to suck me down.

"Mom, he wants me. He wants me to leave Michigan and go west somewhere with him. What do you think? Mom, Ronnie's such a good man, of unquestionable character. A man that cares for people and laughter is a way of life with him. God knows he's a hard worker, with a good head on his shoulders. A man of his word and most of all he loves me, he loves me, ma."

"Whoa! Whoa! Honey, what's wrong with him might be quicker."

I thought for a moment and smiled saying, "he isn't rich, ha, ha. Mom, all I can think of is he's going west and I might not see my family again. My family is important to me, Mom."

"Honey, he's not going to see his family either."

"Oh mama," did that ever hurt, "no I guess he won't."

"Honey, a good man is so hard to come by. Michele, I came out here with your daddy leaving eastern New York State and rode the ferry (the Michigan) to Detroit. We then moved through the woods all the way into Ingham County and finally we made it up here.

Your grandma, my mother, is back in eastern New York State. Honey, if you love him, go. If he turns out to be rich, ha, ha, send for us." We laughed together. This mom of mine had a great sense of humor and understanding.

Later pa and Ransom came in from the barn. They'd been doing the farm chores. "Dad, Ronnie has asked me to marry him, what do you think?"

Ransom piped in, "I guess that proves he's still out of his head with a fever and all. That boy must be really sick. Sis, you can't hold him to it, poor fellow. Don't make him eat crow Michele. Wait until the fever's gone and I'll bet he'll sing a different tune."

At that point I slugged him on the shoulder. He let out a war whoop, "ma, she's beating up on me. Give her a spanking; she's such an ole meanie."

We all had a good laugh. "Pa, he's going out West somewhere and wants me to marry him and go with him to God only knows where, I don't."

"Sugar, I don't ever want you to go and leave us. We love you and want you with us. Sweetheart, think this through, if someone hadn't shot him and he had just eased on out of here, how would you feel then? Would you hurt?"

"Oh daddy, I get lonesome and half sick just thinking about it."

"Then are you going to just let him go on by? Sweetie, think on it. He isn't going anywhere for a while. But to tell you the truth, I don't think he'll be back this way again. If his mind is made up to stay out West, he won't be calling again. Be wise in what you decide to do, either way we will love and support you in your decision."

"Daddy, I would like to stay near you and mom, but I get lonesome just thinking about him leaving. What'll I do?" My dilemma is that both sides of this situation tear at me. Now if he were staying here, in Mid-Michigan, I would accept his proposal in a heartbeat.

I would feel bad if he left me or if I went with him and left Mom, Ransom and you here. I wonder if I could talk him into staying on his homestead. No, I don't think so. Ronnie earlier said, "That was out." If he stayed here and got bushwhacked again and they killed him how would I feel then? "Oh Lord, help me make the right decision. Jesus, talk to Ronnie for me and let him know how I feel about this."

Daddy sent Ransom over to the Holden home place to talk to Ronnie's uncle, Leroy Gross to tell him about Ronnie and see if anyone has found his large wagon yet. Daddy had a hunch it's still in the area somewhere and Ronnie's little wagon just wouldn't do for a long hard trip out West.

Dad said, "Ransom, check along the way and try to locate it. If Ronald is headed west, he'll need that big wagon and the horses. Ransom, be careful who you talk to. I think someone in this area killed Ronald's folks and bushwhacked him. Be on your toes and just talk to people that you know. Whoever is doing this is willing to kill at the drop of a hat."

My dad was a take-charge kind of a man. He would get things worked out somehow. I love how he's working for Ronnie in this situation. I love my papa very much.

Returning to the kitchen, Ronnie was awake for a change. There was pain still showing on his face when he moved. With all the blood that he lost it would be awhile before he could go anywhere. Maybe he wouldn't be able to go this year. It was April 6 already. No, he'll go. I know him. By June he'll be rolling on out of here. That young man will push himself to get back in shape. I like that about him, but on the other hand I don't like him leaving me and heading west on his own.

His eyes followed me everywhere I went. First while setting the table then those hazel eyes were glued on me and it felt good to know for sure that he loves me. Man-oh-man did I like to watch him when he slept. This young man was hard from head to foot. I watched him fight Greg and those hands had blinding speed. Greg, I thought was quick, but that night he looked slow. Ronnie would hit him once, twice and again, then back off, then step in and land a couple more punches. Poor oh Greg knew how fast he was that night. This young man could do about anything he wanted too and Greg couldn't stop him.

Glancing his way again he had his eyes closed and even as pale as this young man was he was still something to look at. I bet he can make great babies. Michele, get your mind up out of the gutter. At this point Ronnie isn't thinking of me in that way, "Lord, help me make the right decision. Help me keep my hand in yours through this situation and don't let me go gallivanting off on my own."

Ma and dad had left for Crystal over on Crystal Lake to sell some butter, milk, cheese, two rabbits and oats to the livery stable, the oats were for the boarded horses. Ma needed flour, baking soda, sugar and a few other things.

Crystal Lake was a beautiful place; the lake was crystal clear and you could see clean to the bottom. The sun on the surface made it shimmer in the sun light. The lake was down below the town. At night the lake sparkled in the moonlight. The sandy beaches make it a wonderful place to have a picnic and swim on Sundays after church.

Eight years ago the first settler settled there and built a log house close to the lake. Enos Drake is a shirttail relative of Ronnie Holden. Three years ago Mr. Drake came in here and installed a sawmill for lumber and to grind grain into flour and soon was producing boards from the timber that grew everywhere and close by. That year (1857) the first frame house was also built in crystal.

We were lucky to have a mid-wife settle in the area back in 1854. Early the very next year they put her to work. Mrs. Burk delivered a boy and a girl and added two more to the population of the settlement of Crystal. We pick up our US mail in Crystal at the small post office. On Wednesdays Alan Snow the postman brought the mail in from Ionia, a town to our south. From Crystal he went to the town of Fred, then on to New Albany (later to be called Shepherd). At first Alan walked his route but now he has a horse to ride.

Four days ago dad had finished planting his oats and soon they would be peeking through the ground. Ransom was even now plowing for corn and later they would plant navy beans for a cash crop. This was bean and potatoes country, here in Mid-Michigan many folks grew them for a cash crop.

The very next day Ronnie's, uncle Leroy, aunt Norma, their boy Danny and his sister, Susan, made their way into our dooryard. They had Ronnie's big wagon and his pretty matched pair of Percheron draft horses harnessed to it. The big horses were a mighty big team, bred for hard work. I knew this team and they were workers."

Leroy said, "The horses and wagon had wandered into the Howard family's yard and Jim had returned the big pair to him." This was a stroke of luck for Ronnie Holden. To make the long hard trip west he would need another team to help with the heavy load. That big dappled gray pair and another team would take him out West and carry all the things he would need for a good life. It was good for him while it left an uneasy feeling inside me. Why? Why should I feel this way?

Mr. Leroy and Miss Norma were talking to Ronnie about his nice farm land. Leroy was looking to purchase all one hundred sixty acres from Ronnie for six hundred and fifty bucks which was a fair price for good land. Ronnie was coherent and quite capable at least enough to say, "No." He only wanted to sell eighty acres and let Leroy use the other eighty, if he thought he needed that much. Ronnie wanted a place he could always come back too if things didn't go well out West.

After much haggling they finally settled on a price of four hundred twenty-five dollars and a good pair of draft horses plus a few other odds and ends. The deal was struck with a handshake. The other team could be picked up at Uncle Leroy's place, in a day or so. As soon as Ronnie could maneuver his body well enough to make it there and back he could pick them up and bring them back here. I wanted him to reside here with us and not stay at his home. Here I felt I could nurse him back to health.

Ronnie wasn't interested in staying with his family on his old home place and that was good. I needed to have him here, with me, so I could communicate with him. I wanted to have him close so I could make a decision about him and our life together.

They stayed for supper and it was near dark when they left for home. Pa cautioned them to be careful on the road. They left with waves of goodbye and Ronnie's light wagon making wheel tracks in the dirt of the road. The Gross's light team was moving at a pretty good clip eastward.

Ronnie was sitting up a little and true to his nature he was exercising his legs and arms. Soon he was on the front porch walking back and forth, in and out of the house, then up and down the steps. He was working hard to get ready for his trip west.

From that day back when he had first talked of marriage until now he had said nothing about it. Sometimes I wished he would. Did he even remember asking me? There were way too many things that were still unclear in my mind about all he said and I felt left out in the dark about some things.

By May 1st, Ronnie was walking around the dooryard pushing himself for his journey west into the Great American Prairie. Yes I knew him so well. Once he made up his mind to do something everything else was left in his wake.

May 7, 1860. He rode his gray mare back home and was gone for three long days visiting with his aunt and uncle. They were locating and staking out the property lines. Late the third day he returned with a four horse team and he looked worn out from all the exercise. The following day he slept until noon and awoke with a sick headache. He was pushing himself for all he was worth to get ready to leave. I hope he isn't over doing it. He seems to be pushing himself way to hard for a man as sick as he was.

When he was able, he worked both teams in dad's fields, getting the horses and himself into shape for the long hard trip west. Just building soft winter muscles into hard ones, on both man and beast. This good looking young man was determined to get as fit as a fiddle. He is a dyed in the wool hard worker.

May 21, it is well over two months since being shot; he came and sat down with me asking, "Have you thought on what we talked about earlier, the proposal of marriage? Have you come to any decision about me? Michele, I love you, and I have for a long, long time. There is no one else in Mid-Michigan that I want to go with me on this trip west, but you.

My hope is you will marry me, go with me and build a life and start a ranch somewhere out there on the prairie. Michele, I will be leaving on the twenty-eighth. If you say yes we have one short week to bring all the loose ends together and get hitched up right, with a church wedding." We sat in the porch swing and talked for a long time about his plans and how I felt about life, his trip and me. I told him about being torn up on the inside, and how I was in a dither not knowing what to do next. I knew it was time to do something or get off the thunder mug (potty) but there were so many things that I needed to work out in my mind.

THE CONCLUSION

I shed many a tear that long lonesome night trying to come to a conclusion on what I needed to do. I loved both Ronnie Holden and my family. This is a classic case of wanting my cake and eating it too. Throughout that long restless night, in my bedroom, I didn't sleep a wink and I tossed and turned all night long. Sometime during the long night I finally came to the conclusion that I had to love someone more than the other. It turned out to be Ronnie Holden. The boy I'd dreamed about all those years.

Okay, I would go with him on his great adventure into the western plains. Now that the decision was made a huge heavy load melted away and I now felt light as a feather with all my indecision gone. At the lifting of that burden, I got up and hurried off to dad and mom's bedroom. "Mom, mom wake up. I'm going to marry that boy out there. Mom, the wedding must be next Sunday. Mama, we have five days to make the arrangements and all the preparations for a trip to only God know where. Now that I've made the decision on what to do, I'm excited about it. Now I've got to go tell Ronnie of my decision."

Mom laughed, "You mean you haven't told Ron yet? That's a first."

Dad even chuckled at that. My dad was a real kidder and cared for me. "Girl, I must say you've got the cart before the horse this time. You should have talked to him first. For some reason he may want to know what you're thinking. To him it could be a big hairy deal."

"Daddy, he loves me and I love him."

"Yes girl, we know. Well little lady get on out of here. You've got things to do."

"Ok! Ok! I love you folks. You're the greatest."

"We know young lady, good night, see you in the morning."

As I left, I could hear my folks talking in their bedroom and ma said, "I knew it."

Ronnie was sound asleep in the living room. "Ronnie, wake up." As soon as the yawns ceased I kissed him. His right arm encircled my neck and he held my lips to his. Whew! If I'd known he was this good I would have done this a long time ago. I quickly felt a stirring inside of me; so I pulled away. "Ronnie, you are going to make me a great husband. I love you so. Yes! Yes! Yes! I'll marry you and go anywhere you want me too. Honey, I'll see you in the morning. Now go back to sleep." a funny look came on his face as I turned to leave.

"Michele."

"Yes dear."

"I love you so and you only will I ever love. Only you will I cherish for as long as I live. Darling, I will watch over you and take care of you as long as breath fills my lungs, as God is my witness. You my fair lady are all I ever wanted. I'm sure we will have many happy years together."

He was in earnest and meant what he said. I could trust him. The next few days were all hustle and bustle getting ready for our wedding, on Sunday, and our trip out west. Ronnie rode to town for a coat, a new pair of trousers and polish for his boots so that he could shine them for our big day.

Daddy planted a small field to corn then stopped all fieldwork. Ransom made long rides telling people of the Sunday wedding of Ronnie and me. We talked to pastor Underwood and everything was set for Sunday. Weddings, on the frontier, were a big deal. People needed some kind of a distraction from the humdrum of daily life and a wedding fit the bill to a tee. It got all their friends and neighbors together in one place and they got all the latest gossip in and what was going on in the neighborhood.

Mom and I got busy and completed a dress and was it ever a showpiece. It fit me to a tee. Cakes and pies were baked. Ten families would bring ice cream makers on Sunday. Wilson's store had an icehouse and he would furnish the ice. We planned a potluck dinner on the grounds, shortly after the wedding which followed the morning service on Sunday. Sumner and the Sumner church would be a busy place with people coming in from everywhere throughout the countryside.

May 27, the Lord's Day was a beautiful day. The weather was warm for late May and white clouds were banked high in the pretty blue sky. Oh it is so beautiful out. A light breeze outside gave us relief from the heat. As we traveled along a Plymouth Rock Rooster sounded, from a split rail fence, as we rolled on by on our way to church.

Dad snapped the buggy whip over the young filly's head, and our horse picked up the pace a bit. By the time we hit the edge of town she had worked up a good lather. This was my day, a day to be remembered the rest of my life. I watched a huge Red Tailed Chicken hawk circle round and round sailing on the slight morning breeze. The morning air whistled softly through the pines, in the church's front yard. Whispering to me he loves you, he loves you and today is your day. Pines trees do that. Say a phrase and the wind will repeat it over and over, in the pines needles just for you. That's how God made it.

In the distance we could see that wagons were still making their way here. A piano played in the church. As I listened to the melody a songbird joined in, it made my day a wonderful time to be alive. We've been up since the crack of dawn. I was so excited even ma was happy for me and dad was so proud. Ransom was even nice to me. Can you imagine that?

But most of all my man loved and wanted me. Yes, this is a good time in my life when everything I wanted was coming together. I was a queen on this special day and people treated me like one. Our marriage ceremony was awesome. People came in from miles around. Folks were everywhere. By ten o'clock there was no room left in the church to even stand and food smells filled every table on the church lawn. Dogs were hanging around so someone had to watch the food and shoo away the flies.

Before Sunday we had our big wagon packed with all we would need to start a new life out West. Ma and dad helped out considerably. They had started life twice on the frontier and now they were helping us. They thought of things we never would have. We would later pile wedding gifts on top of our stuff in the wagon.

We received many of the things given to newlyweds headed for the far frontier. Some old, some new, but all needed. What generous friends our families had. My hope chest had many personal things a woman needed to start a new life with a good man. Yes we were ready to start our trip and our new life out there somewhere. Presents were loaded into our small wagon in the churchyard.

As we got ready to leave many well wishers came to say goodbye and the crying was very contagious. One person caught it and spread it to someone else. You could see it going from person to person as we said our "good-byes." People really did love us and it showed as we boarded our buggy and started that little gray mare on the road to dad's place to the West.

Slipping away from the Sumner church, shortly before the afternoon service, it was a good trip home just my man and me. At times we stopped under shade trees and love showed itself. This boy could kiss and I loved him with all my heart. I think sometimes how I almost didn't make this decision to marry him. My life would be missing the best thing that could have happened to me. Ronnie was the man God had picked out for me, no doubt about it.

Ronnie moved into my bedroom and we started our new life out the right way. We learned together as man and wife. "Thank you Jesus for saving this man for me." This little lady hated what the bushwhacking scum did to my Ronnie, but if they hadn't hurt him would he be here in bed with me now, I think not. My God works in strange ways His wonders to perform. Yes, Jesus can make sweet lemonade out of sour lemons any day of the week and twice on Sunday. At least he did it for us. Thank heaven!

How lucky I am and what a sweet wonderful man God has given me. Together we packed and loaded our things in the large wagon. Then hooking the smaller wagon on behind, we would haul that lighter wagon out West with us.

Warren Drake, a shirttail relation of mine and nephew of Enos Drake the owner of the saw mill in Crystal, had asked to go with us and Warren was included in our plans. His folks,

Mr. and Mrs. Clarence Drake, lived up on the Pine River north of Vestaburg, about seven miles north of Crystal. His folks thought it would be good for him to go with us.

Warren was sixteen and was as excited about the trip west as we were. Warren was a good kid and dependable. A hard worker and we needed him and we were mighty glad to have him come along. Warren would ride Molly and kind of look the country over for us.

There was no space between Michele and I, as the big horses leaned into their collars. The teams made many hoof prints and wheel tracks in the soft dirt of this poor excuse for a road. By noon we were past the settlement of Fred and heading south, the three of us stopped for the night at Pearl Lake.

There was a small settlement there. The big horses were sound and eager to pull. We were eager to put lots and lots of green sod behind us. We were excited about seeing new country as we traveled south toward Indiana. The second night found us on the banks of the Grand River near the settlement of Ionia. The third night we stayed on the banks of the Thornapple River and watched settlers as they traveled north to buy and stake out land claims on some land way up North.

Towns were taking shape everywhere. As soon as dirt farmers settled into an area a store would be built and a few other buildings would spring up and carry on commerce. This trail south was used by homesteaders moving north to find good land and by local residents that had settled in this area and needed a trail into town.

On the fifth day we hit the Sauk Indian Trail that went southwest toward Indiana. We urged the big teams southwest taking the same route the Sauk Indians took when they were pushed west by the whites. The Sauk Indians came through Detroit and moved west then south along Lake Michigan. The

Sauk Indians finally settled farther to the west. I heard they settled west of the Mississippi River somewhere.

Warren and that gray mare stayed on the Sauk Indian trail and headed south westward into Indiana. We saw Lake Michigan from time to time in our passing. This was an all new adventure for the three of us. We made ourselves alert to whatever lay ahead of us.

In Indiana we picked up livestock wherever we found them cheap. With the buying and driving of our new stock our progress was slowed a lot. We needed stock to start our ranch if we found one and we didn't think there would be productive cattle to buy further west. We reasoned that folks further west would need all their breeding stock to build their own ranches out there. I'm sure that steers would be plentiful out there but we needed breeding stock.

To tell you the truth life with this lovely woman was something special. She made it so. We enjoyed each other's company and all our time together. Michele had always been my best friend and now our love life was growing stronger and stronger, day by day and mile by mile as our big teams hauled us westward to our new life somewhere out there on the Great Prairie.

Who would want to be shot? No one I know of, but if I hadn't been life would be a whole lot different for my beautiful wife and me. Life wouldn't be worth much for me but now with Michele at my side it was a new and exciting time for us both. The Bible says, "All things work out for the best to them that love the Lord."

Moving west along the south side of the Illinois River and where the river dog legged to the south, we knew we had to find a way across. The water was high so we needed to take a ferry to navigate the river.

BUREAU'S CROSSING

At Bureau Crossing there was a raft big enough to carry the horses and wagons across, but not with the cattle, all at one time. As I looked around I saw that Bureau Crossing had way too many unsavory looking men just standing around, so I kept Michele close to me and made sure my weapons were loaded and ready if they were needed.

The ferry raft attendant said, "If you leave the cattle here alone, unattended, unguarded they will be gone when you get back. Son, you dare not leave your wife alone over there or anywhere for that matter, or your rigs. These low lives that hang around here can't be trusted one iota, so watch them like a hawk at all times. Son, your wife is a pretty woman and it's an open invitation for big trouble, with this lawless bunch that hang around out here. Son, they prey on unsuspecting folks like you. Stealing what they can. Killing those who won't give up what they want. Son, guard your woman for all your worth, if you want her."

"Sir, what do you suggest I do? We only have the three of us to protect our outfit. What do you think, Sir? How would you do it?"

"Sonny boy, I don't know, they've got you coming or going no matter how you look at it. They have you in a bad spot, Sonny"

Well I'd rather lose the cattle than lose Michele or my wagons. In my mind I made a quick decision of what I should do. I wondered if all these men were untrustworthy. Can anyone here about be trusted? I had to try something; I had money invested in my livestock. Could these men be trusted? Ma would say, "Nothing ventured then nothing will be gained." This plan of mine might save the stock and get us across the Illinois River with our outfit intact.

Scanning the weather beaten faces of the crowd I saw three young men, near my, age standing on the store porch, they didn't seem to be a part of this wild bunch that hovered around the ferry. I pointed my hand up that way. Once they saw me pointing, I waved them down here. At first they looked puzzled then two of them stepped off the porch, into the dust, and moseyed our way. A slender good-looking young man about twenty looked me in the eye and asked, "What's up? Do you want something'?"

"Sir, would you three fellows like a job? It could be dangerous. See these rough tough looking bad men standing around eyeing us? I need some help really bad. These ole boys will want to steal my property and I can't let it happen."

Their response was shock and excitement. "Do we want the job, Sir? You bet we do. What do you want done? Just name it."

"See those cows, about forty-five head of stock and that boy on the gray horse; bring the stock over on the next trip across the Illinois River. There is a bad element here that will try to steal them if I leave them alone very long on this side."

"Sir, we have two wagons and I need money for the ferry. Could I get an advance on our pay? We were looking for a job so we could get both wagons across."

This guy had brass. He hadn't lifted a finger and he wanted money. Maybe his ma said, "Nothing ventured, nothing gained to him also." Looking past him I saw his two rigs beside the store. A young woman was working around a campfire and a teen boy was standing nearby. "What's your name Sir?"

"Jared Jenkins and this is my brother Jeff, my wife and younger brother Kevin are over at the general store by those wagons."

"Well Mr. Jenkins, I was told by the ferry owner not to leave my wife alone around here. So you need to send Jeff back to your wagon with your brother and your lady and we will talk business. First, I don't know you from a hole in the ground, so I will pay the ferry attendant for your fare across the river. Once my wagons, horses and that few head of livestock get across, and your rigs too, maybe we can travel together for awhile for safety sake. With this kind of low-grade trash a hawking our outfits, the more the merrier and the safer we will be.

"Okay, I got it. We want to thank you, Sir; we needed a hand up at this time. Thank you so very much. We'll get you out of this fix, or my name isn't Jared Jenkins."

"Jared, you watch this bunch. The livestock are important but not more important than your life. What you see here could be cold-blooded killers. At least that's what I've been told, so be careful. These rotten riff raff will try to take everything you have from you if you don't watch them closely."

"We're well healed, with guns enough to make these cutthroats sit up and take notice." I passed Jared Jenkins my extra Greener, (double barrel twelve gauge loaded with double 0 buckshot.) "You use this if you need it but be careful. I don't want you and your outfit shot up. We'll give them a show of force. Take Warren Drake, that boy on the gray, and let him help you, he can be depended on in a tight fix.

Warren, will you come on over here? I want you to stay here with Mr. Jenkins for now, for a show of force. Maybe the four of you will keep them from trying anything. No one needs to come across with the beef; just send them across by themselves. Warren you stay alert over here, I've been told these men are real bad hombres.

The ferry man said, "They will try to take whatever we've got if unattended." When we leave get your back up against something and put the gray in front of you for protection, and be ready for anything and everything. Warren if it's too bad, stay out of it. I don't want you dead. Jared the same goes for you also. We can replace the cattle. I don't want to be responsible for you guys getting hurt or killed." I glanced up toward the store, the fire was out at their wagons and they were throwing cooking things into them in haste.

Jeff and the other boy were harnessing the horses and getting ready to roll on out of here. Warren took Molly and moseyed on back to the herd. Placed his back up against a big tree and watched the goings on. There was a post right there so Warren hitched Molly to it. I could see him getting ready for trouble. Jared and Jeff hitched up their big Belgians to their wagons. They were big teams. You could see they were good stock, born to pull. "Lord, watch over them, please. Get them through any difficulties they might face and help them make wise decisions."

Michele and I loaded our equipment onto the river raft, plus a few head of stock. Five men tried to push their horses onto the raft we were on. So I stood in their way. "You men take your turn. We're not over loading this raft for your convenience, so step back. I've got cattle coming over on the next trip. So please clear out." We're already loaded to the gills and are moving these twelve head of cows over with us."

"Listen mister, you've got room for us and we are making the trip with ya."

"No sir, you're not. Pull them nags off this raft and now. You aren't riding with us anywhere, not now, not ever!"

Michele sounded from the wagon, "my man said move, so do it now or I'll unload this 12 gauge shotgun into ya."

One ruffian who Michele couldn't see made his play. I had my shot gun already to fire and my buck shot plowed into his chest. The man went cart wheeling backwards into the river and slipped beneath the surface. One man started his draw as I thumbed back the other hammer and he saw that shotgun come in line. He let loose of his Colt and watched me with hard eyes.

The horses aboard the raft were half wild with fear, with all that was going on and the only way they could go was into the river. I said to the men, "You low grade trash get off our raft and take your turn." They stood still looking first at me, then Michele and back to me again.

The older man said, "Let ole Bill Anderson make this ride if he wants over there so darn bad." They started backing their horses off the raft and onto the dock where they mounted up and rode off toward the store. One man turned and said, "This ain't over yet, bub. You'll get yours. You can be sure we ain't done yet. It's just a matter of time, you young whippersnapper and you'll get yours."

The raft owner hesitated for a moment checking the air and then fastened the cords across the end of the raft. We slipped away from the dock as we started our ride across the Illinois River. As I looked back Jared had the crew move the rest of the livestock and the two wagons up to the ferry landing. He bunched up the cows to keep a better eye on them and got ready for any kind of trouble that just might come their way.

As we watched, a pistol belched smoke and lead, breaking the noonday silence of the river and right on the heels of that

I heard the boom of a shotgun blast. Our eyes were riveted to the scene that lay behind us, on that eastern shore. I saw Jared Jenkins's young wife holding a smoking shotgun. It was aimed and we saw it jump in her hands moving her shoulder backwards. Then it all broke loose back there for about twenty seconds. Suddenly it stopped as quick as it started and it got real quiet back there.

Now all that we heard came from the raft, the jangle of harness chains and the creaks and groans of the raft as we slowly moved west across the Illinois River along with the bellowing of nervous livestock. Michele had caught her breath and now expelled air as a horse shook nervously then snorted as water lapped at the raft. Our shot gun was now reloaded

The horses stamped their hooves and the strain of the rope against the wooden pulley made it creak. Other than that not a sound came to my ears. On the eastern shore I saw Jared and his wife still standing in the first wagon. These young people take their jobs and a handshake quite seriously. I hope they're all okay back there. Trouble could be brewing up a bad storm at any moment, on that eastern shore.

In the back of my mind I wondered where they were headed. They were eager and determined, anyone could see that. It seems that maybe they've been saddled with poverty. Poverty can be a mighty rough row to hoe. With no more money then we have if we ran into any serious trouble we could be in the same fix they were in.

For Michele's sake I will fight trouble to a standstill. For better or worse we said, but I want it to be better, much better, for her sake, in fact a whole lot better than it is right now. My mind jumped back to Jared's wife and that shotgun belching flame and chunks of 00 lead, as she stood by her man. Jared Jenkins looked to be the leader of their young clan and I was impressed with his devotion to his word.

We were a mighty long ways from any real civilization and I said I would keep my woman safe no matter what. That was my vow to her if she would come west with me and I intended to keep it. Michele was nervous holding onto my arm and watching the eastern shoreline because of the trouble that exploded over there. She had a worried look plastered on her pretty face as we took in everything on the far shore.

By three o'clock in the afternoon we were all across the river and making a run for it. After a few miles we moved off the trail and into the woods a fair piece. Jared went back and erased our tracks in the dirt. It was near dark so we halted the big wagons. Up ahead, on a small rise, we made a tight fort up close to a dead fall (downed tree). Then brought the horses inside, for safety sake, and kept the beef in close but outside the circle of our wagons.

We were way to close to the river crossing to be at ease. Those thugs hadn't given up on us yet and we didn't feel all that safe. I hoped they would think we would go as far as we could, on the trail, and hopefully they would ride on by us. We can't outrun them so I hoped this move would out fox them.

Jared Jenkins was close to my age about nineteen. I guess and his wife, Debbie, was about eighteen, Jeff is eighteen, Kevin and Warren are close to the same age, sixteen. What's a bunch of half-baked kids doing way out here with gangsters, gunmen, bushwhackers, drifters, thieves, cutthroats and Indians all trying to make trouble for us?

THE STORY

This land out here makes Michigan look pretty tame. I guess the only answer is we're following the American dream or is it the American nightmare. As we ate a cold supper I asked Jared what happened back there at the Illinois River, while the two of us crossed over on the ferry.

"Well Ron, as you loaded your wagons and teams plus those few cows onto the ferry we saw those riders try to buffalo you just before you started across and one man dyed for their effort. That is when we moved the rest of your beef up close to the dock so we could keep a close eye on them. I could see you were right, those men were watching our women and your livestock pretty closely, and when you shot that fellow on the ferry things began to kick into action where we were.

A long haired whiskery gent came ambling up to our wagon and said, "you there young feller, we want our cattle now. It's time for us to leave here and head on home and we don't want to leave our stock unprotected or unattended."

I said to him, "well sir, go find them. You can bet your knee high-boots they aren't these cows that you see here. These cattle belong to Mr. Holden. He's out there on the ferry boat right now. If you want to buy them you'll have to talk with him first. But I'm pretty sure he won't sell to you or anyone else, he has plans for them."

"Hey there young man what do you mean buy them, they belong to us? What the devil are you talking about? Wake up kid and smell the roses, you half grown whelp. I don't think you understand that all these fleabags left over here belong to us. Those are the standing rules here so those are our fur balls and we're taking them home with us. Have you got that you little pip-squeak?"

"Listen mister, I don't think you understand anything at all. These cows belong to Mr. Holden. He's out there on the raft. They'll be on the other side in just a jiffy; you can talk to him over there if you are of a mind to pay for them. Sir, I'm just a hired hand, so don't talk your tomfoolery with me. Sir, I don't need you feeding me any more crap. Feed it to someone else that wants to listen, but not to me." His face grew dark and strained and his lips got tight over his teeth. This long haired scallywag looked like he was already heating up inside.

"You hear me good, kid. You're way too young to die over a few fleabags that don't even belong to you. Sonny boy, we have plenty of men back up in the pucker brush. Way too many for you to make it across the river with our stock, so ease up will ya? They ain't your beef, so try to be cool about the whole thing."

"Come on old man, you might as well save your breath you ain't getting any of these flea bags, so just take your big mouth and move along." His look was hard and long as he sized up our outfit and my wife.

Dust drifted across the dock area and blew dust into his face and the wind moved the tag on his Bull Durum sack in his shirt pocket. If this came to something, that Bull Durum tag would be my first target the one I would hit first.

The big man closed his eyes and turned his back to the wind. When it blew on by he turned back to face me. The outspoken outlaw rubbed his eyes and said, "remember this kid, when you're dead it's forever and there ain't no exit signs in hell. Once you're there, sonny boy, there's no way out. Think on that."

"Get away from me with your fool talk. I've heard enough of your chin music to last me the rest of my life." Right then Debbie cocked her old twelve gage shotgun and moved it into a better shooting position as the outlaw leader strolled away.

That Drake kid moved that gray horse in front of him. Then cocked the nasty ole Greener of his and got in position, with his horse in front of him and a tree behind him. His shotgun was cocked and slung over his saddle, and aimed at a group of rough looking men that milled around. That young man was more than ready for a fight. I was sure glad he was on our side.

Kevin had his long gun, in his hands, and his shotgun stood against the big Maple Tree. Jeff was in the second wagon. They were both set and ready for any kind of action that might come their way. These two boys were level headed, calm, cool and collected in a scrap of any kind. My lovely wife Debbie had leaned the big bore rifle at my fingertips and it was cocked and ready for action. If it was to come let it be now before they brought in the rest of their outfit. That could put more pressure on us and tip the scales a little further in their favor.

Right then the outlaw leader turned and moved away from us. Dad's old saying came to mind; evil will chase ya only if good men do nothing about it. I was pretty sure of what they were going to do. I could feel it in my bones. With my right hand close to my revolver I loosened it, in its leather resting place, and adjusted it for quick and easy use, if needed. It looked like we were as ready as we would ever be.

The outlaw leader took several steps then stopped, turned and said, "What are you doing this for if these cows aren't your flea-bags that you're watching?"

"The man out on the raft has already paid us and I gave him my word. You probably don't understand that, but we do. Our word is our bond."

"Well I still don't understand this whole thing, just how much money you going to die for? What's it amount to, big money I hope."

"It's none of your business but he paid our way across the river on that ferry raft."

He then looking at our rigs and he laughed a sinister laugh and said, "You'd die for two bucks? Man that's crazy. No, you're a fool doing a fool's job."

"Sir, be careful, if you try anything you'll die for nothing and you said it, 'death is forever' and like you said, 'there are no exit signs in Hell.' Does it sound familiar? You be careful what you start here today. It could get you killed."

He laughed a hardy laugh and turned and walked away. As he passed one of his men the fellow drew his pistol, with good speed, although a little too slow as my 44 slug plowed deep into his chest. His pistol shoved a foot long flame toward the ground as a twisted smile quickly changed into shock and put a puzzled look on his whiskery face. He took two shaky steps backwards sat down, stared at me and then toppled over dead. This little deal had gone bad for him today.

Jeff's shotgun exploded and a man on horseback disappeared from his saddle. Without looking I saw him on the ground shaking all over. Another rider came at a frantic gallop with his handgun loose from leather and Debbie put daylight through him, with a good shot as he rode toward us. The man tumbled to the ground, rolled a couple times and lie still.

Debbie yelled and pointed; a man was sighting over the saddle of his fidgety horse and was ready to fire. Kevin let the hammer drop on his big bore rifle and it spit a fifty caliber slug through the horse and into the gunman. His small buckskin made a terrible noise and flopped over on top of him.

The man, for a moment, was struggling to free himself and then lie still. Several other cow thieves went down in a barrage of gunfire. I lost track of who did what as I worked my own firearms. A bullet whined off the wheel rim. Then all of a sudden the gunfire stopped as quickly as it started.

The last few men stood frozen in place and did nothing foolish that would get them killed. Bill Anderson had tried to run roughshod over us and steal the livestock. Several of these men were dead or dying. Five men didn't draw or lift a finger to help and so avoided death.

Debbie handed me the reloaded shotgun with the ram rod still in the right barrel. She was now reloading the big 50-caliber rifle so it might get back into the action. That sweet lady could reload faster than anyone I knew of.

Jeff said, "You men better make some tracks on out of here before you get us really mad and end up like your friends, dead and buzzard bait. Don't let your greed get you killed." They backed off, mounted their horses and slowly rode off. Warren rounded up the dead men's horses and guns. This would help us on our trip west. We had very little money to spend for anything extra. Debbie watched the men that were leaving over her rifle sights.

The tension began to drain away and a breeze from the river felt fresh and cool on my face, while watching the gang raise dust eastward away from the river. As they rode out of sight I had to smile, not for the dead lying on the ground all around, but one of paw's old sayings was, "one boy is worth one boy, two boys are worth half a boy, three boys are the equivalent to no boys at all." Not today, daddy. These three boys are equal to any three men that I know of. They did a bang up job on this river trash. They did better than most men could have or would have."

Frogs along the river were doing their mating songs and it was easy on the ears. Home came to mind. That same river produced a nice cool breeze, which kept moving fine dust by the docks as we waited for the ferry to return.

Several men watched in silence as we finally put distance between us and the eastern shore line. The ferry owner asked, "How many scaly-wags did you kill? Sonny boy, that's the first time they had their bluff called. You boys now need to be on your guard. Ole Bloody Bill Anderson is one mean hombre to have on your trail.

His wild bunch have killed way too many settlers and for much less than your outfit has. Sonny, keep your eyes on your women. Ole Bloody Bill will want them along with your outfits. A fool can see he has his eyes on your ladies.

"Sir, do you have any idea how many mangy maggots are riding in that pack of thieves?" He inferred that Bloody Bill Anderson had several more dirty rotten scoundrels in his outfit.

"Son, you better be a-worrying about what they will do if they catch up to ya. Bill has about thirty-eight hooligans riding for him and he will be pressing ya real soon. Don't dilly-dally once ya get to the far shore! Ya hear?" "Thanks for the information, mister. We will be concerned but let worry be far from us. Worry makes the young old fast. We'll be ready for Bloody Bill Anderson and his bunch, if they come looking for us.

"Son, me and Bureau Crossing is thankful for what ya did. Bad Bill is still a threat. He won't be here long; he'll be a looking for ya over west of here. Our loss is your gain. I don't envy you boys. Bad Bill Anderson leaves a bloody trail everywhere he goes.

Here we are, now be careful a getting your wagons on the dock. Hope ya do well. Go with God and go quickly while ya can. I'm going to eat my lunch over here and that will help ya some, good bye and good luck."

"Ronald you were asking what do we have planned. Well Ron, I was a hoping to persuade you and Michele to go with us up on the Sioux River and build a life there. There's good grass, good soil and lots and lots of water. It is empty land just waiting for five hard working young men to make something of it."

I thought to myself Ronald was no fool and as we talked he kept looking at his young wife and asking questions. At least he didn't say no. He looked capable enough; his hands showed he wasn't afraid of hard work. They were both intelligent and looking for a good piece of land out here on the frontier some place.

"Not too long ago we talked to an old white haired gentleman that trapped that area fifty years ago. He was a telling us of the good land and where to go if we wanted some. With the falls this land could be irrigated. He believed it would really grow crops. The grass was tall and made the buffalo fat. The man was sure cows would grow fat and sassy eating it.

Jeff, Kevin, Debbie and I are going to take a good look at it and see if it's as good as the old man says it is. We're sure he's on the level because his bubble was slap, dab in the middle.' Ha! Ha! Ha! All kidding aside, we would sure like to have you and your young wife come along with us. With you three along, it would be a whole lot more protection for us all."

Jared was persuasive and we liked what we heard. Michele suggested we think on it. Taking note of these three boys, I wondered, are they really what they seem? We will go with them for a spell for safety's sake, finding out whether they are reliable over the long haul or are they like an ice cream cone. They looked good at first but when heat comes will they melt away to a soft mushy mess?

Although what they did back at Bureau's Crossing speaks volumes to me, but will they hold up over the long haul? At first glance I'd think they are dependable people. This wife of mine was wise beyond her years. Her advice was usually pretty good. This little lady of mine doesn't get caught up in the spirit and excitement of the telling. She thinks it through and analyzes what she hears.

What we need here, honey, are cool heads." Not only did I respect this wife of mine, I really did love her. When I made a decision it would be for the good of my family. All our unborn kids had to be taken into consideration with every decision we make or don't make.

Jeff was out on guard duty and everyone carried a weapon. Michele leaned against me resting her lovely head on my shoulder. We sat together watching smoke drift up through the green leaves. Anyone looking for our camp couldn't smell our cooking fire or smoke for we had moved away from it. They would need to track us and that could be dangerous for them.

This bunch could shoot. These Jenkins boys were really good shooters. I decided I must practice with my sidearm, to be ready for anything. The revolver was the only weapon that would shoot more than twice and it looked like we might need as much firepower as possible if a tough scrape came our way.

At dark we had covered our campfire with dirt and moved our whole kit and caboodle to another campsite. That way if the wild bunch smelled the wood smoke or food smells, while traveling through, we would be long gone from that spot. This was an old Indian trick dad taught me. He said, 'use it in a bad situation', he meant like this situation was.

Western Illinois was that kind of country, in 1860, and bad men roamed the land. Those inhospitable men at the crossing could really make it dangerous for folks out here like us. With these boys lurking around out there it spelled bad news for everyone that came this way.

We kept guards out all night long. On my watch ole Ronnie moved closer to the trail and heard the pounding of many horses' hooves as they rode by in the dark. Was it the rough customers from the boat landing? I assumed it was. Will they be waiting for us up ahead somewhere? Your guess was as good as mine.

You can bank on it, but I'm sure they will not be waiting for us with open arms. That pack of thieves wants it all and killing us wasn't beyond what they would do to get it. I often wondered what made men go bad like that.

To me everything we had was expendable except my wife, Warren and the Jenkins. There's no way my pretty wife would end up at the mercy of Bloody Bill Anderson's wild bunch. I pledged my everything to keep that from happening to Michele.

Darling, I know you can't hear this, but I will be dead before they touch you. That's my pledge to you, honey. This ole Michigander moved a little closer to the four wagons and stood between two trees. From experience I knew that death hurts the ones that are the family. Yes, death hurts. My family is living proof of that. In the past it hurt them, but now the hurt is on my shoulders. Did you ever see God? Well my family has. The only warmth I get from their deaths is they're in a lot better place up in Heaven.

The sky was so clear tonight. You would think you could reach out and touch the stars overhead. All at once I caught my breath someone was moving through the trees, looking and searching. Then I recognized her, it was Michele, I made a barn owl call. She stopped dead in her tracks and scanned the darkness of the shadowy woods. She then waved as she detected my silhouette and slowly she sashayed my way.

Not a sound came to me, from the forest floor, as she made her way slowly toward my position. This lady never ceases to amaze me. "Lord, I thank you so very much for her." As she drew near I asked, in a whisper, "what are ya doing up, darling?"

"Well Honey, I felt for you and you weren't there and I was missing you a whole lot, so I came a-looking for you." She was in a nightgown and a housecoat and she slipped that warm awesome body up close to mine. My little pea picking mind wasn't on my century duties any more, but on Michele, and I struggled with the time left on my watch. All I could think of was the outlaws out there and my sweet wife beside me.

Early the next morning when the gray of false dawn lighted the eastern sky we were moving northwest away from the trail west. We had eaten a cold breakfast not trusting a fire with so many looking for us out there. Our objective was to travel further into the woods, a good distance away from the trail. We traveled through the dense heavy timber and as if that wasn't bad enough the woods were now shrouded in a thick fog. The fog made it hard to scout ahead and not get lost from the wagons.

The slow moving wagons and livestock dragged along behind. The progress was slow. Daylight made it a little better. We traveled at a snail's pace, going nowhere fast. The livestock had a mind of their own. We tied the lead cow to our last wagon and that helped keep the small herd following us as we traveled in a zig zag course back and forth through the trees.

These beautiful frontier women of ours were a big part of this operation, doing their part to keep this wagon train moving. Driving wagons over small logs and on a zig zag course we moved through the woods. Sometimes we had to snake bigger logs out of the way to let the wagons pass on through. About eleven that morning we caught a break, the fog started to dissipate and by noon the sun peeked through. We turned west pushing this outfit hard and long to put distance between us and anyone that might be following.

Five days after turning westward we pulled into the Rock Island area about two miles north of the Rock River on the mighty Mississippi River.

The Sauk and Fox Indians that were driven out of Michigan had settled here and they were not happy campers. The Sauk and Fox Indians helped the British fight the colonials, in the war of 1812 and that left a bitter taste in peoples' mouths.

"The English made a fortification on the island. Later the United States built fort Armstrong there, and then abandoned it. The fort was used in the Black Hawk War. The first white settlements on the mainland were in 1826.

During the war, that would soon come, twelve thousand southern prisoners would be confined here. Two thousand of those soldiers would die in this prison camp fighting for a cause most didn't even understand. At this point the war was just talk in the South but soon it would manifest its self into a full fledge war.

I was so proud of this sweet young wife of mine. She was holding up quite well as we tramped across the country. She wore her wide brimmed sunbonnet as we labored in the warm sun. She was quite a picture of the frontier woman. Our small group took in the magnificent sunset that evening and was it ever beautiful. We watched until the red sun sank lower and lower and finally slipped out of sight. Then darkness chased the sun west and our campfire was our main source of light.

Paddle wheel boats brought many things up the Mississippi river for people like us. This is the place where we decided to buy our supplies to take on west. All the supplies we would need and as many more as we could haul west in our two wagons, to sell. We first purchased another team of big draft horses. That gave Michele and me three teams to pull two wagons full of merchandise across the prairie. We had Molly plus the riding horses Warren picked up at Bureau Crossing.

We talked with many teamsters, mule skinners, bull whackers, plus a lot of early settlers about what we should take west with us to sell. We also hired an older teamster along the way named Benjamin Simeon. He would drive my second wagon west. Ben Simeon had a pretty good knowledge of the West and was slightly familiar with the area up by the Sioux River Falls, in Dakota Territory. This little piece of heaven that we were headed for was a good five hundred seventy-five miles west, northwest from Rock Island; it was a mighty long trip with four wagons and a bunch of kids.

When we could, we built our little herd up to one hundred twenty-five head of bred stock, plus ten bulls. It was a good start to our growing herd.

Michele was excited about this trip west. It was a new adventure into the wild frontier. I'm not happy with the confrontation that took place at the Illinois River and the threat of their presence out here.

Somewhere out there Bloody Bill Anderson was looking for us and that concerned me a whole bunch. There were way too many of them for our small group. Thank God this is a mighty big land to hide in. Jared and Benjamin were good men and I trusted them both, somewhat.

What a wonderful time we were having my man and me. Ronnie let me do about anything I wanted too on this long trip west. He allowed me to ride herd on our new fleabags if I wanted to and it was really interesting for me. I also got to drive the wagons or just ride his horse and investigate the western prairie and I loved it all. He said I must always keep the wagons in sight and not wander too far away. Ronnie was just looking out for me and I loved him for it.

At Rock Island, Ronnie had seen one of those no good pole cats from Bureau Crossing and from a short distance he watched the opportunist until the guy left Rock Island. What worried him was when the guy left town he was in a mighty big hurry to make some tracks south.

Bloody Bill Anderson and his wild bunch were somewhere out here or at least, Ronnie thought they might be. If so, our small party needed to put lots of horse and wagon tracks in the dirt and always be on our guard. I shudder when I think of Bill Anderson trying to kidnap me and haul me off to who knows where. This man was sick in the head and the only thing that would cure him is a chunk of lead in his vital parts.

All of the four wagons that we hauled across the prairie were loaded down with farm equipment and all manner of house wares, coal oil for lamps, pots and pans, harness parts, all manner of food, guns with lots of lead and powder, hoes, shovels and all kinds of odds and ends that might be needed further west, but mostly we carried food.

Ronnie had spent a lot of time selecting merchandise for resale further west. Our hope was after selling our load of merchandise somewhere for a quick profit, we could pick up more fur balls for our ranch. My Ronnie believed we had more than enough money left to build a good home on our land yet this year.

Boy-oh-boy did that sound good to me. A home of our own but where, I guess somewhere out there on the Great Western Prairie. I hope there are people close by when we build. The farther we go the fewer houses we see and we have five hundred plus miles yet to go. There are pockets of people throughout this great western wilderness and I hope we settle near some.

"We heard the plains Indians aren't all that interested in cattle, they can't see all the fuss that the white man makes about beef, but they loved buffalo meat. Now good horse flesh was a whole different story, they desire to have as many ponies as possible to help them carry their belongings as they move from place to place in this vast prairie.

Before dawn we were pulling our freight out of Rock Island. Except for that group of bad men from the Illinois River, I was enjoying our trip as I rode Molly most of the day. I enjoyed being straddle my ole saddle under these gorgeous western skies. Dad taught me to ride when I was a little girl, back in Michigan, on the farm and I enjoyed my time out here alone.

Several long days into our long trip across Iowa I decided to pick up a few more head of livestock to get started with. We'd seen some small ranches and some livestock the night before as we moved on through the area. We sent our wagons on ahead to look for a good campsite as Jared and I scouted out the land. They would fort up as soon as they found a good defensible spot on the river and wait for us there.

We followed a small tributary south and picked up about ten animals, then went up another small stream to a small farm. The house was set back into a hill. As we hailed the house like it was the custom in the West. Three farmers came out with shotguns and aimed them right at us and they didn't look any to friendly. So we were real friendly and minded our p's and q's.

They had made contact with some riders that were looking for a four-wagon outfit. That sounded a lot like us. The riders were getting pushy and these farmers pushed right back with black powder and shot, blasting one man to kingdom come and wounding another. The other riders left real sudden like. The outlaws took a couple pop shots at them from the woods, but didn't hit anything, but no way did these brothers trust us this close to their home.

They were spread out and had their weapons cocked and pointed so they could bring them to bear instantly. One big fellow kept glancing toward the wood lot as if at any time a gang of men might come riding out of there and start blazing away at them. These boys were being real careful with us and we didn't make any false moves. The ten head of young stock we had with us kept them from sending lead deep into our carcasses.

They wanted us to leave, not trusting strangers around their place. If that was Bad Bill's bunch that did this, we had to make tracks and catch up with our outfit and fast. If they caught us out in the open we could be in a peck of trouble. We ran some fat off those yearlings, moving them back along our trail. We hoped this wasn't Bad Bill's bunch out there. But we were pretty sure it was his group and they were poisoned with a hatred for us. It had to be them or why else would they spend so much time a-looking for us?

We saw about ten riders south of where we were and they were moving mighty fast toward us. We could move faster without the livestock so we left them far behind us. We put it in b-for-boogie and high tailed it out of there. Will the problems ever cease? Why is trouble always hot on my heels?

Coming up to a brush filled creek we stopped our horses and holed up for a wee bit to watch the movement of the ten men. We pulled our rifles and hunkered down by the creek bank with our horses standing in knee-deep water and their reins in our hands. We waited and watched as onward they came. We could see dust moving on the wind as we watched.

Over a hill and off a-ways we could hear the drum of their horses' hooves as onward they came.

Jared asked me, "what would you call it, if these ten men were all tied together good and tight and tossed in the deepest part of Lake Michigan.

"Is this some kind of a quiz, I have no idea Jarred. What would you call it?"

"I'd think it would be a good start, don't you?" He gave me a great big smile.

"You my friend come up with the craziest things in times of trouble."

With that said Jared fired his revolver and hit the ground at the feet of the fast moving horses. It didn't slow them down one iota. Every nerve in my body was alert and ready. With my rifle I took the first rider clean off his horse and right on the crack of my rifle, Jared fired his and two riders rolled off backwards like they were clothes lined.

Jared had hit two men with that one shot. He planned it that way and I'd never thought of such a thing. At times this ole kid wondered if he was up to living out here. These young men are thinking way ahead of me. Ron you'd better start thinking a little smarter than you do or you won't be thinking at all.

The outlaws' horses swerved to the right and headed upstream out of our sight. I think they might be trying to dig up a different plan for us. They disappeared around the bend in the stream. As quickly as they disappeared upstream we were on board our mounts and took flight out of there, heading downstream as fast as Molly could move through the wood lots and through open country. Our young stock was forgotten, for now, as we did battle on the open prairie.

In our attempt to break free we stopped, in a small woods, rested our ponies and waited an hour. We saw them about a mile off looking for us, and our horse tracks. As they drifted out of sight we high tailed it out of there in the opposite direction, moving toward the wagons in a roundabout way.

Another ten days into our five hundred seventy mile trip, Kevin Jenkins spotted a dozen men riding parallel to our wagons. Later that afternoon Benjamin Simeon located a good spot on the river with three giant cottonwoods, a couple hackberry trees, and a twelve-foot high bank along the river. We built a fort with our four wagons, putting the horses inside and kept the beef close so they couldn't be stolen or wander off.

We needed all the livestock we had and then some. With the river to our back we had a slight rise, from the front, up to our wagons. It was an ideal spot to defend. That little bunch would pay dearly if they tried to move against this little fort of ours.

Warren Drake saw them again later that afternoon and watched the desperadoes until the sun started giving us a beautiful sunset and then he returned to our little fort on the Iowa River. Warren had been shadowing those boys for the last couple hours. It looked like they were up to no good, following us like they were. We were sure in our minds, that they were part of Anderson's rag tag army. The late evening shadows were getting long and we talked it over as the red and purple sky faded into darkness.

It was so dark you could feel it and Michele came and stood close to me. At full dark, before the moon peeked over the horizon, Jared and I slipped out of camp pointing our horses back the way we'd come. Then circling to find out who these mystery men were for sure and what they were up to.

The grasshoppers in the tall grass made their summer songs and the crickets joined in. That was the only sound out here other than our horses as they moved westward. The slow clip clop of iron shoes were muffled by the long prairie grass.

When we finally found their fire, there were over thirty men in their camp. Some sleeping while most just sat around chewing the fat and shooting the breeze with each other. It looked like one of our ten lost head of young stock would be their evening meal, which was being prepared by two cooks. Jarred and I lay in the prone position until after midnight just watching.

They'd settled in for the night, all except a lone guard. He was out away from the men. I shot a long glance at Jared and said, "let's not dilly dally here any longer, let's head on back. It doesn't seem like they're going to leave here for quite a spell yet." We made our way off the hill and slipped back to our camp and we were challenged by Benjamin Simeon as we came near. "Be alert Ben they're out there with thirty men, maybe more."

Benjamin stared at me for a moment. "Ron, that's a bunch of bad boys, how did you get that many scum bags a following you?"

"We had to coax them with honey and a guarantee of a good time. Ben, they're camped off to the south a-ways. So keep a sharp look out."

"Thirty men, that's an army, Ronald!" Ben was a tough ole dude, a dyed-in-the-wool frontiers man and a wily old buck. He was a tough fighting cock from the old school and he would fight if needs be. That night we all took our turns on guard duty except the ladies. Maybe later we would need them. These ladies worked a lot during the day and needed their rest.

Long before the crack of dawn, Jared and I rode out alone to watch our unwelcome neighbors. Our little wagon train wouldn't be moving today and not until we saw what these vultures were up to, or if we came up with a good plan. Our position was very defensible, with water at our back, with a slew of weapons and all these supplies from Grand Island.

We could hold out for quite a long spell, but we wanted to get up to the falls on the Sioux River. We had so many things to do before winter set in. From a knoll, a quarter of a mile away from their camp and behind a few stunted evergreens, we watched them through the early morning mist, ghost like in their fog shrouded camp.

It didn't look like they were moving today. I guess they were going to take it easy and finish off the roast beef. Their whole crew was hunkered down. They probably figured on waiting us out.

After dawn a rider moved away from their camp. I watched him disappear toward our little fort on the river. At ten o'clock another rider left in the same direction and soon the first horseman returned and spoke with a man in a plaid shirt. I marked him for size, build, clothes, a full black beard and a small brimmed hat. If worse came to worse I would kill this man before any others.

Throughout the long day I chewed jerky, sipped water and stayed belly down in the grass napped a bit until after dark. Their small army didn't move anywhere so I returned to our wagons for the night. We must watch these saddle bums closely. No telling what they had in mind for us, but you can be sure it isn't good for they were spending a lot of time waiting for us to make our move first.

Michele was nervous about me being gone so long. Her tender love showed through as we hugged and enjoyed each other while eating our supper. Newlyweds did this kind of thing although her worried blue eyes stayed glued to me throughout the evening. In bed she asked, "Ronnie, will we ever be free of Bill Anderson and his threats?"

"Honey, Bill is crazy for power and money. He will stay on us until he gets what he wants or we stop him and I'm not sure we can. He has a big outfit sizing us up."

Talking with the group I said, "Truthfully I don't know for sure what they're up to. It's no good you can bet on that. If you ask me, I'd say they want to catch us out in the open prairie. That would make it a whole lot easier to pick us off and they have lots of time to do it if that is their plan. I'm quite sure they are scanning our camp trying to find out what we will do next. They run a loose camp over behind those hills.

They act like they own the whole prairie and with that group they probably could. But acting like that they are playing into our hands. In my mind I'm working on a surprise party for them."

Jared agreed, "Some of those fools out there are from Illinois. From what I see they don't know we know they're out there. That my friend is to our advantage, maybe we ought to shoot up their camp. We could take several of our new muzzle loading rifles and hit them at dawn and shake them up a little bit and make them nervous."

I got my two cents worth in right there. "Jared we should try to steal their horses or run them off and put them a foot. Then hustle on out of here taking all the horses we can with us; that my friend should slow them down considerably.

"Okay Ronald, it sounds like a good idea to me. If we're going to swallow a frog we shouldn't stand around and look at it too long, but get at it right away, maybe tonight."

"Alright Jared, let's get on it tonight, the sooner the better."

Benjamin and the guys had fortified our little campsite by moving logs up around the wagons. We could shoot from behind them if we needed to. It was quite defensible now. Both ladies were a surprise to us. Their fathers had taught them to shoot and shoot well. The unanswered question was could Michele defend herself if it came to a fight. I'm not sure I wanted my wife killing anyone, good or bad. Would it change her sweet disposition? One never knows what shooting someone will do to a person's soul. Would it change her whole outlook on life? To tell you the truth I'm not sure I want to test it out.

Jared, Jeff, Warren and I would plan a big surprise for that evil company out there. First before we left we would need to harness our horses and get ready to move out with the wagons loaded. Then try to steal their horses and shoot up their camp then beat it back here and if all was successful make a mad dash out of here before they could make a try at any of our horses or the ones we steal tonight.

They have worried us long enough with what they might do to our families. If we could put them a foot and throw a scare into them, at the same time, that should give us a chance to flee to the northwest and away from this outlaw menace.

After midnight I kissed Michele with a long embrace and the four of us eased on out of camp like a pack of hungry wolves on the hunt. Long before dawn we moved into a position to make our attack.

"Whoa Jeff, Jarred, Warren, wait up a bit." The hair on my arm stood up and goose bumps covered my arms from my wrist to my shoulder. Standing stock still and straining my ears I heard a hoot owl that didn't sound just right and then a Whipp-er-will's song that was just a bit too loud. Hunkering down we waited to see what was up. We were too far east for Sioux Indians, at least I thought so. It must be Indians, but what were they up to? We all hunkered down on that hill and waited.

All of a sudden we saw shadows below us. We watched them as they moved closer and closer to the outlaw camp. The camp guard was not alert and ended up without a whole lot of hair left on his head. His body must have looked like a pincushion with arrows sticking out all over him.

These Indians, whoever they are, were after the horses. The night guard must have made a noise as he died for the camp came alive in the dark below and loud voices were heard clearly on this cloudy late summer's night. The Indians were moving into Bloody Bill's camp from every direction and the horses were their targets.

At this time we put our two cents worth into this little drama that was unfolding before us. As the Indians moved toward the picket line and released the string of ponies we pumped slug after slug into the outlaws' camp trying to help the Indians make their escape with Anderson's mounts. With the Indians' help this bad bunch would be left afoot way out here in no wheresville.

After firing three rifles each and emptying our revolvers, we mounted up and high tailed it out of there as fast as we could ride. The small army was scattering to the four winds and taking cover, wherever they could find it, as their horses were being driven westward out of their camp. These Indians had helped us and maybe saved our bacon.

Hustling on back to our camp they were ready to depart. We must leave before those cutthroats think of our horses and try to steal them from us. In less than ten minutes we were making wheel, horse and cattle tracks northwest and fast, putting lots of distance between Bloody Bill Anderson and our horses.

Our teams were frisky and wanted to run. Benjamin let them have their heads and we covered some ground in a mighty big hurry. This man was a real horseman and knew the teams. Jeff and Jared worked their teams to keep up, while Warren and Kevin moved the fur balls in pursuit of the wagons. All eyes searched our back trail for signs of Bill and his boys.

We hadn't forgotten those pesky Indians that took the outlaws' horses. Where were they? Ahead, maybe, waiting for our horses and us? I was feeling like meat in a sandwich with the Indians ahead and Bloody Bill's bush whackers behind us and us in the middle. We were truly in kind of a pickle. We must be alert to all the possibilities and keep these wagons moving. Who knows what awaits us as we travel toward Dakota Territory off to the west?

Later that afternoon we saw horses with mounted Indians watching us from a distant high hill, off to the north. Watching us with arms extended. Then after a moment we saw an arm wave then they skedaddled northward over the hill and out of sight.

"Ben, what was that all about?"

"Ron, it appears to me they were a saying, 'thanks' for something or other. Sioux don't often say thanks from a distance."

The Indians had left us eight yearling beef in our path, beef they'd picked up as they departed the outlaw camp, they were our beef. The same young stock we had lost to the outlaws a few days ago.

We spent thirty more long days of travel toward Sioux Falls, when we came upon a skeleton of a wagon that had been looted and stripped of everything of value, two wheels were missing and the other two were without spokes and a metal rims.

This put us on guard again. What had happened here? Seeing this made me want to continue practicing with my colt revolver and try to be ready for any trouble that might come our way. This is a wild and woolly land full of many dangers. What was I getting my wife and me into out here?

This land was full of things that were not quite what I expected to find out here in the territories. How many gangs of cutthroats were out here killing and living off innocent people? Bloody Bill Anderson was way more than this ole kid wanted to come up against here or anywhere.

SIOUX FALLS

Another five long days of hard travel and we sighted the Sioux River below the falls. We drifted north to have a look see at this little settlement in the middle of nowhere. The little town was setting all alone out here on the Great Western Prairie. This small settlement was called Sioux Falls and it was in Dakota Territory. It had a general store, blacksmith-livery and saloon plus five houses.

At one house they served meals and rented two rooms plus space with a bed in a woodshed. At this time they served no meals in Sioux Falls. The small town had little to no food. It had some milk, eggs, flour, buffalo meat, and potatoes and not much else.

This place looked like it was at the end of its rope, and their fingers were slipping. I'd seem busier places in my time that's for sure. As we dismounted it was good to see friendly people way out here. We entered the store to have a look around and the shelves were nearly empty. A young man and his wife greeted us. "Hello. Lovely day isn't it! May we help you with something?"

"No, but maybe we can help you. Our wagons are loaded down with supplies and we're looking to sell most of it. Are you interested in making a purchase?" Lilly and Fred Miller stared at us in unbelief for about thirty seconds without saying a word.

"Sir, we have very little money on hand. Three months ago Fred started east to buy supplies in Des Moines and was robbed of all the money we had, plus the horses and wagon. He was lucky they let him live. Now we have no way to purchase the needed supplies this little settlement of Sioux Falls needs.

We have some money but not enough to restock the shelves of our little store; sorry we have so little on hand. We have neither horses nor wagons to fetch any food with, but have generated some cash, certainly nowhere near enough to keep us afloat. It doesn't look like we'll be able to make it through the winter. As you can see we're close to being out of business here."

Michele had her arm through mine as we talked. Jared kept shooting glances at his wife. Our hearts went out to the Millers and their bad luck. It was clear they needed lots of help. The Millers had extended credit and it was slow coming in.

We left the store wondering if we could somehow help them out. We strolled from house to house and from business to business, talking and getting acquainted with the people. Asking where good land could be had. As we talked about things Michele always brought up the Millers.

The answers to her questions were they are good kids, but way to generous. It was a bad break for the town and them being robbed. Sioux Falls really needed them and the general store to stay in business out here..

As we sat around the campfire that night eating and drinking hot coffee, we discussed what would happen to this burg if it lost the general store, if people had no place to get supplies. Every town needed a good general store. But how could the Millers hang on out here?

Later Michele and I talked of leasing the supplies to Fred and his wife, leaving them at their store, on consignment. Des Moines was four hundred seventy-five miles round trip back east and that's a far piece. Would we even have time enough to make a trip there and back before bad weather set in? Michele and I talked well into the night about what we should or shouldn't do. She wanted to let them use our supplies and pay us later. This softhearted woman would give everything away to those in need. I had a heart, although I wouldn't go that far.

In my heart I knew she was right. We needed a store here in Sioux Falls if we were going to stay on here, that much we knew. She wanted me to accompany Mr. Miller to Des Moines and help protect his load. We needed lumber anyway. This way we could kill two birds with one stone. Make one trip to Des Moines, get supplies for Fred and Lilly and pick up the needed lumber for our house.

This woman of mine had a heart and she lived by the golden rule, 'do unto others as you would have others do into you'. It was a good rule. I guess we needed to practice it a whole lot more. Michele suggested we ask the Millers if they would take these supplies on loan or consignment. "Darling, Debbie Jenkins and I could stay with Lilly while you men make a trip back East.

You could leave Benjamin, Kevin and Warren to help here and watch the livestock. First find a ranch sight and we'll lay a rock foundation for our house while you're gone." Michele had thought this through and it was a real good plan. Everyone agreed we must not let this store go out of business, if we must take it over ourselves. "Well my sweet lady don't you ever take your hands out of God's hand or we could end up a creek"

"Mr. Holden, no big brawny man can pull my hand away from my Lord's. We're both holding on real tight to each other. We must always stay close to Him and love Him for what He did for us and what He is going to do in the future."

The next morning we presented our plan to the Jenkins and Millers. Fred and Lilly listened and she lost it crying uncontrollably. Fred placed an arm around her and the crying got louder. Her unspoken fears had near overwhelmed her and hearing our generous plan she was falling apart from the inside out. This lady down deep inside has one fine heart maybe just a little to tender for the frontier. Now God had sent someone to help them out when all seemed lost. These three young women were like old friends from that day forward.

On our second day at Sioux Falls, by afternoon, the supplies were piled high on the store porch. The three ladies were taking inventory and marking the stock as it was unloaded. They had the younger boys and Fred Miller carrying things inside and putting them on shelves most of the afternoon.

After they finished we left, Sioux Falls, to look for a good piece of land to build our ranch on. As we left town, folks came flocking in to purchase supplies for their families. I guess they had been out of most everything for quite a spell. They would eat well tonight if they had money in their pockets.

Looking up river, with Fred's guidance, we found a great place to build on and start our ranch. We marked out a place to build our new home. Michele fell in love with the great view of the many falls. Jared, Debbie and Jeff located a good piece of land just downstream from us. With a little bit of work both places could be irrigated.

For lack of money and time, this winter everyone would live in our home. Next summer they would, if they could, build their own place. It just might have to be a shoddy. Jared really did come out here on a shoestring. He said he had enough money for a few cows, in the spring.

Debbie keeps saying, "God will supply." Somehow I feel He will. Our plan is to haul enough lumber to build a house and a bunkhouse for the single men.

My hope is to buy more cows after we return with the lumber and supplies from Iowa. We would need help bringing the supplies back to our ranch. These boys were quite willing to help out if they could. The Millers said that the supplies were a whole lot cheaper in De Moines then over at the military post at Fort Pierre. We were happy to go to the cheapest place to buy what we needed.

My lovely wife and I were close and we loved touching. This love affair of ours is good for us and we held hands often. This was a good night for these two love birds. As a lover she was learning how to please her man. My goal in life was to love and cherish her.

This ole Michigander would try hard to provide a good life for her. Oh how I loved this woman of mine. I knew the first few years would be rough getting a working ranch up and producing a good living for us. It just wouldn't happen overnight.

Michele loves this country but misses her family back in Michigan. Contentment is slowly seeping into her soul. In spite of all that's gone wrong, this girl had courage and faced each day with a measure of tranquility in her life.

As we four guys moved out of the Sioux Falls area and headed east, it looked like the sun was climbing out of a huge hole off to the east. It was a clear, warm; sunny day, a good time to be alive. All day long we rolled through the empty prairie toward Des Moines, two hundred thirty-five miles away, we made excellent time with rested horses and three empty wagons.

Each day we pushed our horses eastward always thinking of the cold winters out here on the plains. We grained our horses each day at noon to keep up their strength and stamina. We didn't stop at noon so they couldn't graze, but kept shoving miles and lots of prairie grass behind us. We kept our wagons rumbling and rolling eastward across the wide open prairie.

We were making good time. Jared, Jeff, Fred and I worked well together. Each night we made a small fort with our wagons, usually on a stream. Our big horses were needed quite badly out here. There is nowhere to replace them if they are stolen. We would have to go back East some place to pick up another big team.

The Sioux always needed horses; for the Sioux Indians moved a lot following the buffalo and it took many horses to move a teepee and all their family possessions. Hides and poles were heavy and it took many of them to make a big teepee. A poor family of Sioux that has only a few mustangs will only have a small teepee to live in and very few belongings; in that case everyone would carry something except the braves. Their small mustangs only weighed about six to eight hundred pounds.

The braves out here needed to be fresh and ready for trouble at anytime. A tired brave couldn't put up much of a fight against a fresh enemy. Braves were not lazy, and all worked to stay alive out here. Life is not easy for poor Sioux Indian families. They need to defend their family to the death.

More horses would make life better for the family. Horses would make it possible to have a bigger teepee, plus many more things to make life better. So protecting our horses was a priority out here in Sioux Country. The Sioux Indian wouldn't trade a life for a horse, but you had better keep a close watch on your horseflesh.

In Des Moines after we had finished buying lumber for our house and bunkhouse, and the supplies we needed, our big wagons were loaded to the gills with supplies. We picked up several newspapers, old and new and off we went to visit with the town folks, picking up any other news that we could. In our travels I located some books and purchased fifteen for Michele to read on these long winter nights ahead.

The word was out that some Indians or whites had killed off a whole wagon train south of here and drove away the wagons while leaving bodies, with throats cut, scalped and women raped and killed, all over the battle area. The sheriff and several men rode down there to have a look see and buried them. He said to us, "Whoever it was, they somehow gained admittance to their wagon train camp and ended up murdering men, women and children.

They then drove off with what looked like five wagons and all their horses and livestock. It was a pretty messy place with blood everywhere and people rotting in the late summer sun. The buzzards had been feasting on the dead carcasses when the posse found them. The sheriff thought it must be whites, but he said, "Why would whites do such an appalling thing?" Stopping into his office I told him all about our little episode with that gang of thugs at the Illinois River and later as they followed us west. "Sir, these animals would do about anything to get gain".

The sheriff wasn't so sure. I thought to myself, what did Indians want with wagons, firewood maybe, so I told him so? It didn't sound like Indians to me. Even greenhorn settlers wouldn't let several Indians into their midst. No way could I come up to his way of thinking. No, it didn't sound all that much like Indians to me. It sounded like the white man's work to me and Bloody Bill Anderson was my prime suspect.

At least that group was a low down bunch of men, on the dodge, like those in Illinois. These men would kill, rape, steal and scalp folks for their own gain. Those inconsiderate, lowdown, no good white men would prey on people anywhere they found them. The thought came to me; did we contribute to this massacre by helping the Sioux steal their horses? I hope not. Or would they have done this dastardly deed anyway?

A bad hombre like Bad Bill Anderson and his bunch would use any excuse to do their dirty work. Yes, Bloody Bill was my prime suspect in this colossal catastrophe. We must be on guard for they are mounted again and out doing their contemptible work. Their cold-blooded attacks are being perpetrated on decent folks. They're outrageous to say the least. We must be alert and prepared for them, for they are out there.

I'm real tired of those treacherous thugs working us over. Just how long will they be allowed to do their dirty deeds unhindered? They had me kind of worried now. "Oh Lord when will this all end?"

I informed the guys of my thoughts and with haste we shoved off from Des Moines making our way toward home. Our ninth day out of town, we noticed a lone rider waiting for us up ahead on a small hill. I got that feeling again, as the hair on my arms stood up and goose bumps popped up all over my arms and neck giving me the heebie-jeebies.

Raising an arm in warning I rode my gray to within a hundred and fifty yards of him, stopped the gray and waited with Hawkins in hand. My double barrel was at my fingertips. The rider stayed put for a long moment then slowly ventured off the hill, riding our way. Ole Ron was like a bowstring strung a bit too tight, but this kid was ready, with his pistol loose in its holster he waited. Okay Ron loosen up a little. Come on relax.

As the lone rider came near I looked him over pretty good. He was white and I didn't remember seeing him back in Illinois. He rode to within twenty feet so I shifted my rifle to my left hand and placed my right hand close to my colt revolver. I would save the Hawkins; I might need it for long range shooting. Could someone be behind that hill waiting for us?

With a quick glance I checked each and every cap on each nipple. The hill was too far away to kill someone with anything but my rifle. I was ready for whatever he might try to do. The man came to a stop, looked at me and said, "Howdy."

"Howdy." The man had a thin mustache and a couple days growth of face whiskers, twenty-five years old, maybe younger with a pleasant look about him. A chewed stub of an unlit cigar was in his mouth. He looked to the left and spit an amber stream of juice onto the ground.

"Where ya headed, son?"

"Back home."

"Where's that?"

"Why do you ask?"

"Well our outfit is headed the same direction as you are and I wondered if we could move our wagons in with yours and travel together for safety sake? As you know this is Iowa and it is full of Indians and unsavory people who would do a man harm."

"Sir, where are you from?"

"I'm from Indiana, the southern part."

"What's your name?"

"They call me Doc, Doc Barns. What's yours?"

"Ronald." I was still being evasive.

"Well Ronald, what do you think?"

"I don't think so Doc. You see back in town we heard someone had stolen a wagon train and killed off everyone, men, women and kids and I…"

"Did they? Wow! All the more reason we should travel together for your safety and ours, with dangerous people like that sneaking around stealing and killing. What's this world coming too? It's getting so you can't trust anyone."

The man read my mind. This kid watched him closely and said, "Doc, I don't know you. I don't know if your guilty or not." He furrowed his brow, and moved that dead cigar to the other side of his mouth, while shifting in his saddle, and then nervously he chewed on that unlit stogy and then spit again. He then got out a match and lit the nasty thing. Then like magic his frown turned upside down into a big ole grin.

"Well son, if we can't join you may we tag along, oh say a quarter mile behind ya? Then if we get attacked we could join up and fight them off."

"No Sir! You go your way and we'll go ours. We'll take no chances with you or anyone else for that matter." For a long moment he looked at me making a decision in his mind, what it might be I did not know.

"Okay Ronald, I understand, nice meeting ya anyway. Have a good day." He whirled his buckskin and at a gallop, off he went to the south. I stayed put as he rode out of sight, and then I whirled my gray and returned to the three freight wagons.

This Doc Barns whoever he is, is one smooth gent. I wanted to believe him but no way could I, not with what we knew about the massacre that took place south of here awhile back. We have too much at stake to make a foolish mistake like that. Michele is waiting for me and I will see her again. If it means I must start killing Bad Bill's bunch on sight.

Turning our wagons more to the north we picked up the pace somewhat. and moved our big wagons long after dark with Jared on horseback scouting ahead. When Jared returned to the wagons we decided I should ride south and scout out their wagons, down there, and see if I could find them, and see if Doc was on the level or playing a con game on us.

Long before dawn's early light I had eaten and was raising dust searching for the other wagon train to our south. By noon, with great care, I sighted their campfire smoke way off in the distance. They were not moving. My suspicions were well founded. There were no females or children to be seen. While I watched several men left the encampment, some on riding horses and some on workhorses, most rode bare back. Twelve riders in all were moving north.

Returning to my horse with haste I followed the twelve, staying well back and out of sight until they came upon our wagon tracks. Then they followed our wagon tracks, so I skirted to the east coming up on their flank and from a small hill; I shot one of their riding horses dead where it stood.

To my surprise six men on saddle horses sunk spurs deep into their mounts. Their ponies dug dirt as they pursued me, frantically making their way toward my position. Molly left that knoll in a flat out run. I urged her on for I was kind of anxious to leave that place myself.

My single shot rifle was empty and their long guns were still loaded. I did have my shotgun and revolver, but for long range shooting I needed my muzzle loader rifle. Trying to load on the run was an exercise in futility. Putting gun powder down the barrel was okay, but putting a chunk of lead and a silk patch down the barrel was a test.

Coming over the crest of a hill I stopped the gray to blow. Got the cap in place, sighted in the lead rider and touched it off. The lead rider swayed then grabbed the front of his saddle and held on, as his horse swerved to the left. He handled that okay, but when his mount dug in his heals trying to stop, his rider tumbled from his seat and lay still in the tall grass. They slowed to watch this but then spurred their horses onward again.

I turned Molly and hot-footed it out of there loading my rifle as I went. What a hard tedious job from the back of a fast moving horse. Over three hills I could see a line of brush.

There must be water there and some kind of cover. If I could find a place of concealment where they had to come in close, my double barrel shot gun could be brought into this action then.

My gray mare was doing fine. She'd been rode a lot and her muscles were in good shape. She had wind for this kind of work. Topping the second hill it looked, to the outlaws, like I had gotten my rifle reloaded again. Pulling my gray girl to a stop I turned my horse to face them. Then the riders went every which way and hurried back behind their hilltop.

Slipping over the hill so that only my head and shoulders could be seen I waited as Molly caught her breath and I finished reloading my rifle. These men had a healthy respect for my shooting ability and I took advantage of it. When the gray mare was ready to run we left that hill and headed for that stream up ahead. When I crested the next hill the outlaws were nowhere to be seen. These boys thought I was ready to shoot and that was all it took to put a scare into them.

Ole Ronnie slipped that gray lady into the brush and waited and watched. Soon the riders were on the hill just south of this line of trees. Some of the yellow leaves were on the ground. But there were plenty still hanging on the limbs, enough to conceal Molly and me down here in this creek bed. I held her nose so she wouldn't make a noise and reveal our position.

They split up two going upstream, two down and one stayed on the hill with just his head showing, scanning the little valley up and down the creek. A quarter of a mile up and downstream both pairs of men separated. One on either side of the stream and were slowly, ever so slowly making their move toward each other and my position. Soon I would have no place to go without at least three men seeing me and only one shot in my muzzle loader.

Downstream the banks were higher so through the water we plodded heading that way. Then all of a sudden I aroused a sleeping black bear and he headed downstream, in a mighty big hurry, right at the two men coming my way on the creek banks. This was my chance so I mounted and followed that black fellow as fast as Molly would let me pursue him.

Molly didn't want to be anywhere near that critter and she was acting up herself. She didn't want to get to close to the black bear, but with reins slapping and my heels kicking her she reluctantly followed with ears up and running sideways most of the time fighting her bit. Her tail was in the air as she ran on.

The two outlaws downstream were having problems of their own. One rider was on the ground and his horse was making a run for it. The other rider should have joined the rodeo. As I looked back his horse was sun fishing and his rider was hanging on for dear life. Around a bend, in the creek, I came up out of that streambed and rounded a hill.

The gray lady had run a fair piece so I slowed her to a ground eating pace then to a trot for awhile. As I rode toward our wagons I kept watching for any pursuit. Momentarily I had forgotten about the rest of that bunch, but they hadn't forgotten me, not one iota.

As I broke over a hill I heard a rifle shot and poor Molly made a trail of dust heading for the wagons that were up ahead somewhere. This kid was riding hard and fast and those boys were pushing me for all they were worth. Then seeing the wagons up ahead I headed for that small opening and dropped to the ground inside the circled of wagons.

I had run amuck with those outlaws and had somehow slipped free. Molly had quickened her pace on her own. As I looked back I counted my blessings many times over. I was trapped with no place to run and that bear had sprung me free.

I'd gotten back to the wagons and my chances looked a whole lot better than they did a short while ago. Jared stood watching, rifle in hand, then took a quick shot and they scrambled to get out of firing range.

A discussion quickly took place, inside the enclosure. We decided that four men could hold them off for a bit and make them pay dearly. But these twelve could hold us in this place until the whole gang caught up to us. No way did we like the situation we were in.

To leave the four big wagons here would put our community in danger of running out of food this winter and that was not acceptable. What's a man to do? We sat right smack dab between a rock and a hard place.

Michele was always on my mind and I wanted what was best for her. My wife needed me to look after her and build that home to raise our kids in. She was always eager to pull her own weight in any situation. This women of mine is more than just a wife, she is a friend and a lover. Down deep she has a fine heart and love flows out to me at all times. It's true I needed this woman a whole lot.

Our immediate decision was to fight this group of outlaws. We set up our temporary fort on a hill near a small stream, and took time to fill our water barrels. We were now ready for a three or four day siege. I wasn't all that happy with the way things were shaping up but we had to make do with what we had.

With our three wagons in a fairly tight triangle, except for a place for a horse to squeeze in and out, we waited with rocks piled up for a barricade to fire from. We also dug pits to add to our protection. We opened a box of twelve rifles. That gave us four rifles each. First we cleaned them, loaded each one and checked our shotguns and handguns.

After building a fire, we ate a good meal, while we could. That Fred was a great cook. The food was always tasty. Breakfast consisted of cackle berries (eggs), prairie trout (bacon), flapjacks (pancakes) and hot black brew (coffee).

This time around we were a lighthouse for all to see, high on a hill. About three eighths of a mile away we saw them glassing us from a hilltop. All that day they didn't come. What in the world was holding them up? At noon and six we watered our horses at the creek, saving our drinking water for later. This would extend our time to do battle.

Early the next morning Doc Barns came riding our way. "Hey you boys, what's up? Was that you that was a-firing at some of our men folks? They thought you were outlaws out to kill them. That's why they chased ya. One ole boy got shot, why did you do that?"

"Doc, what is your outfit doing this far north?"

"We're a-following you. We're going to live where you live, if its good land. We don't mean any harm. We're just folks looking for some good land to settle on."

"Doc, we don't want your murdering bunch anywhere around us so just high tail it on out of here, before someone gets hurt bad. I told ya already we didn't want your company. Doc, if you want to know the truth we don't trust your outfit one iota. A wagon train with thirty men and no women just isn't the kind of people we want or need living in our area." (I didn't want to say town.)

"Okay boys, if that's the way you want it. We were only looking for a good place to call home. Some place with good grass and water. After we get settled we will send back East for our women folks."

"Don't give us that bull crap Doc, just find a place out here and stake a claim. Don't be a bugging us or following us as we move across the country. Go find your own land." Doc left our hill and an hour later the gang started sniping at us. Their shots didn't come all that close, although they stayed at it for nearly an hour. The jig was up and out in the open now. No more pretense of being good people.

Later that night I slipped out of camp to check out their intentions. About two miles south they had circled their wagons and posted two guards. I'm guessing when they lost their horses to the Indians, awhile back, it had made them a bit more cautious.

The horses were inside their wagon enclosure and hobbled so they couldn't run off. There would be no driving these horses off this time. Are our lives ever going to get straighten out for us? It's been one thing right after another.

As I looked back on our past it all started at that barn dance way back in March. Seems like all this trouble stems from that Grange Barn Dance back in Mid-Michigan. It hasn't been all bad; Michele has been good for me. I guess I've got to take the good with the bad; she's a wonderful part of my life now. As I day dreamed about that awesome wife of mine, a horseman left the outlaw wagons and was beating a path in the direction of our camp. I wondered now what?

Jared Jenkins would be on guard duty so I didn't worry all that much. Jared was one man who could take care of himself in most any situation. Of all the men I knew I would pick him in a tight spot. That pistol of his was faster than greased lighting and true to its mark.

I was getting good but I don't think I'll ever be that fast. But with a rifle no one I know can shoot with more skill then this ole country boy can. Dad did a good job and taught me well. He said, "I was good even better than he was." I wish he were here now to lend us a hand.

Easing on off the hill I loaded leather, kicked my horse into motion and slipped quickly away, following the man, keeping him in sight as best as I could. He ended up on a hill close to our camp. I found a good spot, on a hill, a short distance from him and with binoculars I watched the onlooker and searched the surrounding summits for more scumbags.

The early morning sun was killing the dark of night and lighting up the eastern sky as his relief came he left the hilltop. The rising sun spilled its morning light onto the western hills and it was warm on my back as I lay on my stomach, eye-balling the enemy.

Later I moved, staying under cover while circling and came into our camp from the opposite direction. As we talked things over, our new plan was for me to take out the night watchers and that would allow our big wagons to make a beeline north, north east as fast and as far as possible.

When the guys saw trouble a coming they could move into another defensible spot as quickly as possible. We needed to try a different approach and make something happen if we could. This ole dude slept the day away. It was pitch black as I slipped out of camp and headed in a roundabout direction toward the lone gunman that watched our camp from the hill top.

Our plan was to get rid of the outlaw that watched us and send the wagons a high tailing it on out of here, with me as a rear guard. We wouldn't move toward home but head north first. We wouldn't lead this riff raff toward our ranch. We must do something but nothing foolhardy.

It was Doc Barnes that was hunkered down a watching our camp. He never heard me so with my revolver I clunked him alongside his head and took a five foot leather lace and tied his hands behind his back, then with a phosphorus match, I signaled our camp and they signaled me back. By the dim light of night, they left their hilltop camp and fled the scene.

Retrieving Doc's horse, I headed downhill and tied Doc to some brush and warned him not to make a sound. I decided to gag him anyway, and then warned him again, "If you try to give me away or make any trouble I'll put a bullet in ya, that much you can count on. If you make noise I'll believe you are trying to get me killed and then you will find out if your friends care enough to help you survive. My guess is they'll let you die out here.

Think about it Doc would your family like to see you again, would you care to see your mother before death comes to you. Doc, 'If you don't want to be counseled then there is no way you can be helped.' It's a time to listen Doc Barns, because I'm tired of messing around."

I'm glad it was dark out; my family invaded my mind as my Adam's apple stuck in my throat, tears flooded my eyes and pain tore at my heart. Man-oh-man did I hurt! Will I ever get through this? Michele was all I had left out here and she needed me and people would die before I would leave her alone to shift for herself.

It was easy to see I hadn't put my family away yet. They just wouldn't stay in their graves. They were still wandering around in my mind singing, dancing and fellowshipping in there. I still loved them but I needed my peace to grow and fill my whole being. "Lord, please take from me this troubled mind, put me at ease and get me back to my wife safe and sound."

One hour before dawn I left Doc and on foot headed up the hill to watch for the next night guard to come. Half an hour before daylight he came slowly toward the hill, head moving left, then right, searching for Doc. Fifty yards from the top he stopped and in a low voice he said, "Hey Doc." When Doc didn't answer he began scanning the hilltop. His eyes located the scrub pines and he stopped for a long moment and said, "Hey Doc, you asleep?"

He paused a moment more, took a few steps, stopped again, fixed his eyes on the pines with a long hard scrutiny, then quick as you please up came his rifle and he sighted it on me.

That's when I touched mine off. The slug took him in the chest. I heard my lead strike flesh and he was dead when he hit the grass. Killing wasn't in my nature. It didn't come easy for me like it did for some men. I have to stop thinking about it, but the poor man is dead never to see his loved ones again.

Straitening up, I squared my shoulders and pulled myself together, then loaded the guy on his horse all the time checking to see if someone might be coming. Tears slid down my cheeks. I would wipe them away with my coat sleeve and they would reappear like magic.

I got everything loaded on his horse and took him down slope to where Doc Barns was located. In the meager light he stared a long time at me as I covered this man with rocks from the dry wash.

DOC BARNS

As I watched ole Ronald Holden filled his leather saddle with his backside and followed after the three wagons, out aloud he said, "Why must life be like this? Why do men turn out this way?" I slowly urged my horse and my friend's horse up beside Ron's and cleared my throat.

I took a long glance his way and said, "It's because we sin continually. It turns our hearts to stone and away from God. He has a plan for us, but we don't want Him to interfere with our lives so we turn our back on Him."

My eyes focused on Doc Barns for a bit. How did this man know about God? If he knew the ways of God, why was he out here doing what he was doing? The man must be confused. His folks would really be sad if they knew what he was up to. I found myself just staring at him and I turned my head back to the front.

I watched Ronald's back as he rode ahead of me in the late afternoon sun. The high hills were basking in a red glow of the bright sun. Oh the magic of those beautiful western sunsets. The sight was awesome; you could see fantastic colors in the prairie grass on the eastern side of the hills. This lovely land had its share of these beautiful but lonely sunsets. They were lonely when you had no one special to share them with.

Ronald and I watched a Red Tailed Hawk over head. It was making its late afternoon swoop for food. Soon the sun would drag the darkness onto the wide prairie and the stars and moon would light our way. All of a sudden a White Tail buck exploded from the brush by the creek. What I saw, I wouldn't have believed if you would have told me. That six-gun jumped from its resting place on his hip and a slug hit the buck in the head on his second jump, was it luck or was this kid that good?

Before I saw it happen I would have laughed at you, for the telling of it. Even now after seeing it, it puzzled and befuddled me. Who was this kid anyway? With those tears, surely not a hardened killer. He was stern but also had a soft spot in his heart. This kid was determined to do what he must for his friends and his family and I kind of admired that of him.

I thought back to our first meeting. How I'd thought of drawing on him. This ole boy would be gone to the happy or unhappy hunting grounds, just a pushing up yellow flowers. All thoughts of escape now vanished from my mind. This kid would have killed me on the spot and I would have lain dead there on the ground, never to see my family again.

What was I doing out here anyway? Ma taught me better than this. Oh the terrible things men do when they're hungry and away from home. Man-oh-man how easily I let myself be led into this life of crime. I'm glad ma couldn't see me the way I am now.

Thinking to myself, I remembered saying, "One job, get some money and scram on out of here. Pressure and threats keep men in line and now it's been way to long. I hated what I did. I've killed no one while going along for the ride. This little trip with, what's his name, just may be my only way out. I can't turn the clock back, yesterday is gone. What would dad say about it? I'm oh so glad ma can't see me living like I am. She would cry her eyes out and this kid wouldn't be able to look my folks in the eyes.

This kid, what's his name, John, no Ronald? He was good with a knife. He had the deer skinned and boned in about half an hour, while I sat my horse. He was even now loading it into a gunnysack with a ground sheet over it. He hummed a song as he worked. I remembered that song he sang from church as a little boy. What was it? Ah yes. "Jesus loves me this I know." Oh how long it's been since I thought of those simple words that mean so much when you're so far from God.

It seemed like we were not trying to catch up with the wagons. He would set his horse high on a side hill with just his head over the top scanning our back trail. Death would come to anyone following us I knew that now. For this man had three rifles, a shotgun and a revolver loaded and on his horse. It also looked like he had an extra cylinder for his sidearm. That deadly, lighting fast revolver was slung on his hip and ready for action.

Thinking back I felt sad, the only enjoyable time I had was the solitary moments I spent away from that bad element I rode with. It was the only peace I had in my life. Well I've saddled this bronc and now I don't want to ride him anymore.

With darkness coming on, the kid did a strange thing. He left the trail, for about a mile, went into a pucker brush thicket, along a creek, and built a fire of fair size. The kid laid dead Cottonwood logs across it to make it last and then left. It was a decoy for Bloody Bill Anderson and his bunch, if they came this way. Bloody Bill Anderson is turning this expedition into

Iowa, into a bloody killing spree and I wanted out before he finds out I was just faking it and haven't killed anyone.

"If you hear me talking Lord, please help me find my way out of this mess, I've got myself into. I know I have no right to ask you for anything with the life I've been living. I'm sorry Lord. Protect these boys Bloody Bill Anderson wants dead. These boys are working hard to make something of their lives and Bill wants to destroy it.

Bill and his gang will try to kill them and take it away and then squander it all away on wine, women and cards." It's like Pa used to say, "If it comes too easy, then it will go easy. Easy to come then easy to go, if you work for it, then you will appreciate it." It isn't right but these young men with Bill Anderson will probably die out here and whoever is waiting for them will never know what happened to them. After the Turkey Buzzards get through with them all that will be left will be dry bleached out bones in the prairie grass somewhere.

Bad Bill Anderson will make it look like Indians did it, scalping and mutilating their bodies. But I know something he doesn't know. He may have a little trouble killing these kids. They're not green or foolish, not by a long shot. Bill is an evil, evil man. He desires it all, livestock, wagons, cows, ranch and for sure those two good looking ladies.

They are driving him to spend a lot of time chasing this outfit. He talks and talks about those two young women at the river crossing. I feel sorry for them if he ever gets his hands on them. My hope is that these boys get away scot free from ole Bloody Bill and his bunch. If I get free I ought to just ride off and try to make it to some place, find a good job and start over. Buy as many cows as I can. This life of crime is no life for anyone.

I should but the Lord knows I won't. I should've done something a long time ago. Well should have just doesn't get it done. This mixed up ole dude exhaled a long breath of air and pushed away that wishful thinking. Bill Anderson was a mean, cantankerous, no good killer and this ole boy isn't going to cross him. No I'll keep my place and live. Bill has way too many men to be stopped by these four farm boys.

These boys were somewhat west wise; their wagons were circled up tight. Bill knew he would lose way too many men if he tried to pry them out of there. He saw that kid, Jared, in action at the river crossing in Illinois. That boy is going to be hard to kill. He will take a lot of men with him and now that I saw this Ronald in action, for sure our outfit will lose half their men. If I was in charge, which I ain't, but if I was, I would move our wagons and all the men up close and hem them in. Lefty got a beating for speaking his piece. No, I'll do as I'm ordered and when I get a good payday I'll leave this wild bunch behind some night and strike out on my own and disappear into the distant grass. The West is a mighty big place to hide in.

Thinking back about what happened earlier, back on that hill, I was enjoying my time alone just watching the kid's camp. It was cloudy and the wind was moving dark clouds across the night sky and at times you could see stars peeking through. A coyote, on a nearby hill, sang a song and some others further away joined in.

Once I saw that big ole moon for about a minute. What was that, Ouch! Stars exploded in my head and all went black. Slowly consciousness crept back into my brain. Oh the headache I had. That lean hard kid I saw earlier had my hands tied behind me and he lit a phosphorus match. Oh the stink that the match made. It must be some kind of a signal to his friends. Yep, they did it in return. I saw their lit match on that hill to the north. What were they going to do now?

He half dragged me off the hill and later gagged me. Soon he was gone, as the sky took on a light gray in the east. As time passed it begin to break daylight then rifle fire split the stillness of the early morning calm. In five minutes poor ole Lefty came down the hill lying across his horse. Larry (Lefty) Norton was no slouch with a long gun, but he laid dead, a hole dead center in his chest. In the chest or in the head, dead is dead. Lefty wouldn't bother these boys ever again.

Poor Lefty is what I would call a hard as nails man. This tough kid had a soft spot in his heart. Maybe that's why I'm still alive. Maybe God hasn't left me or should I say He still loves me, after all I've done. I remember when He used to answer my prayers. But that was oh so long ago. As I watched him tears made tracks on Ron's face and it smelled like he had vomited. This young man didn't like killing not even no-good trash like us. The West was seeing more and more men like him. It was a good thing to see, good honest folks coming west, honest men would do what they had to do to make a place safe for their families.

If he killed Lefty, I'm glad he didn't throw down on me. Now I know just how fast this kid really is. I felt he was fast. But I never dreamed he was lighting quick on the draw too. Lefty Norton like me was just a good man gone bad. That could have been me back there, on that hill, dead and on my way to Hell. I remember what that man said way back in my Sunday school days, when I was a kid. Ole Mr. Brown was a talking to me across those years. Now this ole dude was concealing his tears. My memory of Mr. Brown's words pricked my wicked heart and I thought of my mom.

Ronald kept drifting northward parallel to the tracks of their freight wagons. It was quite dark as we came upon them. He hailed the wagons and they answered, "Come on in Ron. We've been keeping an eye out for ya."

Now I remember, Ronald was his name, as we slipped between the wagons a shotgun looked big as they stuck it in my face. I made sure that I made no fast or false moves. These boys were playing for keeps. Sitting my horse in silence I waited to be pulled down, instead they untied me. Mmmm, was that a mistake on their part

Many hours in leather with my hands tied behind my back, I couldn't get down myself. Rubbing my hands I worked to get the circulation back in my hands and feet. Finally I slipped from my buckskin and was handed a big tin cup of beans and some hard tack. It was near midnight and this was my second meal today. Two big tin cups full of good tasting food were filling, along with some hot coffee.

They doused the fire, hitched up the big horses to the wagons and loaded their camp equipment. They told me to get on my horse, then said, "Stay twenty-five feet from the wagons and in their line of sight, or pay the consequences, and away we went. To my surprise there were no tie ropes on my hands or feet. Without a gun they cared not if I escaped. We traveled throughout the night north and a little bit to the west.

About ten a.m. we passed through the small settlement of Spencer. For some reason Ron hired an older gentleman, from that Podunk place, to drive a wagon. The man looked very capable with the double teams. As we traveled north at night, off in the distance we saw many red glows and by day columns of smoke behind us.

This made Ronald worry some. Knowing Bloody Bill as I did, I was sure he was destroying small ranches along his pathway. He would be killing, raping and stealing everything he came across. Bloody Bill Anderson seemed to enjoy this kind of life. Without his murdering gang he would be powerless.

Knowing I had a part in his greedy plans hurt me as I stand and look back at all this destruction. There's no way I can go back and be a part of his ruthless plans. I felt so sorry for all those poor souls back there.

Ronald and Jared Jenkins picked up a nice saddle horse in Spencer and they were loaded to the gills with guns. Lefty's mare, as a pack animal, was loaded down with many, many camping things.

Ronald and Jared pulled out of town. Those two started along our back trail. Now what were they up to? Death was a riding with them but whose side was he on?

A younger kid named Jeff Jenkins took control of the freight wagons aiming them north and making a run for it; heading deeper and deeper into Indian country, moving through the silent emptiness, surrounded only by lots and lots of prairie grass.

The first day out of Spencer a cold hard October rain poured down on us. Jeff turned straight west for the duration of the four-hour downpour. As the storm slacked up a bit, but before the sun peeked through, he turned slightly north.

That was a good move. Anderson would spend a lot of time locating them that is if he ever could. That afternoon we saw a large herd of buffalo in the distance and he crossed in front of them and turned south. That monster herd would obliterate all signs of our passing. The next day it rained pitch forks and hammer handles again and Jeff did the unexpected, he turned west again. At this point they gave me a shotgun, a horn of powder, a hand full of double 00 buckshot, and some percussion caps, and then sent me packing.

That kid looked at me and said "Doc Barns you're unworthy of any real trust so move along. We don't want to see your face again. If we do we'll know you've come to kill us and we'll act accordingly. I gave them no argument of any kind and high-tailed it on out of there on my buckskin. If this kid was half as good as his brother was then I wanted no part of him. A man could end up dead messing with them boys. I was kind of anxious to make some tracks south away from all the trouble that I saw ahead.

What were Jared and Ronald up too? Those two were mighty good men with their weapons. But two men against so many what could they possibly hope to accomplish? These boys were bent on doing the right thing no matter what the consequences. But in their minds what was the right thing to do? To me it was to cut and run and run hard.

My thoughts were on the innocent people, back there, being butchered along our back trail. They were mostly unsuspecting clod hoppers (farmers) that were trying to make a good life for their families. Bill often turned his nose up at sod busters and belittled all that worked the ground for a living. It would take an army to stop ole Bloody Bill Anderson and keep him from destroying the homes and lives of the settlers. Robbing and raping was a trademark of his gang. No way did I want to be a part of that, ever again.

My mother would cry her eyes out if she knew I was a bystander to what was going on out here. Even at my age paw would take me out to the woodshed and try to beat some sense into me. Paw always corrected me in love. Anger and rage were not his friends and they never went to the woodshed together. Those were not good times for me but I learned right from wrong in that woodshed.

SPENCER

Jared Jenkins and I stayed off our old wagon tracks as we trotted our mounts south looking for Bloody Bills outfit. Jared looked chilled to the bone and his teeth were chattering. The cold hard rain this late in the fall was bone chilling. With our slickers on we sat under a big old Cottonwood tree. The slicker helped to hold out the wind and rain as we waited.

Some of the yellow leaves that still clung to the tree came drifting down with the wind and raindrops. The water in a near-by creek took many and floated them downstream to who knows where. The creek was rising and soon would be overflowing its banks; man-oh-man what a miserable day this is.

After a wee bit we moved out, staying off our washed out wagon tracks. Mud sucked on our horses' hooves as we traveled south in search of the gang. The rain finally stopped and we located a thick patch of pucker brush. We worked our way inside and pitched the tent in the middle of it and built a good warm fire.

We had no idea where Bad Bill's murdering marauders were. There wouldn't be any tracks until they moved their whole kit and caboodle. Even our old wagon tracks were washed away. We stayed put for a full day and two nights waiting for them to move and make some tracks in the deep mud.

There was no smoke in the sky to pin point their location. In a way that was good for the lack of smoke meant no fires. Early the next day the two of us loaded our stuff on our horses, filled leather and headed out looking for their tracks in the soft earth. Unbeknownst' to us we'd brought real bad trouble down on the settlement of Spencer and someone had to help them out of it. We hated how things were shaping up and not really knowing how to end it, without gunplay.

Jared located their tracks first in the soggy soil. It looked like a herd of buffalo had come through churning up the ground. We placed our tracks in their tracks and pursued them as they made their way north. Apparently they were stealing livestock from homesteaders as they raised havoc and destruction on all that stood in their way. Before we caught up to them they'd entered the village of Spencer, that same small town on the Sioux River that we had left just two days ago. The bushwhackers took over the only tavern upon their arrival in the settlement.

They were making a mess of the place with their wild party and heavy drinking. This was a tiny town without any real law. The town consisted of about ten or so adult males against so many outlaws. Bad Bill's gang numbered over thirty men and they ruled the roost here, bullying the town folks who wanted no trouble. We tried to organize the men of Spencer but they had families that needed protection.

So first the women and kids were shipped out of town to a small ranch to the southeast away from the direction the bushwhackers were headed. We hoped this would keep them away from trouble. But it is hard to tell if this move would keep them safe or not.

We told the men in town of the difficulties we have had with this criminal element and what they had done to the civilian population to the south of town. The folks living in Spencer didn't know quite what to do. We were asked if we would like to be the law in their town. The answer was "no." We weren't planning on staying in Spencer any longer then the outlaws did. Only long enough to rid this small town of this wild bunch and then we would be on our way."

As we studied Anderson's operation we noted Bill kept about a dozen guards sober at all times, plus he posted the guards and two men to care for the livestock and watch the wagons with their ill-gotten gains. All together the guards numbered around a dozen and a half men. The wagons, cattle and all they had stolen, were all taken from the settlers along their path way. The wagons were filled with all kinds of loot from dead settlers to the south.

In town we watched their every move. We all stayed clear of Bill and his bushwhackers as best we could. On the third day something changed, Bill sent fifteen men to harness and saddle the horses in the livery and to steal the town's livestock. They were loading hay into two wagons, I thought to myself why? What's up?

They then moved the wagons up to the saloon and they slipped out of the tavern and placed the remaining booze into a wagon. They then moved quickly up the street. That same afternoon his whole army took over the general store and helped themselves to all the remaining food and merchandise on the shelves.

We had gotten rid of the weapons, ammo and things of high value and sent them out of town. They stole what wagons there were from the town and removed everything. They filled the wagons with things from the houses in town. They nearly stripped this place bare. Everything of worth was loaded into the stolen wagons.

Bloody Bill's dastardly deeds almost put this newly formed town down for keeps. It was only their will to survive and their determination that helped them to prevail in this ordeal. The town folks didn't put up a fight; they just stayed out of the bushwhacker's way.

After Bill's boys left town the rains came again washing away any and all traces of our three wagons. Thank Heaven for that. Jeff Jenkins should be close to home by now. While tracking them north the rain turned to ice and then snow. The winds whipped across the prairie and numbed us to the bone. The tall dead grass broke off with the weight of the ice and the wind. We tucked our heads down into our coats and followed them north toward Minnesota.

I wondered how Michele was making out. I missed her so much. Would I ever like to be home with her again? I felt I must stay on the job because I want my family and other families to be safe from men like this, but what can I do? People live to far apart to help each other. All they could do is flee from their family farms and ranches to some place of safety away from Anderson's reign of death and destruction.

As we traveled north we saw destruction everywhere. We rode on ahead of Bill's outfit trying to warn people of the coming of Bill's bunch and many escaped his wrath and many, many suffered loss of some kind. Anything the wild bunch wanted, stock, wagons and things from the buildings they just took it and burned their buildings to the ground. Some folks stayed to defend their farms and paid with their lives

In a month Bill slipped into Minnesota and started trading with the Sioux and settlers for hard cash. Selling and trading whiskey, guns, horses, pots and pans. Just about anything they might need. With trade goods Bill's bunch filled ten wagons high with furs and buffalo robes. The sad part was they killed anyone, whites or Sioux that wouldn't trade and give him a good deal. Then taking what they wanted from their dead bodies, stealing horses, cows and what have ya, Bill left a wide trail of blood, death and destruction as he headed further into Santee Sioux country. Winter was upon us with blowing freezing cold winds and lots of pretty white snow.

We rode hard to warn settlers and Indians alike, zigzagging back and forth across the prairie, working our horses to a frazzle to keep ahead of Bill and his boys. Long hair grew on our tired horses and on our faces. One cabin we came to was a long robe missionary; this man could talk the Sioux talk. With his help we located a large Sioux village that lay to the north.

Without any enthusiasm they listened to our sad story then fed us from their meager food supplies and provided us with a warm place to sleep. At dawn fifty braves, Jared, the missionary and I with guns and other war tools headed southwest to intercept Bloody Bill Anderson's wild bunch. We were finding folks along the way that were willing to lend a helping hand after hearing what Bill had done and help us put a stop to what he was going to do. We were a small army on the move with one mission in mind. Stop bloody Bill Anderson and his gang.

The Santee Sioux counted us as friends for what we were doing. A young brave that spoke English inquired of us the location of our ranch. I was reluctant to tell him at first, but the missionary said, "They would know soon anyway." So we revealed our location to them, on the Sioux River. I asked him if it was possible to purchases the land from the Santee Sioux that we had settled on. He directed me to a chief that decided he would take it up with the elders when they returned to their village on the Minnesota River.

As we moved, I slept some in the saddle. My body was about run ragged. My hair and my whiskers were way to long. I missed my wife more than you know. Her face was growing dim in my tired mind. I needed that beautiful body close up to me and her luscious lips pressing on mine. This ole bum has got to get home and soon. I am cold most of the time now. Exhaustion was riding with me on the same tired horse.

We finally engaged Bloody Bill's bushwhackers in battle. They were tired out from running from us but our Indian friends and settlers put the hurts on them and it took a heavy toll on Bill's wild bunch.

When Bill's boys held up somewhere Jared and I would pick them off one at a time from a long distance, as they showed themselves. At night they would make a run for it and during the day they would hold up and hunker down. They were fighting a rear action as they traveled south toward the Iowa line. Five days of this kind of warfare and Bill was down to two wagons and four teams as he was making an attempt at escaping.

The Sioux Indians were jubilant taking many, many furs, horses, cattle for food and lots of supplies. We were glad that Bill's killing of settlers had finally ceased. Now he was only interested in his own skin. I wished we had put an end to Bill himself and his activity. I was sure that he might just take it up again and starting his killing of folks again.

Bad Bill made it out of Minnesota and way down deep into Iowa with just one single wagon and about five men. His gang left dead bodies littering the countryside as they made their run south. The settlers killed by Bad Bill's bunch lay dead for over a hundred miles.

I heard in the next two years Bill restarted his operation in southern Missouri and Kansas. When I look back I feel sorry that we didn't finish him off here in Iowa. People would die because of our neglect. We can't let animals like that continually roam the countryside and do their dirty work as they darn well pleased. We were both tired and cold and that swayed our decision as we traveled toward the Sioux River. I pictured in my mind our new home there.

After the long chase was over, Jared and I slept a long, long night in a settler's cabin. Their place was okay, but we needed to be heading home to our wives. My home and family was at Sioux Falls and they were heavy on my mind. Bright and early in the morning we said our good-byes and headed for our horses and that long ride home. Once I got into that leather seat, I pushed poor Molly hard for home. Michele occupied my mind nearly all the time now.

I hope my sweet wonderful lady is waiting for me to come home. It's been quite a spell since we left Sioux Falls, back in September. Too many settlers died in this small war with Bloody Bill Andersons. I have slept so many nights away from my wife I feel almost single again and I didn't like it one darn bit.

Man-oh-man I hope she is expecting me and is eager for me to get home. I know that happiness is where you find it. My happiness is at Sioux Falls on the Sioux River. Ma said, "Take your love with you or it won't be there when you get there, Man oh man that was kind of deep if you ask me."

MICHELE'S DIARY

December 15, 1860. Winter has hit us hard and cold weather froze everything solid. It has been ninety-one days since Ronnie left for Des Moines, Iowa and my heart is breaking without him. Dear sweet Ronnie are you alive somewhere out there? My heart says you're dead. I wish I had never asked you to go to Des Moines, but it seemed like the right thing to do at the time.

What hurts me most, it was my idea for you to travel east to get lumber and supplies. It sounded so good and so noble, helping out the Millers and getting lumber for our house at the same time. I think now I would rather live in a sod dugout then not have you around. Honey, I need you here and close to me.

Jeff and the three wagons have been back here for well over a month and there is not a sign of you or Jared. Ronnie please come on home I need you. Ronnie Honey, please don't die on me I need you here to help fulfill my life and my dreams. Honey, where are our kids? The kids I wanted with you. I wanted so many, Darling. You my love are my dream and my life. Why aren't you back home where you belong?

Christmas is just ten days off and no one is showing any real joy. Ronnie, you are my man and I want and need you here to make our family complete and our lives worth living. Tell me where are the boys that look like you and the girls that look like me? You can't leave me yet. Please come on home, honey. "Oh Sweet Jesus, where, oh where is he?" My ever present prayer is "Lord, stay close and continue to watch over him. Lay a protective hand over him, build that hedge of protection around him and bring him home to me."

Poor Debbie is carrying a heavy load of troubles. Her life is falling apart without Jared. I've tried to comfort her although it seems to make it worse. She is pregnant and Jared doesn't even know it. She has never been separated from him for more than a few days since their wedding and I sometimes think she sees him as bad hurt or dead some place out on the Prairie.

There are so many dangers out there waiting to ensnare some unsuspecting soul. Did they do battle with that gang of ruffians? Questions, questions, questions with no answers for anyone, all we are left with our doubts and confusion?

My heart goes out to my friend Debbie, in her struggle with doubts. She mourns with her great needs, while I cry for Ronnie's and mine. I miss him and the thrill of his loving touch. This trip out West is much more than I ever bargained for.

Reading from my diary, I wrote of Ronnie so long ago, when I was a little girl in pigtails. He would stick up for me and include me in all the boys' games that they played at recess, even mumbly peg. Ronnie let me use his pocketknife and I was pretty good flipping it off hands, arms, knees, and shoulders and sticking it into the ground.

He even let me win sometimes. We played marbles and ennie-I-over the schoolhouse plus soft ball. We would swing together. He would take me oh so high when the swing came down I would freeze in that swing seat. We played tag, hide-n-go-seek, kick the can and many other games we made up, at our one room schoolhouse back there on Klees Road. Those days are gone but I still remember them.

I always thought of him as my boy friend, even though I was only his good friend. As long as we were young friends all went well. We would ice skate together and hold hands while playing crack the whip. He would jump logs in the pond and he would push me so I could skate backwards. He could skate backwards all by himself and he taught me how to. Oh the great fun we had together.

I remember a few times that we had a sliding party over on Pugsley's hill near Henelmire Lake. Yes, I do remember all those good times with him. I would ride downhill with him as much as possible. We were such good friends.

Was that all over now? Would we ever be that close again? As I read, those books he bought for me at De Moines, I felt the impulse to cry and I struggled to check myself and lost. It was tearing me apart on the inside as I thought of Ronnie and the good times in our youth.

When I was a foolish young teen, I hoped my dreams would come alive and Ronnie would come and sweep me off my feet and carry me off on his pure white horse or watch him battle some knight and win it all just for me and carry my hankie over his heart into battle. Slaying all the bad guys and then come and take me off to some fine dining place, him all dressed up and me in my white gown. I saw myself dancing to a band in a large ballroom just him and me with all the people cheering us on or him in a fine red surrey pulled by sleek black horses prancing and dancing down the cobblestone streets in some large city.

Is this all gone also? All I have is wants and dreams to lean on. I'm where I always dreamed I would be, but now my good man is missing. Is he lost out there or dead under some snow bank? My diary says, "Life would be oh so wonderful with Ronnie at my side. Alas, as time went on I hoped this boy would come to love me and one day I would be married to him and bare his children. But I was just a friend he liked having around just one of the guys so to speak.

The hard part was once we graduated from that one room country school, on Klees Road and he started working on his father's farm I saw very little of him and loneliness for him crept into my life. As he meandered in and out of my mind, my heart took a beating.

In his absence many, many prayers were sent up for him and our lives together. It didn't seem to help. Then like now I faced the same dilemma longing to be held close by a man that wasn't anywhere around, to be kissed and feel his tender touch while my unspoken fears had a bear hug on me and wouldn't let go no matter what I did.

A cold shiver consumed me for a moment and I was cold all over. I must keep the faith. He is alive! I know it! He is alive! My ma said, "Love your man more than anything else." I have loved him ever since the seventh grade in that one room school way back in Mid-Michigan.

The Bible says, 'Whatsoever a person soweth that shall he also reap' and I'm sowing seeds of love into that man of mine. I must believe Ronnie is okay and will return. "Lord please keep me from sowing seeds of doubt and unbelief."

I remember that night at the barn dance. I went with Greg while Ronnie was on my mind. I watched him from across the barn floor, seeing him happy as always. Laughing and kidding around with the other guys and my heart ached for him even back then. How could I get him to think of me and want to be with me? Why-oh-why was he so slow and shy?

As I watched him he looked to be deep in thought, he felt someone staring and glanced up. His eyes searched the crowd and rested on me and that half frown turned instantly to a face lighting smile. It thrilled my heart and I responded with a big ole smile just for him. You bet I longed to be held close in his arms and having him pull me closer and closer to him. It was a place I had never been, but I desired to be there.

How could this girl get there? Oh how my body yearned to be there that night. Gregory was off somewhere talking with some of his friends. Slowly and cautiously I ambled across the barn floor, fighting that feeling I shouldn't be doing this. If I had my druthers, I would rather not do it but I had to get him to notice me again. As I approached he was leaning back in his chair against the wall. When I said, "Hello Ronnie," A look of surprise captured his face as he tilted his chair forward on four legs and then jumped up.

"Hello Miss Stevens." Ronnie was always polite and friendly. "How are you tonight, Michele? You look really nice."

"Thank you, I'm pretty fair Ronnie. How are you?"

"Tolerable Michele," He reached out and took my hand and I felt it all the way to my heart. He looked into my eyes and I glanced away for an instant. Next he asked about my family and what was Ransom up too. At that point the conversation grew stiff. Oh how shy we were. I felt perspiration sliding down my back as I racked my mind searching for something nice to say.

There was so much I wanted to say. But it wasn't the way of a lady and Ronnie was way too shy. Just then someone started plunking on the piano. Then strings joined in, then a banjo helped out and out it came, "Will you dance with me, Ronnie?"

His mouth dropped open and he stared at me for an instant. Then quick as a flash that winning smile captured my heart once again. His warm hand took mine leading me out onto the barn floor and my heart skipped a beat as his arm encircled my waist. Something welled up inside of me and I shook at his touch. I tried to look composed while falling apart in his arms.

No one ever did this to me. I remember saying to myself, "Oh Lord, I must make this man mine somehow." The ecstasy that invaded my being shook me and I trembled in his arms. I thought of no one like I think of you Ronnie. What am I going to do? Then the dance ended, for us, there was a violent jerk as Gregory hammered him with a hard punch to his face and down he went. I wanted to scream as my hand covered my mouth choking it off.

With his elbows on the wood floor he looked surprised then his surprised look turned to a half smile. As he rolled over Gregory kicked him in the ribs and I heard the pain jump from his lips. Pushing, with his hands, on the floor he bounced to his feet. Moving like a big wild cat still eyeing Gregory and Greg backed up. He knew Ronnie was fast, strong and could he ever fight. Ronnie just loved to wrestle and box. I remember how the boy used to horse around in school.

Now I stood in indecision, Gregory had brought me to the dance while I now had other thoughts. They were of Ronnie. Man-oh-man was I ever fidgety wanting to root for Ronnie. Yes, I did on the inside. With his blinding speed he had Gregory hurting, in a big hurry. Greg did connect with an uppercut and it did stop Ronnie for a moment, but he quickly recovered and that big smile found its way back on to his face.

Gregory said something to him then and Ronnie smiled a big smile just for him. After a furious flurry of punches thrown by Ronnie I noticed Gregory's knees buckle and down he went.

Oh my goodness his head smashed hard on the wood floor and he wasn't moving. I could see that Greg needed help.

I rushed to Greg's side; I saw and still remember Ronnie's face as I cradled Gregory's head on my lap. He had a hurt look and maybe a bit bewildered. He stood there looking at me, that sweet, magnificent, adorable man. I felt only love for Ronnie. How could a person be in two places at once? Wanting to be with Ronnie and needing to be where I was, at Greg's side. Thinking back to that night, wasn't I the one who really caused that fight to take place last spring? Even if no one said so I knew it in my heart. Dancing with Ronnie, the fight and maybe all the bad things that happened to Ronnie's family, their deaths and all; I didn't want to think about it that way but it was still there in my mind. It was way to troubling to ponder. It was disturbing to think that it worked out so good for me with Ronnie.

Before the decision to come out here mama said, "Ronald wouldn't see his family again, either," oh that hurt clear to my heart. "Lord, forgive me for those transgressions." I didn't want Ronnie at such an expense. Yes, I did want him, but not like that. He only came back into my life after his family was murdered.

My heart is breaking for my man and what I might have brought into his life. A twinge of sadness held me. What strange turns life can take sometimes. This young man has had it all happen to him and now maybe he is dead out there somewhere himself. At this time, I didn't know if he is alive or what. All I have out here in Iowa is my loneliness and my God. My God is more than enough I know. Struggling with my bad thoughts I oft times see Ronnie lying dead in the snow with blood everywhere.

The month after Jeff and Fred Miller pulled in we kept busy. With the town folks helping us, our house was up and the roof is completed and he still isn't here. Today we moved all our things into our new home. We have done a good stroke of business here at the ranch. When Ronnie gets here he will be pleasantly surprised.

As I move and worked I feel Ronnie's presence so I'm watching the hills to no avail. Tears flow way too often. A stiff upper lip is the order of the day for Debbie's sake. At night it's another matter. Oh how lonely I am here in eastern Dakota Territory.

Longing to be held and fighting back tears most every night; yes, I find time to cry no matter how busy I am. They just come without any prompting. It is a lonely time for me. Everyone tries to cheer us up and for them I smile a lot. But I don't feel like it on the inside.

The fireplace is built and the cook stove was operational. The bunkhouse is completed now. The men have been real busy working every day and the cold weather makes it rough on them. They had been sleeping in tents. But now they're up off the ground and happy to leave the tents behind. Jeff, Kevin, Ben and Warren Drake now sleep in a warm bunk house.

Debbie and I have separate bedrooms with fine straw tick mattresses to cry on and feather pillows that hold our tears. The weather adds to our misery for our men folks. If they are alive they must be suffering out in the cold. The nights are extra cold with snow covering the ground. There's a foot of the white stuff everywhere covering the landscape in all directions.

If Ronnie were here I would think it was beautiful. At night when the moon shines on it, a jillion sparkling diamonds give off a thrilling sight to see. The cold weather condition makes the white stuff crunch under our feet as we go about our daily lives.

The men folk are now building an extra large pole corral to hold our livestock. Ronnie will be surprised if or when he gets home with all that's been done. If we have to feed our livestock we have four large haystacks by the corral. If we get lots and lots of snow the plan is to bring the cows into the corral and feed them hay while it lasts.

Ben was a joker with many funny sayings like, "Over the fence I threw the horse, some hay." What a play on words. Benjamin Simeon could always cheer us up for a bit. He told about the Indian that dreamed most every night. He said one night he dreamed he was an Indian wigwam out on the prairie. I didn't get it at first, the next night he dreamed he was an Indian teepee and this went on for several nights like that. So finally one day he went to see the medicine man and told him about his dreams and asked what does it mean? "Well Buffalo Rump it seems to me that you're two tents (tense)." I liked this good man a lot. He was a treasure to have around, we were lucky to have gotten him.

It's been over forty days since Jeff Jenkins arrived home and still Ronnie and Jared don't come. Around me the men are brave, but I can see they have given up hope of their return. That's all I have is hope. My faith and prayers are weak and without power. My ma use to tell me seven days without prayer makes one weak so I pray all the time for my man.

Knowing down deep in my heart, Ronnie is gone. Each night I ask the same question. "Are you dead out there somewhere?" We're trying to be brave for Debbie's sake. Although in her heart she is burying Jared also. That sweet girl walks the house expressionless and void of all emotions. I wonder what lies ahead for us. It's an unknown future and it's bothersome to me, because my heart has no feeling. Life without Ronnie has lost its appeal and I'm numb all over. I'm just going through the motion, and like Debbie, no way can I rest easy at night.

I'm like a bowstring strung way to tight. In the back of my mind I've started thinking of Michigan and my folks, although it's so far away for a woman traveling alone. Without my man this place can never be home. My life is headed to only God knows where. Christmas is just three days away and I struggled to work up some kind of Christmas spirit for the others. We've decorated the house with colored paper, popcorn strings and popcorn balls and still there's no life in me. I wish I was pregnant like Debbie, and then I would see something in my future. Part of Ronnie would be here with me. But alas I'm not.

December 22, it has been ninety-five long days since they left for Des Moines, Iowa. It has been ninety-five long days without him by my side. It was nearing noon. Debbie and I were fixing dinner. I sat in a rocker watching Debbie Jenkins moping around trying to help. A long curl hung down out of place, without any life I watched her stick it behind her ear. She loaded the cook stove with good size chunks of wood and the flames poked up through the stove lid hole as she slid the cast iron lid back in place.

We were engaged in lighthearted conversation, "when out in the yard there arose such a clatter," horses hooves making noise on the hard frozen ground and the red rock of the area. It demanded our attention at once. So I cracked the front door a couple of inches to investigate the hubbub that was coming to us from outside. Through the crack, that I made, the noonday sun and cold breeze came inside. The sun was bright on the white snow and my eyes had to adjust to the glare.

I could see and hear men outside in the yard talking loudly and with what sounded like excitement. My pulse started racing way ahead of me. Oh Lord it's Ronnie. My breath left my lungs and tears flowed at the same time. In a guarded voice I said, "Ronnie" and a scream escaped my open mouth, as I was certain of it. I flung the door wide and without a coat or hat I ran as fast as I could toward the corral crying uncontrollably and slammed into the open arms of my man driving him into his horse. I couldn't talk I was crying to hard.

I heard Debbie behind me repeating Jared's name over and over. Ronnie's long arms wrapped around me and his cold lips closed on mine. Inside I hurt so bad and was having trouble catching my breath. It came in gasps and my knees gave way. Ronnie held me up close to him and all I could say was, "Darling! Oh Darling! Then oh Ronnie I love you!" and again he put his sweet cool lips on mine and my ears were ringing way too loud and I thought I was going to collapse into the snow.

Gasping for air, I couldn't breathe well. All I wanted was my lips pressing on his and feeling his body snuggled up against mine. "Oh my Lord Jesus, I thank you for saving my man for me. He was dead and now he is alive again." Waves of joy raced through me and my heart was pounding oh so hard. This is what I needed, his presence and being wrapped snugly in his arms. The ringing got louder in my ears. My eyes were seeing black spots and I couldn't walk.

My knees were weak and I lost consciousness for just a brief moment. My man scooped me up and I felt myself being carried toward the house. Going through the door way into the house I looked behind me and saw Debbie and Jared. She had knocked him to the ground and they lay in the snow getting reacquainted. It looked like she was trying to smother him with kisses. Yes, without a doubt they did love each other.

She didn't care who saw it. Her man was home alive and those three long months of not knowing had beaten both of us down. Our fears were eating us both alive and it showed. Debbie held him tight and love now came flooding out on him. I saw no more of her and Jared as my man closed the door, all the time holding his lips against mine.

Ronnie set my feet on the floor but my legs were as weak as a newborn filly and I almost slipped from his grasp. My legs still wouldn't carry me. I shook all over. I listened to myself. Ronnie must have thought I was babbling. He didn't let go or I would have hit the floor. My wobbly legs had no strength at all. My head was spinning. My ears were making a loud ringing noise, and then darkness swallowed up everything.

Waking up on my bed with Ronnie and Debbie in the room working on me, Ronnie had a cold wet rag in his hand, wiping my face and neck. He said, "Hello Darling" He looked worried and touched my face and I shuddered. He then ran his fingers through my hair and along my scalp. I thought to myself, oh Lord my man is home.

Looking at me he said, "Honey, you're so thin. Haven't you been eating? He kissed both eyes and again on my mouth and I couldn't get enough of him. My mouth discovered his lips and bliss swallowed me. His strong arms eased under me and pulled me up snug to him.

He looked down into my eyes and said, "You are my woman you're all I care for, all the rest is as nothing. My love for you is all that I really think about or care about. You and only you, Honey! Michele, I couldn't love you anymore than I do right now. Darling, I love you so very much."

My heart fluttered at his words and warmth flooded my soul. His words started to register down inside. "Ronnie, I love you with all that I am."

He looked deep into my eyes and said it again, "Darling, I love you so very much. I've missed you more than you know. I've been away from you way to long. It's been way, way longer than I ever dreamed it would be. I didn't want to stay out there that long, but I had to, folks needed us."

"I know Honey; it's been way to long." At his words I started to cry. "Oh Ronnie, I love you so much and I need you here with me." Not letting me go he lifted me again. Leaving our bedroom he set me in a chair, at the table, and then sat down beside me. "Ronnie darling, I thought you might be dead" and when I said, 'dead,' a pain tore at my chest.

"I'm sorry Darling, I gave up on you." He smiled and kissed me then kissed me again.

"You silly willy, oh how I've missed you." Then he pulled me close to him again.

Debbie and Jared were talking, as I looked deep into Ronnie's hazel eyes. Tears made tracks on his handsome face. Feeling his great love for me, all I felt like doing was crying. I placed my hands on his face and kissed him again and again. Oh it's good to have him home. "I praise you and thank you Lord for all this love we have for each other."

Burying my head into his chest, he rubbed my shoulders and neck. It started releasing the tension throughout my whole body. Whew! Oh how I needed that. Yes, it's true my man was home and my life is good again.

My face was sore from his whiskers, but who cares my man was home with me and I knew how much I really missed him and his good love. Oh it's good to see how much he loves me. "Honey, I thought you were lost to me. Just give me some time and I'll be okay."

"You bet you will Michele, you've always been okay."

I had no idea I was this distraught. He must think me a frail little thing passing out like this in front of everyone here. Believing I could now walk I asked, "Honey, would you like something to eat?" He jumped up and quickly tried to load the cook stove, but Debbie already had that little chore done. I guess that means yes. Debbie filled the coffee pot and placed it on the heat. A pan with dinner in it was still setting on the back of the wood stove waiting for the men to come and get it.

Debbie didn't stray very far or long from Jared's lap. Her face was bright red from whisker burns. I could feel my face, but like Debbie I didn't care. My life was here beside me and it was good again. It's wonderful how a good man can change things in such a hurry.

The guys from outside peeked in and saw all was well; they then filed into the house. Soon coffee and cookies were served up. Later dinner was enjoyed by our whole family.

I sat really close not letting go of my man's arm, as the men talked, telling of their trip into Indian country and their Indian friends. Also their meeting with a young brave who knew us from their horse raid on Bloody Bill's horses. He said, "They looked our camp over and decided they couldn't get our horses without loss so they picked on Anderson and his horses instead."

The day wore on as we talked of many, many things. His eyes kept returning to my face. His arm encircled my shoulders and I held his other hand. I was quite content where I was for now my world was all right again. Jarred Jenkins and Ronnie loved what was done here, in the last three and a half months, the house, the corral, the bunkhouse and what we girls did with the inside of our home.

Melvin Lars, who drove the wagons out of Spencer, went on to a place called Edgewood in western Dakota, Territory, over by the Black Hills.

They talked of our livestock, ranch and all that had transpired since they left. They loved everything about the house and all the hard work that was done while they were out playing around with Bloody Bill Anderson and his bushwhackers. All too quickly darkness crept into the area and it wasn't long and all the single men left for the settlement, of Sioux Falls, and didn't return to the house that night. Every last one of them slept in their own beds in the bunkhouse.

Ronnie shaved and we took a birdbath together and he cleaned up good as new. He was my man and loving him was my plan. Not for just a little while but all my life. Then Ronnie slipped under the covers with me and all was well in my world once again. In a soft voice he whispered, in my ear, "I love you, my woman, and have since we were in school, but never like I do now, this very minute."

Morning came early at Sioux Falls. Tomorrow was Christmas Day. Ronnie and I headed into town to buy a few things and do some visiting. My life came alive and Christmas was exciting again. I received my Christmas gift two days early, it was Ronnie coming home. I couldn't let him out of my sight and I couldn't keep my hands off him.

Fred Miller met us at the door, of his little store, and I asked him, "how's business?"

"People were coming in from everywhere and business was brisk. With careful management he would be able to pay off most of his debt to us and still be able to buy the needed supplies later. He assured us he would never be able to repay us for all our generosity.

You folks didn't know us from a hole in the ground. One thing I would like to know is how did a bunch of greenhorns like you know what to buy for a store way out here in the West?" Fred we had Ben to help us and a lot of other people were eager to help.

CHRISTMAS 1860

Remember this Fred we had Michele too, she helped out with her womanly touch and that helped us considerably."

Jared and I were back home again with our wives and that made a world of difference to our wives and us. Michele was oh so good to have next to me again and I couldn't keep my hands off of her. This is just where ole Ronald wanted to be. Close to his women and near his friends.

Christmas was a good time for our outfit. Michele and I had gone to Sioux Falls and picked up presents for the families, a lariat for Kevin and one for Warren. Warren Drake was my second cousin, who is secretly my favorite, who loves people and is a hard worker.

They both were surprised and happy with the gifts they received. They really wanted those lariats to learn roping. It would help in the months ahead with our ranching. Good ropers would be needed and the boys got really good with their braided leather ropes.

Benjamin Simeon, the only hired help, got on great with us boys; he was kind of a father figure for us. He was more like the foreman and us the hired help. We were mighty lucky to have him as part of our family. Ben needed a new pipe and a couple of large tins of tobacco, which we picked up for him. We all needed red flannel long johns and a heavy shirt to wear in cold weather. Benjamin was fast becoming a substitute for my real dad.

For my lady, I purchased a pretty flower print dress, made back East. It was like the one I bought for my mother before she died, and some nice under clothes. The men got new blue store bought pants to wear to town on Sunday when we went to Sioux Falls for church services.

Benjamin shot a big tom turkey for Christmas dinner and we made short work of it on Christmas Day. This was a time of togetherness for us. We were like one big happy family. The girls did a great job of preparing the big Christmas dinner. These two ladies worked well together around the house. They were becoming good friends.

They had so much in common, first with this long trip out west and both being young married women, but most of all that long ninety days with each trying to comfort the other. That time together resulted in a lifelong friendship. These two ladies loved and cared for each other when understanding was needed. I thought to myself, "When you needed a friend in the worst way and they came through for you, then they were a friend indeed." That is a good saying and oh so true.

Debbie had Jared and Jeff, Kevin and Warren had each other. Ben was the odd man out. Benjamin had us all and he really did love us. By spring we were a well-knit family. When it came to running a ranch, Ben knew many things that made this place work a whole lot better. He was a good man with lots of experience in the West.

We needed to generate some more cash. For without money we were stalemated and bogged down in our cattle business. I thought on it, Michele and I came up with the solution, we hoped would get us through the hard times we saw ahead of us.

Fred Miller said, "He would repay most of what he borrowed last fall and that would help." If that was true we would be okay for awhile. In early February we dug up every penny we had and Fred Miller came up with a hundred and fifty dollars that we could use to buy livestock.

February 14, 1861. Fred Miller, Jeff and Kevin Jenkins and a young man that lived a couple of miles from Sioux Falls left with the Jenkins wagons and started for Yankton in Dakota Territory, on the Missouri River, to replace the needed supplies for his store. The steamboats were making regular runs with supplies up north way beyond the army post at Fort Pierre.

The supplies were plentiful over in Yankton and it was a whole lot closer than Des Moines. The bad part is it took them deeper into Indian country and the prices were a wee bit higher there. For safety sake they took plenty of rifles and ammo with them.

Jared and I came up with a fairly good plan for purchasing more livestock. We would head north on the Sioux River, then as we traveled south toward home we would buy as many head of breeding stock as we could for the smallest amount of money. At least that was our plan, but our plans got changed as we rode north up the river. Folks had steers for sale real cheap but were hanging on to their breeding stock to build their own herds. By the campfire one night we hit upon another plan that was even better than the first one.

Jared had stashed away about sixty bucks to start a herd. He had guarded it like it was his own blood. Our plan now was to buy steers cheap, drive them to Des Moines and sell high. A good plan, if it worked. While we were there last fall we checked the cattle prices on good beef going to market. It was quoted to us at seven to ten dollars a head.

As we talked of leaving the ranch after being home only two months, it put Michele in a dither. After many explanations on my part she finally agreed, reluctantly. It was partly her plan and she understood, but she didn't like it much. Cattle were needed to grow a ranch. Without beef sales we couldn't make it out here. Sales of beef had to be made to keep a ranch afloat.

We talked about having faith in God. "Honey, faith is believing God and not doubting His Word and what you pray for. Faith believes that it will come to pass when common sense says it can't be so."

As I rode out I looked back at her and waved. She stood by the corral fence and looked at me, then waved goodbye. She looked as if she had as much starch in her as a wet dishrag. It was February 20, 1861. It was cold out as we made the trip north leaving Ben and Warren to work the ranch in our absence.

We still had six inches of snow on the ground in late February. People out here were easy to find, primarily everyone lived along the rivers and we could see their chimney smoke from a long ways off. Until the last ten years no one lived out here at all. Before that it was Indian land so all whites were relatively newcomers, with just a few settlers dotting the landscape.

Cattle outfits were small mostly under twenty-five or thirty head. Most ranchers did some farming on the side. The Sioux hated sodbusters, (farmers), and tensions were present as they broke ground with a plow. Most of these ranches were small family operated and driving just a few, no more than three to ten head of stock. For them to drive a few cows a hundred and fifty miles was out of the question for most didn't trust the

Indians. They were happy to find a market and a little cash for their steers or unneeded stock.

Our success excited us. We ended up with sixty-one head of steers. Forty-five were mine and Jared had 21. That herd was a small start for us. At seven-fifty a head, in Des Moines, that would start a cash flow for us. It would make $157.00 for Jared and $337.00 for me. It would make a great start for us our first time out.

Jared was a wheeler-dealer that was easy to see. He spent every penny he had on livestock for this drive. We moved the stock onto our place and spent the next couple of days putting road brands on our new stock.

The new green grass put some pounds on our small herd and on April 15 Warren, Jared and I moved sixty-six head of livestock plus eight horses east. It was a long haul and we pushed them hard to be the first ones to market, in Des Moines. As we traveled we tried hard not run the fat off them. These fat boys were range stock and they did well on just grass.

Someone said, "Be to market first and we would get a real good price for our fur balls." A month later we could see the lights of our destination twinkling and blinking in the distance. The steers had even put some weight on during our long drive east.

A peculiar thing happened as we neared De Moines. Buyers came out to meet us and they got into a bidding war for our beef. This didn't make a lick of sense to me. The closer we got to town the more they offered us for our livestock. "Why, what was going on out here?"

We finally settled on $20.50 a head, an unheard of price. What was happening? How could they pay this exorbitant price for steers and make any money? It was uncharacteristic of how it usually happened but as we got into town it became clear to us.

Speculators were buying all the beef they could get their hands on. Unbeknownst to us, while we were out there away from all the newspapers, it happened, the state of South Carolina had succeeded from the Union, on December 20, of last year. January 9, through February 1, six more states had left the Union, joining the rebellion.

April 12, 1861. President Lincoln called for seventy-five thousand troops for three months of service." By the end of February, eleven states had quit the Union. It looked like the great civil war was in swing and the beef buyers saw an opportunity to make big money and they were taking advantage of it right now. Now I could see a better picture on what was going on.

Seventy-five thousand troops needed lots and lots of meat and speculators were going to cash in on the war that would soon follow. I wondered what that meant to the nation and the people back home. Civil War can raise havoc on a country. Would seventy-five thousand troops be enough to fight that many rebellious states? I think not.

The war speculators needed more fur balls so we headed for home to see what we could rustle up for them, with lots of moolah [money] in our pockets. Fred was talking to every customer that came into his store and located more livestock to move east. We paid three dollars a head and promised another dollar if the prices were still high when we got to Des Moines.

I had seven cows that didn't produce a calf this spring and we threw them in with the trail herd. Soon we were pushing one hundred twenty-seven head to market.

Michele took $330.00 from the first sale and hid it under the floorboards, by the outside wall, in a tin box, in our bedroom. She didn't think anyone would look there. This was a security blanket, for her, if anything ever happened to me, or if it was needed, our bank under the bed could be opened.

June 15, 1861. Kevin, Jeff, Fred, Jared, Warren and I made this trip together. Kevin, Jeff and Fred Miller drove the wagons to bring back more lumber and supplies. The lumber was for the Jenkins's home and supplies, for the Fred Miller's store and our stock. We changed off, driving the wagon, every other day as we traveled eastward to market. My big concern was that we had only one man at the home ranch for protection from any hostiles. That made me concerned for my wife.

Ben was a mighty good man. Thinking about that situation kept prayers going up every day. The girls could shoot and that eased my mind somewhat. This kept me pushing the boys to deliver these four-legged fleabags to market, in Des Moines, and then return home.

The exciting surprise we got was the price had jumped just a bit. The boy's were really excited because of our good fortune. I could hardly believe the amount. I had to figure it again. Holy cow! Jared jumped and clicked his heels together and the whole crew had a fit and fell in it. Joy was the tone for the rest of our stay in Des Moines. We guarded our money at all times like it was all the money in the world, and it was for a bunch of farm boys, and to us it was a fortune.

I told Warren Drake he would be driving his own herd of cattle the next time we came this way. His mouth dropped open, just before his smile changed all that. Excitement and joy pushed a loud yaw-who through his lips. This young man was a real good kid, working in a man's world and willing to do a man's job. After the sale Jeff, Warren and Kevin stayed with me. Jared and Fred took the supplies back home to Sioux Falls.

We four would buy as many fur balls as we could drive. We moved straight west until we picked up the Rock River, then north, picking up just over a hundred head of breeding stock. Plus one hundred and ninety steers. Warren took ownership on twenty-five cows, fifty steers and five good bulls. I picked up sixty cows and ten big bulls, plus steers. That left one hundred five steers for Jared and me to sell in the spring. Our ranch now had a good cash flow, if the prices of beef stayed high.

September 5, 1861. We moved the cattle onto our home place. No one was home at the time; the place looked deserted with no horses or people around. A note on our front door said, they were building a house on the Jenkins' ranch. Come and help us if you can. Right away Kevin and Jeff headed south for their ranch.

We put the cattle into the corral and started branding them with running irons. A red hot rod you spell out the brand, on the hide. Michele' and I had picked out for our brand M-R. (M bar R) Warren used W-D for his brand. (Warren bar Drake.)

The rest of the outfit rode in just before dark. They turned in at the corral and Michele stepped down from the wagon and my arms snatched a lot of woman up off the ground and spun her around. I didn't set her down until after our lips met and held tight for a long sweet embrace. It was sure good to be home. I thought about that for a moment, yes, it was home.

Her face was bright and glowing as I sat her down and I didn't let her go. I held her close to me and our lips kept finding each others. It took a good long while for us to reach the porch and the front door.

The sun was low in the western sky as we sat on the porch watching the beautiful sky changing colors. It was putting on a miraculous show for us; Michele snuggled up close with my right arm holding her shoulders my left hand had her hand. We had been married fourteen months and her stomach was just starting to say I'm pregnant. We were both excited about it. A good woman like Michele was a real asset to her man and her kisses still stirred me.

Her long lovely hair was in a ponytail and I liked it that way. This sweet lady can and did show me the joy of living. We were truly happy out here. Down deep she had one fine heart and we made a good team, her and I. This ole boy always knew we would.

It was dark when we left the mosquito-infested porch and ambled inside. The lamps that set on either end of the dining table lit the room. Half a dozen flowers set in a quart jar between the coal oil lamps. This was some of Michele's handy work. We all used the house until bedtime, when the single men left for the bunkhouse.

From the new and the old newspapers, we picked up in Des Moines, we read of the war back East. "April 19, 1861. "For three weeks Washington D. C. was in real danger. It was cut off from the North as the rebels occupied Baltimore, MD." The South controlled the railroads and communications along the East coast. This was a scary time for the North with the nation's capital cut off from the rest of the Union. It was a real serious situation and work was a foot to regain control of Washington DC, the hub of most activity on the east coast.

Eleven angry southern states now opposed the Unionist North.

"Lincoln ordered Confederate ports blockaded. He also called for forty-two thousand three year volunteers plus forty thousand regular army and navy troops." It looks like it was building into a full-scale war. It doesn't look like three months will get the hostilities settled not the way things were building up. Men from our area were leaving to join the action in the East.

I can't see where we can leave our ranches and families and travel over a thousand miles to join in the action. Killing Johnnie Rebs isn't what it's cracked up to be. War is brutal, a real cruel thing. Besides we already had our little war with Bloody Bill Anderson. Warfare is bad news anyway you look at it. At this point any suggestions that I head east to help out were going to get doused with a bucket of cold water.

This is Indian country after all. What would Michele do if there was trouble here or if I died of disease or was killed in action? This is one little go round this boy from Michigan isn't going to get involved in. War is war and dead is dead and I don't want any part of it.

Could I make a difference back there? I doubt it very much. I must do what is right for my soon coming child and that is to stay home and sell beef to feed the army of the North. A job someone had to do and this little outfit was gearing up to send a lot of beef back East.

In bed that night we talked about the war. I assured Michele I wouldn't leave her alone out here and go gallivanting across country to fight in a war back East. "Michele, I couldn't leave all this and go traipsing across the country to only God knows where. Honey, look around you, we are already seeing deserters, drifting through this area. The war isn't six months old yet and soldiers are deserting and fleeing to the West.

In late October we scoured the farms and ranches for any livestock we could find for our early spring drive. So many men had left, for the East, to fight in that war. Women and kids were left alone to operate the home front in Indian country, with little or no money to live on. They must feed and care for livestock from the meager haystacks they had put up last summer. To me it wasn't fair to do this to a family but someone needed to fight those Southern boys.

We paid the women that were left out here alone; five to six bucks a head. When the frontier had little or no money and they needed the money to put food on their tables, buy clothes and odds and ends. Most families were at wits end without any cash coming in and ole Ronald saw the effects on many faces.

We promised a dollar more, to be picked up, at the store if the beef prices were still up, in the spring sales. Jared Jenkins kept the books on who we bought stock from. Most men in the army promised to send money home to their families but the twelve dollars a month the army paid wasn't much. Money did come into the Miller's store from men who did send some cash home.

The Santee Sioux were on edge in Minnesota. The Union Army was occupied in the East and the Santee grew bolder and braver. It was a terrible time for the Santee Sioux in our area. The buffalo herds had been decimated in Minnesota or driven further west.

In 1850, white hunters had gotten into the buffalo killing business and in ten years obliterate most of them in this area and destroying the migration routes of the existing herds. The Sioux had to leave lands that they knew and loved to find food. Then people, like us here in Sioux Falls, moved in and stole a bit of their hunting ground. Wherever the whites are established, the buffalo disappear. Our group ate wild meat most every meal deer, rabbits, turkey birds or buffalo this way we could save our stock for resale. But where did that leave the Santee Sioux? It left them on reservations and hungry.

The Santee Sioux's gripes were justified. The worst part of it was the Indian agents were cheating and starving the Indians on the reservation. Because the beef prices were sky high and the agents got very little pay they would resell the Indians' beef and keep the big profits.

Indian agents could make good money reselling reservation beef on the open market. Life was real bad for the Santee Sioux in Minnesota. It makes me stop and think what would I do if my wife and future family were starving because of the Government and the white man? I could see why they're so angry. Their whole world was being turned upside down because of the white man's greed.

This was often on my mind and bothered me to think about it. Seeing how much I was troubled, Michele suggested we take some livestock over to the reservation and help feed the Sioux. Having talked it over with the Jenkins family we decided to move at least twenty or so steers northeast to the Santee Sioux Indian Reservation. On January 1, 1862, Jared and I pushed our twenty head toward the Indian reservation, on the Minnesota River. We searched out the long robe, missionary, the one we used a year or so ago and asked him to help us distribute the small herd to the Santee Sioux.

We took a meal with this fine gentleman and his family and stayed the night. The next morning we moved into the Sioux village and to my surprise things were worse than I could have ever dreamed! They eyed our fur balls and many crowded around them. We had way underestimated the conditions and the number of Santee Sioux here. Were we ever greenhorns! Our whole herd wouldn't have lasted long, in this encampment, with seventeen hundred hungry Sioux. When I saw the conditions, it made me want to cry. This bunch wouldn't last long here.

What were we doing to the red man out here? Do we have the right to take their land even if the U.S. government gave it to us? I know they don't use it like we think it should be used? Was it ours to take? Look at all the buffalo that have been slaughtered just for their hides.

Those nice sounding words, like it's our manifest destiny, doesn't mean a whole lot to this hungry group of Santee Sioux Indians. I apologized to the Santee Sioux Chief for not bringing more beef for their hungry families.

Every year there are more and more, white settler's taking up land along the rivers of the Great Western Prairie. When the civil war is over I feel that young men and their families will be flocking into the west to get a quarter section of land, if all they have to do is settle there.

"Well, One-That-Warns, it is well that you came. This is two times you have come to help your Sioux friends. It would be good if all men would live like you two and the long robes do. Your friends, the Santee Sioux, will not forget your generosity as you live on our land. Your heart is big for your Sioux brothers. The Sioux will not forget your kindness toward us. May the Great Holy Spirit look after you and make your way easy and pleasant as you travel our land."

I thought this would be a good time to ask about the land at Sioux Falls and see if the Sioux would sell us the portion of land that we have settled on. They accepted these beef and another small herd as payment for the land we would need for our families.

After we left the Santee Sioux encampment Jared Jenkins came up with fifty bucks and I had thirty-five which we gave to the Methodist missionary. After we left for home his church people added to it and they purchased more beef for the hungry reservation Sioux.

We went to the Indian agent's store to acquire food enough to keep us until we could buy food in some small store on our long trip home. We talked to the Indian agent about the conditions on the Santee Sioux reservation. You could see that it was a touchy subject with him and he didn't want to talk about it. We shot the bull for a bit and that man got my dander up.

That misfit got my goat and his parting words were, "If they're so damn hungry they can eat grass." We could see just how much he cared for the people he was a servant to. He said of the Santee Sioux, "Let them eat grass." Those were harsh words for a servant of the people.

January 23, 1862. It was good to be home. Michele was big with child and she was having trouble getting up and down. She put her hands on the chair back and eased her big, out of shape, body into and out of it. She would smile and say, "You did this to me."

I'd say something like, "You've got to stop eating so much ice cream." I'm staying in shape turning the crank handle on the ice cream maker. "Honey, I told you all those pickles and ice cream would have an effect on you." Oh the good times we had kidding around. Her attitude was good and her great love motivated her to show love to all.

Warren Drake called her, "Mrs. Duck." The waddle was noticeable. A duck was a good name for it. My lovely wife was the instigator of all such conversation. What a delightful woman she was. Michele had to go to the outhouse about every twenty minutes in the later part of her pregnancy.

January was way too cold to sit in that cold outhouse and do her business that often. I took out the cane bottom of a chair and fixed it up with a thunder mug under it for her to use. Oh how I loved her and oh how she loved that chair. We placed it in the bedroom. You should have heard the fuss. Everyone wanted one just like it. But they didn't get one. That chair and chamber pot was passed from one pregnant lady to another in the next few years.

Other than all the discomfort she felt fine. She had a radiance and loving warmth that was noticeable. Her condition didn't leave her ornery at all. Oh how I cared for this wonderful lady. Even in her present condition she was sexy looking; at least she was to me. Although she didn't want to hear that kind of talk.

On February 5, 1862 she gave birth to a fine looking boy of eight pounds. We named him Wendell Lyman Holden, using his dead Grandpa's name for a middle name. He was handsome, as babies go and healthy in every way. For two weeks I waited on her hand and foot. First making it as easy as I could for this lady of mine and second I needed to be near her. I needed her hands and lips on me.

The Jenkins, Warren and Simeon were out buying more steers and breeding stock for the ranch. The herd was of good size. Those boys worked hard and the beef cost us more per head. Many people knew that the price of beef was up, in the East, and wanted a bigger part of the pie which I understood.

March 3, they rode in with two hundred seventeen head, plus the one hundred thirty-seven fur balls we picked up last fall. Four days later we started our drive heading east to the market in Iowa. It was a long, long ways to push that many bullheaded steers.

My cousin Warren Drake owned fifty-seven steers and fifty-seven cows and had thirty-six new born calves already this spring. This hard working boy was a rancher and fast becoming a man at near eighteen years of age. The frontier would grow a boy up real fast or he wouldn't make it at all. This young man had a good idea and a good plan. I loved him like a brother and we were great friends.

Warren had lots of skills and a knack for cutting and polishing the red rock of this area. With these red rocks he was building a fence in front of the house and around in back. People were impressed with the quality of the work and the stones. One man came by and bought a wagonload and said he would be back later for more.

Warren had many samples of his work in the big wagon, to show people in the Des Moines area. I'm thinking he will pick up a whole slew of customers in the big city, for his work was truly exceptional, and the red rock was beautiful.

Kevin and Ben stayed on the home place with the ladies, until we returned, just for safety sake. This ole cow puncher didn't relish leaving Michele at all with that new baby boy of ours.

The price they gave us for our beef was outrageous. Just how high would the war push up the prices? Twenty-five dollars a head, made our heads swim and we thanked God for our good fortune. The cattle buyers were hungry for all the steers we could get to market. They asked if we could bring in another herd yet this year. My question was would the prices still be the same? Two buyers guaranteed me at least twenty-three dollars on our return trip to Des Moines, Iowa.

The war was lasting a whole lot longer than anyone expected it too and it was escalating all the time. The Unionist North were throwing more and more men into battle and all those Union soldiers were gobbling up the fresh meat faster than people back East could grow cattle and deliver them to market.

The farmers in the East had sold off almost everything they had and now buyers wanted western beef. The Union troops had to be fed and the army had built up forces almost beyond reason. We put together some different plans for the return trip. Most people knew that beef prices had gone sky high. So our purchase prices were a lot higher.

Many people held out for a whole lot more money because of it. Some folks we told that we had to make a profit or we would just have to forget their stock. Some families would meet our price but others held out for more and we had to pass them by. As it was we had to pay the higher prices if we wanted the livestock.

We needed to make a quick trip back to Des Moines with another herd so we sent Jeff on home to get Kevin and then return. The war could end soon so we needed to make hay while the sun shines.

There was a bad element out here in the West that was trying to waylay cattlemen as they pushed their livestock to market; stealing cattle was big business because of the big money to be made. I had Jeff inform our ladies that they should stay in town because there was safety in numbers.

Many, many rancher's wives would live in towns when their men folks were gone just for safety sake. Many built small shacks in town to stay in when they needed to. The bad element that now roamed the West made it unsafe for them to be left alone on farms or ranches when their men folks were gone. Ranchers had to be wary for there were always bad men looking for a grub stake.

You guys tell Ben to stay on the home place and watch things as we worked purchasing the livestock. Please tell him to be careful.

UNWELCOME GUEST

Kevin and Jeff would meet us as soon as possible at a predetermined place. We would travel south on the west fork of the Little Sioux River, then north on the Little Sioux buying beef as we went. They found us near the river fork just north of Turin's Outpost Store. We had purchased sixty-eight head of stock so far. We were doing quite well, I thought.

At Turin's Store the three of us separated from Jeff and Jared Jenkins and the three of us moved north on the Little Sioux River. Warren, Kevin and I latched on to the Maple River and headed north. With all our new stock we moved along fairly well until our herd reached about one hundred twenty head of livestock and then they became a handful.

North of Ida Grove store about ten miles, six men watched from a hilltop, a half mile east of us our position. We camped early that night on a small rise and kept the stock in close. Others had trouble with outlaws but this was our first real contact with rustlers on the trail. We stayed alert as the three of us ate a hot meal.

After dark I left the boys and slipped off to see what our unwelcome visitors were up to. At a distance I watched the shadowy figures riding toward our camp. They came in single file with just the click of shod hooves on stone to tell of their presence.

The distance between us and them closed to a point blank range. My right hand gripped tightly to the walnut handle of my revolver as I slipped it free from leather. The twelve gauge shotgun was cradled in my left hand. The dark shadows of a big Oak Tree and some brush kept me hid until they were up close to me, then I sang out. "Howdy boys, how are you fellows doing tonight?"

Surprise and shock gripped them for a moment and confusion ruled. Needless to say they were surprised that anyone was around. When they got control of their mounts, they acted kind of nervous. They were young slightly younger than I. One man seemed older than the rest.

As the leader talked I knew who he was. "How you been, Doc?" He stiffened and peered long and hard into the dark shadows where I sat my horse. "You back to stealing and maybe killing again? I thought you were through with that kind of malarkey, Doc."

He hesitated not knowing just what to do or say. "Who are you? How do you know me?" His horse was in the moonlight at the edge of the dark shadows of the big Oak tree. He moved uneasy in his saddle as he peered hard into the darkness where I sat my bay. I said with a stern voice, "You boys sit loose now.

Doc, I thought if you got a brake you might go straight. You told us you were going to see your folks, so why are you out here doing what you're doing'? You could almost hear the wheels turning in his head.

"Is that you ah, ah," he thought a moment and then said, "Ron? We're just out a riding."

"Ya, you bet. Night riding is what we call it."

"Ron is that your livestock we saw?"

"Ya, they're ours. What's your intention, Doc?"

"Why, what do you mean Ron? We're just out riding."

"Ha, ha! That's a good one Doc. Just out riding huh? Are you partial to the dark, Doc? It does hide a whole lot of crime, doesn't it? You boys been shadowing us most of the day and now you're headed toward our herd and our night camp.

What am I to think? Doc, I'm no fool. You know me Doc and what I'm about, but I had hopes that you would turn away from crime." His lips grew tighter in indecision as he sat in silence for a moment. He knew I knew what they intended to do.

"Look Ronald, we had no idea this was your herd." He sounded sincere as he talked. I still remembered how he had a way with words and could put a person off guard. This man had a mighty slick way about him.

My hand had not let up on the pistol grip as we conversed. I'm glad I was sitting in the dark shadows of the big Oak tree. As he talked I watched all six while my eyes were fixed mainly on Doc. He was the key to this gang and its gunplay. It would start with him, if it came at all. He was a thinker and must digest all the ins and outs of what was going on. He knew I was jiffy quick and accurate with this revolver.

That must be put in his scales and weighed. But he wanted our stock. As he weighed it, he was in the middle of indecision and annoyed by my intrusion into his little cattle stealing game. Our cattle occupied his thoughts. They were being weighed along with everything else.

My mind was clear and this ole dude was ready. Dad's words came to me, through the night, "in a tight spot always be alert and keep your wits about you." Fear isn't fun and will mess with your mind. "What am I going to do with you, Doc? You get a chance and throw it away like it was a rotten potato."

"That's a good one and he chuckled just for me! The question is what are we going to do with you Ronald, my boy." His gaze was hard and steady; peering into the shadows.

I was wired and ready for whatever he had for me. "Well Doc, hammer away, but don't start something you can't finish. You, my friend, are my first target. You know it doesn't have to be this way. But it'll be whatever you make of it. So what is on your mind Doc.? Go to it my friend; hammer away if you feel comfortable doing it."

"Ronald Holden, It's time to quit jawing." He gigged his horse forward until he had one of his young riders between him and me.

"Are you now ready Doc, is it time for you to have at it." He squirmed a little bit and shifted in his saddle, feeling a bit awkward. He squared his broad shoulders as determination came into his voice. He seemed so cocksure of himself with five men backing his play and one young rider hiding him.

Then a friendly voice, that I knew so well, drifted to my ears in the nick of time, it was Warren Drake. He said "Hello Doc. Don't turn around or this shotgun just might make hamburger out of you." You could see the whole bunch stiffen at his words.

The boys were out there but I couldn't see hide nor hair of them. From off to the side, Kevin said, "It's time for you boys to get shuck of your hardware or receive a dose of double 00 buck and maybe lead poison. Today it's free; there isn't any charge, just raise your hand if you don't want a double portion."

Doc Barns was back to awkwardness again, which wasn't in his nature. Warren Drake's shotgun hammers clicked; people froze in their saddles. They were really nervous about the way things had changed so quickly. Kevin said, "Do it now or die, we ain't got all night, I'm sleepy. So get shuck of your hardware and do it now!"

"Doc, you know me and you know we will." I leveled my revolver lining it up on his outfit. "Doc, don't get any ideas that will get you and your boys killed."

He took on the expression of defeat and slowly dropped his revolver pulled his shotgun and dropped it and slid his rifle free of its resting place. He leaned over and let it drop to the ground. Then one at a time they let loose of their firearms, dismounted and moved away from their horses. I said to him, "Doc, what are we going to do with you? You had a good chance and went back to your old dirty tricks. If you had stolen our cattle tonight, we would have hanged ya. The army is too busy with the war and can't take time to run you down.

Back at our camp with all their hardware in a pile, we tied their hands in back of them and sat them all down in a group, by the fire. "You boys, I'm going to let you leave tomorrow, but without your horses or guns. It's a good long walk back to any place from here."

"Wait a moment, what if we need our guns to defend ourselves?"

"Sir, you had better start praying you can outrun your friends. You didn't worry about us so why should we be concerned about you? Besides that you boys haven't got anything to steal. You were more than anxious to cause us trouble, a few minutes ago. Look hard and hide well and just maybe you can stay away from any pesky Indians that might want your hides or scalps. These guns and nags now belong to us. The walk will do you good." The ruckus they made didn't sway me one iota.

"You mean you're going to steal our horses? You're no better than we are. You're nothing but a thief, a no good horse thief." That made Kevin and Warren give out with a fake laugh that all could hear.

"Take your horses, you betcha! Listen boys, this is a lot better than going to jail and spending ten years or so in some overcrowded cell. Now if ya want to go to jail with Doc you can ride along." The protesting slowed down and then stopped altogether. We tied one loose rope around the whole bunch and said, "If anyone slips out of there before dawn we'll just fire a couple of shotgun blast into the whole group."

I smiled to myself this was group peer pressure for them not to move. With many eyes I was scrutinized. Would I do it, you betcha?

Doc said, "I know this man. He killed a man I use to ride with up north. So do as he says, boys. He has lots of integrity."

"Doc, what's integrity?"

"He's honest and trustworthy Tim. He'll do just what he says he'll do. Tim, this is just how he is whether people are watching or not. He's always the same. That's how we should be. You boys have heard of Bloody Bill Anderson and his killing, robbing, cutthroats, that are burning places and raising all kind of Hell down in Missouri? This boy defeated Bloody Bill Anderson and sent him skedaddling on back to Missouri, with his tail tucked between his legs."

That statement was far from being right but I saw no reason to correct it for them. Let these boys believe whatever he says. It may cut down on the trouble later on. I didn't want to kill anyone out here, not now or ever. But a man has got to do what a man has got to do.

Warren Drake and Kevin Jenkins slept up the hill from our campfire. About two o'clock I woke them to circle the stock back up by our camp. As soon as they finished they crawled back into their bedrolls for just a little more shut eye. As the gray light of predawn broke the eastern sky Warren and Kevin rolled up their bedrolls, saddled up their horses and tied their bedrolls behind the saddles. Kevin added wood to the cook fire. "Ron, do we feed these bad boys?"

"No Kevin, just lay aside a knife when we leave. They can cook their own meal. Kevin pulled a frying pan and some tin plates off their horses and left them by the fire." We loaded Doc on his mount, tied his feet under his horse and handed him a large steak sandwich and a hot cup of black coffee. I backed off a little bit and began loading their horses and camp things on our packhorse.

As I did Doc retrieved his reins and kicked his horse into a flat out run. I pulled my revolver and fired twice, just over his head, as his horse stirred up plenty of dust, heading east at full speed. A smile touched my lips as he moved on out of sight.

"There, I hope he goes straight this time. "Lord, please be with him and help him resist temptation. Help him to be some good to someone and help him get home safely to his family. He could be an asset, a real good citizen if he got his life straightened out." Watching him disappear over a slight rise, I then stepped to my horse, picked up the reins, mounted and sped away quickly catching up with the herd.

To my surprise the first place we stopped we purchased ten nice steers at five bucks a head. The second farm we picked up two more, at this rate we would have our biggest herd ever.

There were a lot more farms, with livestock, as we progressed east. I wondered how Jared and Jeff Jenkins were doing over on the Little Sioux River.

I didn't have to wait long to find out. Jared and Jeff were waiting for us up on the Maple River, west of the settlement of Cherokee. It was just another small Podunk place in the middle of nowhere. The guys had been waiting there for over a day, and they had a tent set up and a big kettle of beans on a cooking and did they ever smell good. The wind was right and we could smell them a half a mile away.

They'd picked up one hundred nineteen head, with our one hundred ninety-seven head for a grand total of three hundred twenty. It was a real good count for a little less than a month of hard work. Our buying price averaged out to a little over four dollars and ninety-five cents a head.

If the prices were still up in De Moines, it would be a great payday for us. God was really blessing us out here. Des Moines was east of us about a hundred and fifty miles, if we had no real trouble, in about fourteen days we'd be pushing our stock into town.

When we finally pulled into Des Moines, with our beef the price was up by fifty cents a head. We all pitched in and gave Jeff and Kevin three hundred dollars to buy stock with. They could now start a herd of their own. Owning cattle would tie them to the land which was what I wanted for them.

With all their hard work they had earned it. The five of us headed on home after two spring cattle sales with big bucks in our pockets. We worked our way home purchasing many productive cows along the way. The new cows were mostly bred stock so we should have a good calf crop in the spring.

In Des Moines, Warren Drake, had earlier ordered stone cutting tools from a catalog. He had purchased many, many tools and equipment to cut and polish the red rocks of our area. Then he bought a big ore wagon and hired a teamster to deliver the equipment over on the Sioux River. The stones he had taken east earlier had generated a great many orders. Once the equipment was delivered he would use the wagon to deliver the polished rock.

It was the beginning of a business that would be known around the world. After the big war and the paddle boats started again his business would grow by leaps and bounds. The Warren Drake Works made a huge amount of money in the next twenty years. Selling his product around the world, he would also polish rocks from the petrified forest of Arizona and ship them everywhere, until the United States Government clamped down and put a stop to the removal of the petrified wood from Arizona.

June 20 we approached the ranch house, and then corralled our new cows. Our calf crop was ninety-eight per cent last spring and calves were everywhere. The spread was working like a well-oiled watch, thanks to Ben.

That sweet wife of mine had her slender figure almost back and she was a sight for sore eyes. With Wendell Lyman in her arms she ran to the corral and our ritual was performed right in the dooryard. Most men on the frontier wouldn't hug or kiss their wives in front of others. They thought it might excite the hired men but thank God my wife didn't hold to that. We both needed those hugs and kisses, especially after a long absence of a month or so. My whole life was wrapped around this sweet woman and now my family. Why wouldn't I want to show it?

The bad part was this ranch work was eating into my love affair with Michele. I wasn't very happy about it either. In a year or two there will be no more chasing down steers for resale. We would start shipping from our own herds and that would give us a lot more evenings and nights together.

Warren Drake had staked out his spread next to mine and went to raising cows. That young man seemed to have the magic touch on everything he put his hands too and he was making a good deal of money.

Back in 1861 the battle around the little town of Carthage, in southwest Missouri was the first and probably one of the most important battles of the early war. Missouri was a pivotal state and the outcome of the war could hinge on whether Missouri went to the Southern camp or to the North.

Many smaller encounters preceded this larger land battle that took place southeast of Carthage and then spilled into the city itself. This battle was important although it didn't decide what Missouri would do in this war. Other things had an influence on how that came out.

Well armed union sympathizers from St. Louis, 1,100 strong had marched southwest to meet the challenge of Governor Claiborne Jackson and his Missouri State guardsmen. Governor Jackson led a force of around six thousand troops into battle there.

The Yanks, under Colonel Franz Sigel, marched into battle with about 1,100 troops. Their missions were to route out Governor Jackson and stop his move to make Missouri a slave state. The Confederacy in the end routed out Col. Sigel and sent him packing back to St. Louis.

Throughout the long struggle, in Missouri, Jasper County would dwindle from almost 7,000 residences before the war to less than forty people at war's end. Many residences were killed and many more left this hot bed to escape death.

The papers told us that on "July 16, 1861, eleven days after the battle at Carthage, the first Battle for Manasseh Junction took place, at the bridge on the creek called Bull Run. General Beauregard and McDowell battled it out. General McDowell used ninety day volunteers and ends up fleeing back to Washington DC.

On July 21, the Federal troops fighting at Henry Hill were defeated. The Union troops retreat to Centerville and fear follows close on their heels. The Federal troops were not ready for the ferocity of the Confederate soldiers. The Federal soldiers have suffered defeat in all of their skirmishes with the Confederate troops.

McClellan is now general of the Union Army on the eastern front. President Abe Lincoln tries to get General George McClellan to move on Richmond, Virginia but George dilly dallies in DC. The question everyone is asking is why?

President Lincoln devised a three prong attack. First the eastern forces would push toward Richmond. Next the western front would attack Kentucky and Tennessee then push into the heart of the South. Lastly they must clear the Mississippi River and blockade the U.S. coast choking off the Southern supply lines that are coming in from abroad.

The sale of cotton was their number one export. Europe wants and needs the cheap cotton which the South produces in abundance with slave labor. Everyone needed the South's inexpensive cotton but didn't receive it. They receive it in limited supplies from other places.

General Grant and Sherman the only officers to win a battle for the Union are both relieved of active duty. "The reason is Grant had asked for two hundred thousand more troops and McClellan said, "Sherman was a little daft in the head."

"February 1, 1862. McClellan called President Lincoln a baboon and then refers to that big ape up on Capitol Hill."

Lincoln said, "If McClellan has no use for the Eastern army, he'd like to borrow them for a spell. President Lincoln finally gets serious and orders McClellan to march on Richmond, but McClellan wouldn't budge, he got sick instead."

"In the fall of 1861 the C.S.A. Merrimac, the most powerful ship the Confederates have, and in order to break the Union blockade, they overlaid the Merrimac with iron plates. The South has no real Navy to fight with and this is their one great hope.

They needed to open one sea port to export their cotton which is piled high on the docks and stored in warehouses. Their expectations were extremely high that they could succeed in opening this one harbor to trade with Europe."

To combat the Merrimac, (which was called the Virginia by the South) the north built a completely iron ship called the Monitor, which sailed south to engage the Merrimac in battle. March 8, the South's Merrimac rams the Cumberland then sank her. Then engages the USS Congress, which is set afire and it burns, but doesn't sink. They then pursue the USS Minnesota and run her aground."

These three engagements took place in one day's siege. It looks mighty bad for the North. Can the north stop the South's exports and imports now? That's the question that is going around.

The following day, as the tide moved in, the Merrimac returned to finish its work on the Union fleet. But earlier that morning the Union's Monitor had arrived in port, a flat top boat with a cheese box turret on top. (From which 2 guns are fired.)

The battle rages for over four hours. From close range they pounded each other; finally the south backs off and skedaddled south. Two months later the Merrimac crews sinks her rather than surrender that magnificent ship to the Union Navy.

March of 1862, Grant returns to active duty. He captures Fort Henry. Then confronts Fort Donnellson and captures it also. At long last, McClellan moves toward Richmond with one hundred twenty-one thousand troops and eleven hundred fifty wagons to finally wage all out war on Richmond. For some reason McClellan thinks the whole Confederate army is ahead of him so he digs in and waits. His fellow officers bestow on him the name, "The Virginia Creeper."

April 9, 1862. On the western front at Shiloh (which means a place of peace) on the Tennessee River General Johnston, C.S.A., with the sixth Mississippi, engages Gen. Grant in combat.

Sherman was assigned a division. General Grant attacks with 42,000 troops. Johnston is killed here. He was one of the South's best commanders. General Beauregard assumes command of the sixth Mississippi and engages Grant. Many thousands die on both sides.

The next day with 70,000 troops by way of reinforcements Grant defeats the Mississippi boys and Gen. Beauregard in a blood bath on the Tennessee River. In two days of hard fighting 23,000 men die in this battle for Shiloh, (A place of peace.)"

Can our country continue to lose good men on both sides to this crazy war? "Lord, where is this great nation headed? Can we lose so many and still stand?" Am I ever glad we are way out here and not involved in that terrible war, in the East. The paper says, "More men are dying of sickness and disease than are dying in battle." Why do some men want to lord it over others? I have trouble seeing the sense in any war.

This summer is a great time for us. The last of June and July we spent many happy and most wonderful hours together, fishing, haying and doing all those things we did on our ranch with my woman there by my side.

The first week of August I filed on our section of land. Jared Jenkins and I went down to Yankton to do so. I hired a man and his wife to work for us. She would do the cooking, for all, and work in the house. He would help with the ranch work. The Reads were good folks.

Pat and Wesley Read were a good team. Wesley, a part time blacksmith and freight driver, was a good worker, a real asset to our ranch. We really needed this man and his wife when we were out moving stock. Pat and Wesley were on hard times, in Yankton, and were happy to have the job.

MINNESOTA MASSACRE

Michele and I planned a trip to Sioux City for our belated honeymoon. It's been over two years since that wonderful day back in Mid-Michigan when she said, "yes." I needed some time alone with my woman away from the ranch. So we packed our things for a long stay in that city to the south.

Michele was all excited and down deep so was I. Our vague plan was to leave in our light wagon with springs on the axles and a spring seat for an easier ride south to Sioux City.

We could go at our own pace and sleep in the wagon bed at night. We put a canvas over the top plus we had a small tent. We packed all kinds of things, I was sure we wouldn't need. Michele went ahead and packed what she thought we three would need for a long month. Since we set no timetable to return we would just play it by ear and do the town up right.

August 19, the day we were to leave, a Santee Indian brave rode a lathered mustang into our dooryard with news that the

Santee Sioux were on the war path. He was warning friends, of the Santee, of an attack by Sioux warriors. I sent Warren Drake on into Sioux Falls to warn them of the uprising and the trouble headed our way. I guess we were classified as friends.

The Santee Sioux under Little Crow were killing whites up and down the frontier. Many war parties were out. They were waging war against unsuspecting families in the area, men, women and children. Many men were off fighting in the war of the Rebellion and their families were dying without male protection.

Most settlers didn't know the Indians were at war and were easily killed while out doing summer farm and ranch work. I left Warren Drake in charge of the ranch until we returned. I asked them "To stay well armed and close to the buildings until this thing was over. If trouble came to our area, use the root cellar for defense. Work in pairs always, never ride out alone.

Benjamin, help Warren out until we return. Warren, listen to these men but be wise in what you do. Cows and buildings can be replaced, human lives can't." Wesley hitched up our wagon to a good team of horses and I tied a good saddle horse on behind. Benjamin made one last plea, of concern, for us not to venture out on the trail with the Sioux on the warpath.

I explained that most of the Santee Sioux braves knew and respected me and called me friend. Benjamin, my friend, I fought side by side with many of the Santee Sioux Warriors. But before I make a final decision I'll see what's happening in Sioux Falls. I'm sure many families will be leaving and we'll join up with some family and head south together.

As we rode into Sioux Falls the town was being evacuated, as I supposed. What did surprise me was the store supplies were almost all loaded into three wagons and they were nearly ready to travel. Most folks had already left. They were heading south toward Sioux City, on the Sioux River a place with a whole lot more citizens. The Millers were seeking more protection than Sioux Falls could offer.

Michele started helping by loading things into the Miller's wagons. Lilly had a wild look on her face and ran around in a dither giving orders. Fred was throwing things into their wagons just any ole way. A town family would accompany the Millers out of town and drive two of their wagons for them. Michele and I talked it over and we decided to drift south with them to Sioux City. I felt that maybe I could help Fred and Lilly get to Sioux City alive.

I felt really sorry for Mrs. Miller all this time out here had been a rough period in her life. Her fears had near overwhelmed her. If it hadn't been for Debbie and Michele she could have had a nervous breakdown long ago. She was a sweet soul but not made of the right fiber for the frontier life. In my mind I said, "She won't be back." If she were my wife no way would I ever bring her back out here to this wild potentially dangerous place in Dakota Territory.

By two p.m. we were pulling our freight southward. Fred kept urging his big teams to step lively and we were making good time. There was not a soul left in the town of Sioux Falls. It had become a ghost town in half a day. Only six years old and it died without a whimper or a struggle. It shriveled up and died in less than four hours.

No permanent settlement would be re-established again until 1867, five years from now. At which time the Reads would open a small store for the ranches in the area and he would run a livery and blacksmith shop. He was the one that really put this little town back on the map. Pat, his wife backed him in all he did. They were a family that just needed a hand up and the people of Sioux Falls did that for them.

As we rolled south we saw one war party of young Santee bucks headed south. We quickly made a fort with our wagons and they saw how well organized we were and they left moving ahead in a faint stir of dust. Nine, hard riding leather clad braves bent on destruction and death had gone on by. Their yells were making the hair on my arms stand tall.

Michele said “look.”

As I looked back toward Sioux Falls a lots of black smoke was drifting skyward where Sioux Falls once stood. A sad feeling captured me as I thought what a waste. As we slowed our pace we saw big columns of black smoke ahead as settlers, on the Sioux River, were being burned out and maybe killed.

The long green prairie grass stretched out as far as the eye could see and it danced and swayed in the prairie wind. I was alert and my eyes scanned the terrain in every direction for an unseen enemy. The Santee Sioux were not interested in us. It would cost them way too much. They were looking for unsuspecting homesteaders easy targets to raise havoc on.

A little bit later while riding my saddle horse and leading our little wagon train we came across a burned out wagon that had left from Sioux Falls earlier. The family was lying on the ground dead and scalped. We knew this family well; the woman had been raped and then murdered.

The cruelty of the red man showed up today in their dirty deeds. The Millers knew this family well, we all did. Mrs. Miller started going to pieces as she surveyed the scene before us. Fred quickly moved his wagons ahead of the others so Lilly couldn’t see the burned out wagon or what went on there. This terrible scene was too much for her. My thoughtful wife Michele stepped down from our wagon and comforted her as best she could.

We saw black smoke off to the south and east as we moved southward. I felt bad for what the Sioux were doing. What could I do while my wife and little boy were beside me? I couldn’t help save anyone but them that were with us. There’s no way I could leave my family alone out here I'm not sure I would get to them in time to help anyway.

Most of the settlers out here were living along the rivers and it was easy for the Santee Sioux to locate their homesteads and small ranches and do their dirty deeds.

Following the rivers they could find and kill unsuspecting homesteaders. Most families had little to no protection from the Sioux and were living out here without their men folks to help protect them. These frontier ladies took the brunt of the Sioux rages and died because others weren't doing what they should. The U.S. Government and the bad Indian agents were shorting the Indians on their food rations and now the settlers were paying with their lives.

The buffalo in this area were nearly all killed off and the Sioux food supply from the government was coming to them short of what it was supposed to be. As I think about it, it makes me sick to my stomach.

After two days in Sioux City we posted a letter to Warren of our change of plan. On our trip south I asked Michele "if she would like to see her folks?" With all the hugs and kisses I received I could see she really wanted to go. There is no reason why we couldn't do what we wanted, we had money enough. We sold the team, the wagon, and the riding horse in Sioux City.

We rode the paddle wheeler south to Omaha then the stage east to Des Moines, Iowa City, Davenport and Chicago, Illinois. Fifty-five miles east of Chicago my wife and I left the stage and bought a heavy-duty buggy for our trip on home.

Then traveled northeast on the Sauk Indian Trail to Battle Creek, Michigan and then north to the little town of Fred and east to the Steven's farm. The reunion was a crying, laughing, hugging, happy homecoming. I smiled at the reception Michele received and watched as this loving family made over each other. They had missed us as bad as Michele missed them. What a great reunion we had in their dooryard.

Ransom was missing from this homecoming, and a call was made to him to join in the good fun. Later we found out he had just two months earlier enlisted in the U.S. army. He enlisted with some of his friends from this area. They got into a tough outfit, the 23rd Brigade.

Wendell Lyman Holden, that big boy of mine, was a hit and grandma scooped him up. He wanted his mama but Grandma wouldn't let go. Wendell was eight months of age now. Grandma knew of him but she didn't know him. Now she was getting acquainted with her only grandson. Grandma thought this was the greatest. Wendell wasn't so sure.

It took a lot less time coming back to the Steven's place then it did going west in 1860. Travel was getting better on the frontier as more and more people were moving west. More and more businesses were moving west and that brought freight wagons and many more people. Better trails came into existence and travel became easier, like the stage line that went into Omaha and on west. Our first trip west was faced with all kinds of snags to slow us up. Bloody Bill was the biggest snag of them all.

Dad Stevens had harvested all his crops except his corn. The next three days we worked together hauling shocks of corn up to the corncrib and spent lots of time together, husking out many nice ears and tossing them into the corn crib to dry a little more. The time I spent with Mr. Stevens was enjoyable for me. I remembered doing this same kind of work with my Dad and now it all came flooding back to me.

This ole cow puncher swallowed hard a few times and then finally he had to get out of there. "Lord is it going to be like this all winter long?" All these heart breaking memories of my family still had a bear hug on me and didn't seem to want to let go.

At the supper table I asked, "If they had found out anything about my family and who might have killed them?" They didn't know anything, although another man north of here died last spring of a gunshot wound in the back. That incident put folks on edge. "He was shot in the back like you and your dad were, Ronald.

The guy was just driving on the road heading for home near Vestaburg. We now knew it was someone in this area, but whom? We didn't know that part for sure, but dad had an idea."

Sunday is a special day for us. We were going to Sumner to church, it was a good place to see all our good friends at once. In our Sunday best we arrived a half hour early and visited with Pastor Underwood. What a good Christian man he is. We had a short visit with him and the people as they came into the churchyard. Bill Pugsley hugged me and his Misses hugged and kissed Michele and me. They were glad to see that the three of us had come back home. Bill asked, "How ya doing out West, Ronald? Are you home for good?"

"We're doing fine, Mr. Pugsley, and no were only home for the winter. Uncle Leroy, Aunt Norma, Susan and Danny came rolling in. Leroy jumped from their buggy and hugged me and then Michele. He then took Wendell and held him and then Norma took her turn. Oh what great people they are. This family of mine was great. Yes, my kin folks were awesome.

As we mounted the steps I saw Greg and his mother's buggy coming up the road at a pretty good clip. People swept us into a pew near the front of the church and very soon the music started. The Sunday school was commencing with singing and lots of hand clapping. Shortly the kids left for their classes. Our class was taught by Pastor Underwood it was about a woman who touched Jesus' clothes and was healed and why.

Between services Greg came to see us and we talked. Mrs. Howard came forward with a big smile and was her old wonderful self. Something caught my eye. It looked like one of Ma's new dresses. I couldn't be sure. It's been over two years. I would keep it to myself for now. It was the one I purchased for Mom's birthday. Mom hadn't even worn it yet. I looked her over real good as we talked and I saw nothing else that I remembered.

The Pastor's sermon was wasted on me. I was thinking of many other things that took place in my life. I thought of my ma, the kids and about dad going to the Howard's and how they found him dead on the roadway.

What if, they didn't find him dead? What if? MMM, it couldn't be Greg doing this, he was still recovering. Where did she get that dress? Was it really mom's dress? I got to thinking on it real hard. "Oh Lord, help me figure this one out. It's been way to long without any real results in this case." Lord how long must we sit on pins and needles.

Michele who never missed anything about me focused her beautiful blue eye on me and a bewildered look captured her pretty face. Her hands slipped under and around my arm, slipped down and held my hand. Her gaze came to an end as Wendell started fussing. Michele bounced him a couple times slipping her arm free and hugged him. A smile of joy came to my face while sadness filled me. What a paradox joy and sadness at the same time.

Her unspoken words said, "I love you, Ronnie." It would be tough to slide a piece of paper between us. Our love for each other was still mighty strong. This sweet wonderful woman was my life and this kid was fast becoming my best friend.

I had to tell someone. Michele was my confidant and I could tell her my innermost secrets and she never laughed, or told anyone. She always had good ideas to help me out. Sometimes I wouldn't tell her because I didn't want to load her down with worry. She wouldn't like it much when she found out. My wife wanted to share the good and the bad with me. "Ronnie, we are a team you and I."

Sometimes I play the fool for she had excellent insight into most problems. Common sense is a rare thing in this old world and most valuable to those who have it. My sweet wonderful wife was loaded down with it and shared it with those who would accept it from her.

My life was good with Michele in it. She is the one that makes it all worthwhile. I think of life without her sometimes. No, I don't want to think that way. My goal in this ole life is to scatter seeds of love and kindness around her.

"Give me that peace that only you can give, Jesus." I really haven't buried my family yet. My bereavement was still chasing me and now it was catching up. Sadness was coming in like a flood, trying to overwhelm me.

The Bible says, "Whatsoever a man soweth that shall he also reap." That's what I'm sowing, seeds of love and I'm getting a bumper crop from her. By golly it's oh so wonderful to know the love of a good woman. The service came to an end and people were filing out to go home, (the church only had one service when the days grew short, so farmers could do chores before it got dark) many friends and neighbors stopped to talk and it was great to have so many friends crowding around us.

Pastor Owen Underwood invited us to have Sunday dinner with his family. They lived in Sumner on Main Street. What a great family they were. Two of the girls played piano and after dinner we sang and sang about the Lord.

Pastor Underwood asked me about the West and my ranch out there, of the Indians that were on the warpath and why? About my gunshot wound, the death of my folks and did I have a clue to who did this dastardly deed?

Some people have an evil nature and killing comes easy to them. You say you killed Mr. Howard after he shot at you several times and when you were on your front porch. It took place shortly after Greg and you had that fight. Your dad went to take Mr. Howard's body home and your dad came home later shot gunned in the back. Then your family was murdered and burned up with him. Lastly you were shot in the back. I guess I am pointing my finger. My suspicion is one thing proof is another? What I think won't hold up in a court of law."

While traveling west toward the Steven's home the sunset was giving us a show, with reds, oranges, gold and blue colors before us in the evening sky. As we rolled on home Michele questioned me about the service and what Pastor Underwood said. She looked at me and said, "Darling, what do you think?"

"It is too soon to say, Honey. I will be seeing more of the Howard's in the months to come and that might tell us something."

"Darling, be careful, if they killed before they can kill again if they think they need to. If they had done harm to your family and tried to murder you, maybe they aren't through yet. They could be still aiming to get at you. Honey, please be careful, we need you."

Tuesday in the late afternoon I went alone to visit with the Howard's and have a look around. I took my pistol along and kept my rifle covered up in our buggy. This ole boy wasn't taking any chances this time around. Gregory and Mrs. Howard sat in the parlor eating homemade donuts and did they ever taste good, (out west they called them bear signs) and we sipped sweet cider to wash them down. The talk was quite pleasant. It was of the Great Western Prairie and our life out there.

We talked about the lovely dress, the one she wore in church Sunday? She loved it so much and wore it a lot in the summer. She said "I think, I like it the best, of any I own."

Then I asked, "Where she'd purchased it?"

She said, "The boys got it for me for my birthday."

"Greg, where did you get that lovely dress for your mother?"

"Don and Jerry picked it up in Carson City on one of their trips down there. They bought it brand new. Jerry and Don have jobs down there and they bring home something almost every week, some used, some new, but all good things." Ma Howard said, "I sometimes wonder how those two boys can afford to purchases all those things for us. I guess they really love their momma very much. I got to say it, my boys are really good boys."

Greg asked, "How is Michele? She looks well. It's hard to picture you two as mother and dad. Ron you're a mighty lucky man. Michele is a very lovely lady and a good person which you already know by now."

"You know it Greg; I'm a mighty lucky man to have her for my own. Life is so good with Michele by my side and now with little Wendell around; it is fantastic. I never dreamed it would turn out this good"

"Ron, how are things shaping up out West? Is it really good grass? Is it as wild and woolly as they say? I guess I'm envious of you making the move and getting in on the ground floor. We heard the Santee Sioux went on the warpath out by you folks. Was it bad? I've heard so much about the Sioux. Is the Santee Sioux a tough lot like we hear, or what? The papers say the Sioux are skilled hunters and great warriors, is it true."

We talked and I answered all their questions as best I could.

He finally said, "that isn't my cup of tea, I'm sure glad I'm still here in Michigan where the Indians are civilized. "

I then added, "Any place west of the Mississippi River is wild country." Dakota Territory is wild and full of many dangerous men, both good and bad. Sometimes when the winter storms blow in it can destroy a herd of cattle and kill anyone that is caught unprepared. Out there you need a support team or you can't make it."

Finally they asked that question, "Did you find out anything about the death of your folks? Do you have any idea who killed your family or shot you?"

Mrs. Howard had been praying hard for Michele and me for quite a spell, that the killers would be caught. I thanked her for it. I thought to myself, what if it was one of her three kids that did this, how would she pray then? This gentle sweet woman loved the Lord and wanted the killers brought to justice.

They invited Michele and me for supper on Saturday night. They wanted us to come early and bring Wendell. I accepted their invitation for the only clue I had was right here at the Howard's farm. The Howard brothers would be home then. I wouldn't ransack their house, although I did want to see as much as I could and find out as much as I could, by watching what Ma Howard and the guys wore.

On Wednesday Michele, Wendell and I slipped out in mid-morning and headed over to Uncle Leroy's and Aunt Norma's. It was a wonderful day. They had kept up the small gravesite and it looked pretty good. It was so much better than when I left for the West. The split rails were still in place just where I'd left them and white wash made them look great. There were flowers everywhere.

Aunt Norma loved flowers and they grew close up around their new home. Leroy had enlarged the gravesite to accommodate their family. Mama's roses still clung to the rail fence and did they ever look and smell good. Even this late in the fall they had blossoms.

It was chore time when we left; it was a very satisfying day. I even went through seeing the home place and the gravesite without eye troubles. On the inside it was a little rough, while on the outside I looked composed. All the tension drained from me as Michele slid her hand into mine. "Lord please don't let me ever take this magnificent lady for granted or her wonderful love. Help me keep it burning with my love and keep it burning bright."

On Sunday I saw a broach on Mrs. Howard that looked like Ma's. "Oh Lord was the hangman's noose coming down over the Howard boys' neck." The cold-blooded murderers deserved to end up on the gallows. What would it do to Mrs. Howard, if her two boys hung for killing my family? It looked like they weren't through yet. They'd killed that man up by Vestaburg, a short while ago or at least someone in this area bushwhacked him.

Over the course of the next couple months many things transpired. Mrs. Howard used a hankie with the letter H in the corner. Something that I knew without a doubt had belonged to ma. The H stood for Holden not Howard.

The law confronted the Howard boys and was closing in on them. Jerry and Don disappeared in the middle of the night. We heard they headed south and enlisted in the army. The law found a large trunk, in the hayloft, with a lot of our family's things in it.

The sheriff bungled the case really bad. Now our problem would be someone else's problem. There was no evidence that would stick on Jim or Gregory Howard. But Jerry and Don were as guilty as all get out. I had hoped that they would swing for their dirty deeds. But no luck there! They slipped their guilty heads out of the hangman's noose and left the country.

TIME TO LEAVE

President Lincoln, last year, passed a bill that would allow any adult to file on one hundred and twenty acres of land if they stayed on it for five years and would improved it by putting buildings on it and farming it. Mister Stevens felt that this bill would send thousands of poor folks out West looking for free land.

The Stevens were a lonely pair without their children around. The fact that they missed Michele plus seeing how good we were doing financially made up their minds. They sold their farm and loaded up their belongings into two wagons and left their home in Mid-Michigan far behind.

We read in the local paper where the Sioux had been rounded up and the army had them in camps. So they felt that, that problem was solved, so Michele's folks would head for Dakota Territory in March. They were as impulsive as I was in leaving Michigan, back a couple years ago. The two of them had made up their minds to go west and set about leaving their old homestead in the spring.

I left in February ahead of the family. Cold weather kept Michele with her folks, at home. Wendell was now a year old, a little bit too young to travel this early in the year. The weather was the biggest reason for them to come west later. This ole cow puncher wanted to be home to help with the spring cattle drive.

I was needed in two places at once, with my family and back home working the ranch. Michele suggested I go on ahead and she would come later with her mom and dad when they came west. "Honey we will be fine just you wait and see." Before this kid left for the West he hired a young man from the Sumner Church, Matthew Roberts, an older teen, and Richie Parker, a single man about thirty years old, to go with the Stevens and help out. I've known Rich and Matt and their families for several years.

This dude was apprehensive about his family traveling without more protection. Matt could shoot and was a strapping lad and Richie Parker knew horses as well as anyone. They would do what was needed to defend my family and help with the livestock.

They would stay on the stage road all the way to Des Moines. We had planned it out well. When I got the cattle sold in Des Moines I would hustle on east to find them.

I found out much later that there was an extremely bad element in Missouri. Bad men were roaming the countryside along the Mississippi River and on west preying on people, wagon trains and stage coaches. This area had produced gangs of thugs, robbing and killing. It was a lot worse than when we came out here a year ago. Most were Civil War deserters mixed in with southern sympathizers who couldn't go home. Men who took up crime to survive and doing things they would never do back home on their farms, like fighting guerrilla warfare and hindering the North anyway they could.

I made a bee-line for home as fast as I could. I sold the surrey for a good profit, purchased a good saddle and two good mares, loaded one with a pack saddle and headed for home. I say home. It really wasn't home without Michele being there.

I knew that all too well as I traveled west. My heart and thoughts were often of my wife and that little one of ours. Was this a good idea? They thought so, but I'm not so sure. This being apart was for the birds and it was one thing I didn't need.

March, of '63, the ranch lay just ahead. Warren Drake had the ranch working really well. The guys said Warren was a slave driver. He had his rock polishing business up and running and doing well. The beef were bunched up south of the ranch buildings and ready to go. The crew had been buying steers all winter long. We had nearly eleven hundred sixty critters going east to market.

People that feared the goings on in this area were bringing all kinds of stock into our ranch for us to sell. They were paid and many left for larger cities where there were more people. I guess I understand what they were going through

The ranch hands purchased cows, calves and steers of all sizes all through the winter. Six hundred head were mine. Sixty head of steers were from my own herd, from my original cows. A hundred and twenty-five head of breeding stock, from the bunch I brought west in "60". This little spread was starting to show some profits of its own, finally. Being anxious to get back to my wife, we finished branding and in three days we were headed east with all our fleabags.

Benjamin made the trip with us this time for he had livestock of his own in the drive. Wesley and his wife, Pat, stayed on the ranch while the rest of us headed east. Debbie and little Jared came and stayed, with the Reads, as we rode east with the cattle, to market.

On April 16, we sold our mammoth herd for twenty-four dollars a head. These cowhands of mine were making me lots and lots of money so I must help them out. Now I made Ben a full-fledged rancher with a gift of three hundred dollars. Ben and Warren would buy livestock on their way back home, or if they wanted to make another trip back to De Moines with steers, then they could do that also. If you want to, make a swing up into Minnesota then go ahead. As they worked their way home, I took two extra horses and headed east in the direction of my family and Michele's folks.

The people in Des Moines gave me the scoop on what had happened here last August and the beginning of the Sioux war. On August 17 four Santee Sioux Braves took some eggs from a farmer's hen house, after a hunt. One brave was accused by another of being afraid of the white man. To prove he wasn't, with a bow and arrow and war club, he killed the family and stole their horses. This would lead to big trouble.

Later in a war council the Sioux leaders asked, "What should the tribe do, return the four to stand trial, or what?" The final decision was to wage war against the whites. Little Crow, the Santee war chief was against war. He knew the blue coats would come.

There is no way to beat the white man in an all out war. Some argued the whites were at war with the South and couldn't come and we must take back our land now while we can. Against his better judgment Little Crow struck the war post and joined those who would kill the whites. That night the killing began. Without any warning they killed unsuspecting settlers on their land. Many whites were off to war and no one was prepared for a brutal Indian attack and few whites were spared. Only friends of the Santee were spared. Only people that did a good turn for the Sioux. Many long robes, who worked with the Sioux, had to flee, because many Sioux resented them being there teaching the red men some new religion and trying to do away with the old ways. No one was really safe out here on the Great Western Prairie.

The first morning the Sioux hit the Indian agency store at Redwood Falls, killing the agent there. He looked like a pincushion with arrows sticking out all over him. His mouth was crammed full of grass when they found him dead outside the agency. It looked like the Sioux might have made sport of him before they killed him. This cruel man made his bed and now he must sleep in it. The sad thing was many others died for what a few money hungry men did.

When the Santee Sioux were in great need of food he said, "Let them eat grass." The great cruelty of this one man caused the death of so many people. The Government now decided to take a good long look at their Indian policies in the West.

Many long robes were saved, being warned by converted Indians, in advance of the Santee killing spree. Missionaries had to high tail it out of there. Many escaped east with what they wore on their backs and what they could carry. These men of God had to scramble to save their lives and the lives of their families. Eighteen sixty two was a bad time in Minnesota.

A story was told of a young boy who carried his younger brother nearly sixty miles through Indian country. His paw and older brothers were killed, in their fields, as they worked the land. The boy's mother was wounded. The mother and the two kids found each other later." Life can be tough for women folk without their men to help out. The folks in Des Moines said the Santee Sioux uprising lasted about a month and the Indians killed over seven hundred fifty settlers and wounded many others.

"Colonel Henry Sibley took raw recruits into the field and defeated the red skins. Three hundred or so Sioux braves were sentenced to death for their devilish deeds in Minnesota. Bishop Henry Whipple, a Methodist minister, a good man of God, went to Washington DC pleading for clemency for the red men. He argued the biggest blame rested with the bad Indian system of the Government." President Abraham Lincoln acknowledged it and agreed to do something about it.

"The President commuted most of the Indian's sentences. He said, "Death to the leaders and proven rapists and murders, no matter who they were."

"December 26, 1862. In just over four months from "August 17 thirty-eight Santee Sioux Warriors were hanged for the dastardly crimes they perpetrated." Thirty-eight braves were sent on their way to the happy hunting ground. I felt a little distressed and perplexed about the whole thing. My hands were tied and I felt sad. But what's done is done.

Little Crow and two other Sioux leaders escaped to Canada. Later I heard the war chief Little Crow was shot by a homesteader, who knew him, while he picked berries in a wood lot. The other two braves were dragged back to Minnesota, in the dead of night, and hung for their crimes. The sad part is that for the actions of some, the whole Santee nation and all Sioux suffered. The feelings were bad against the Sioux Indians and all Indians. From that day on a saying came about, from that Minnesota Massacre, "that the only good Indian is a dead Indian."

In 1863, seventeen hundred Santee Sioux, who hadn't been part of the uprising or the slaughter that took place out here, were driven onto a reservation farther to the west in Dakota Territory. As I heard this frightful news about my newfound friends, my heart sank. I know hunger was a bad thing the winter before the uprising. It was really bad and many Sioux families were starving to death for what the white man did to them, and tempers were near the breaking point even back then.

Forgiveness and mercy doesn't come all that easy from Indians, especially when hunger is in control. Settlers took the brunt of what the crooked Indian agents did to the Santee Sioux. I felt the lesson to be learned is when the Government promises handouts you must give up some of your rights.

The question is will you get the handouts? Who knows, they reneged on the Indians. They did it to blacks, plus Mexicans in "46." When will it be the white man's turn? I hope we never concede any of our God given rights ever. What will they want to take from us, if that time ever comes?

Right now the Federal Government needs us to take this land for them. Don't give up you firearms or freedom of speech. Watch the Government closely at all times. They seem only to look out for themselves. What is their hidden agenda and how will it affect us? All these feelings make me sad and thoughtful as I traveled the stage road east looking for my family and the Stevens.

In a Podunk place called Newton, Iowa, in a general store, I found something that excited me. It was a new fan dangled rifle that was called a repeater. It wasn't a muzzle loader. The new spiffy looking rifle fired a lead bullet with a brass casing, developed in 1858 just five years ago. The Henry was a rifle that the South said, "you could load it on Sunday and fire it all week long." If you ask me it was a beautiful piece of equipment. This ole boy wasted no time and purchased a rifle and two hundred fifty rounds of ammo. Not knowing if I could buy ammo for it somewhere else. What will man think of next? The Henry Repeating Rifle will revolutionize weapons' fire. If we'd only had these against Bill Anderson back in 1860 it would have really helped out.

BAD TROUBLE

The town of Newton,.Iowa had not seen my family so I started east checking as I went. Three and a half days later, in a wide spot in the road called Williamsburg, I found dad's two wagons by the livery stable with no one around. I located his big teams inside in the horse stalls but not their two saddle horses. The two Morgan's were missing from their things. What had happened here was someone out riding them?

The stable hand said, "Check at the boarding house up the street a block. So on horseback I stirred dust up to the Sleep and Dine Boarding House on Main Street and checked with the owners. I found out that Mr. and Mrs. Stevens had rented room #2 at the top of the stairs, first door on the left and the big room overlooked Main Street.

I found dad stretched out in a bed with a bullet hole in his side and mom sat in a rocking chair, at his side, with a bad leg. It was broken. My family was missing; Michele, Wendell, Matthew Roberts and Richie Parker were gone. I found out that my wife and son were kidnapped by a gang of killers about four miles east of town by a stream.

Mom filled me in about what had happened. She was suffering with lots of pain from a badly broken leg all the time fighting back tears as we talked. A few miles east of town a dozen highwaymen ambushed us; shot Mr. Stevens in the back. They killed Richie Parker on the spot but Matthew escaped on horseback to warn the sheriff here in town. They're out there right now trying to get our family back before something bad happens to them.

My slow burn started when I saw the two wagons by the livery barn. Mom fanned that slow burn with some bad news. It then exploded into some mighty hot flames like a fire in a blacksmith's forge. I was hot under the collar and ready to do something. First I paid for a month of room and board at the boarding house for mom and dad.

This ole man didn't wait for Dad Stevens to wake up. After mom's information about my wife and child this kid said his good-bye and made a beeline for the general store here in town. There I purchased another Henry and more ammo and loaded my packhorse. It looked like I was going to start another Civil War with all my armament. This fidgety father bought another saddle, bridle, halter, and scabbard for his horse plus an extra Henry Rifle, some saddlebags and some food to eat on the run.

Then this ole boy skedaddled on out of there as fast as my three nags could carry me, all the time urging my mares toward the ambush spot on the trail ahead. This worry wart fought to keep a cool head and think this thing through.

My family's lives were at stake so a cool head must prevail as my horses pushed plenty of dirt behind us. The sheriff assumed the crooks were deserters from the military or men on the dodge. Matthew, the sheriff and about a dozen deputies took out after them chasing them south toward Missouri.

The red hot flame of fire returned to a slow burn as I reached the ambush spot. My mind was working at full speed as I raced south. Twenty-five riders plus packhorses had headed south on this trail ahead of me. Half were in pursuit of the twelve or so drygulchers. The sheriff's posse tracks were clear in the dirt at my feet.

This hothead put the hooves of his three horses on the beat up path, churned up by so many horses, and followed the two groups at a ground eating pace, following the outlaws south. This ole follower didn't worry much about an ambush with the law dogs between the marauders and me. Speed was my only goal as I shifted from one horse to another trying to keep them semi-fresh, in my long chase.

I would go crazy if I lost Michele and Wendell. "Lord, I can't lose her; she is all that makes any difference in my life. What I do on this trip sweet Jesus is for Wendell and his mommy and maybe for me." Man-oh-man I feel lost, lost like last year's Easter eggs. I'm not worth a whole lot without them. This caused me to get really mad all over. If anything happens to my wife, they had better kill me quickly.

This lovebird was carrying a bad feeling that never invaded me before; not even with the death of my folks. With my folks, sisters and brother I felt a great loss and sick to my stomach but this mood was black as a thundercloud. Right now this ole Michigander is probably as dangerous as I've ever been in my life. My mood is intolerant for what was done to my little family and me. I'm jumpier than a fox in a hen house and strung as tight as a piano string. You might say that I'm a loose cannon, primed and ready. It would only take a spark to set me off. So kidnappers beware.

When I think of Michele my spirit drains from me and I am half numb with the thought of her in the hands of these outlaws and their reign of terror. If they touch or violate her in any way it will be Hades to pay for the perpetrators of this terrible crime. They had better run fast and hard.

The second day down this trail I saw a flash of movement up ahead. So I slipped off the tracks and pulled that new Henry from its resting place. With my horses behind cover, I waited for them. Shortly several men on horseback drifted into view. As they drew near I saw what looked like badges pinned to their coats.

Slowly this heartsick dude eased the three big horses out of the brush and rested with his horse crossways of the trail. With that mean Henry of mine at the ready I confronted the group with my drawn rifle. My colt 44 revolver pistol set light in the holster on my hip. There were about a dozen men in this bunch. It was the sheriff and his posse on their way back to Williamsburg. They had not completely caught up with the outlaws and the kidnappers were still headed south. I took time to introduce myself as, Ronald Holden. For a spell we talked about what had transpired in the last few days as they tried to catch up to the outlaws ahead of them. The sheriff said we got close enough to be shot at. The outlaw gang went on and skedaddled across the county line.

"We gave them a run for their money, but other than that we didn't accomplish very much, I'm sorry to say. Sonny, I wish we could have done more for ya than we did.

"Ronald, your hired lad did a stroke of business. He rode into town and got help for your father-in-law and mother-in-law. Your father-in-law was shot up and your mother-in-law had a badly broken leg and the other hired man was kilt up on the trail. Shot in the back of the head and he lived 'bout three minutes I'm guessing'."

Mathew said "About a dozen men stopped at the wagons and robbed the Stevens, then emptied the wagons of their valuable merchandise. It seems like they took your wife as an afterthought. Your baby boy is with her. The outlaws are a dragging the whole bunch south with them. We formed this here posse and rode south after them.

They ambushed us in the woods and wounded these two family men. Nine of us stayed on their trail and continued to chase them to the county line where our authority ended. Before leaving Williamsburg we telegraphed the sheriff in Washington County and he's a looking for them to come through down there."

"Sir, do you fellows have any idea who they are or what they wanted? I'm new to this area and I don't have a handle on things yet. Those worthless excuses for men are moving south toward Mount Pleasant, heading for the brushy hill country along the Mississippi River. That is still wild country down there. They've got to pass through Washington into Henry or Jefferson Counties. They are probably headed south for the Missouri line where other gangs are hold up.

That young feller of yours is a good lad. Matthew Robert and your friend Mr. Clayborn Barnard pushed us all the way. Matt and Clayborn are right now following them on into Washington County. If they can they will notify the sheriff down there who are also looking for the bushwhackers to come through.

Those boys are doing all that's possible to cut them off. I wish ya the best of luck in finding your lady. We'll pray for ya, that ya have a good hunt. Use good judgment when ya get close. Those snakes are killers and who knows what they will do next. We'll let ya go and lots of luck to you in outwitting them, and getting your lady back. Look sharp and go with God."

I'd heard all the chin music I wanted to for now. What I wanted was to be hot on those sleaze balls tracks. As the sheriff drifted north I raced south pushing my horses in hot pursuit of those up ahead. The tracks were easy to see even in the moonlight. I worked my three ponies hard trying to catch up. I took time for them to eat and I grained them well and slept.

Then off we went again chasing the border gang south. I ate and drank on horseback following the trail that lay in the dirt before me.

Late the second night, by moonlight, I came upon Matthew's camp. Glowing coals in a pit gave it away. I saw no bedrolls at first. Matthew Roberts challenged me and I sang out who I was and we talked a short spell. His friend Clayborn Barnard was unknown to me and I didn't have time to get acquainted. I needed sleep and I needed it now. Quickly I crawled into my bedroll after I watered my three horses and then staked them out to feed on the good grass.

"Michele, Honey, keep your courage up. I'm coming for ya." Thoughts of my wife merged into darkness and soon I slept. A poke in my backside made me jump. I awoke with a start and sat up. It was Matthew.

"Up and at em Ron, it's daylight in the swamp and times a wasting." Without a word I scrambled out, rolled up my bedroll and placed it on the back of my saddle. Then after saddling my other horses I took a plate of food. Repacked some of my stuff and let Matt use my packhorse.

After wolfing down my breakfast I grabbed leather and skedaddled on out of there to the drumming of my horse's hooves, pounding the ground, moving at an easy gallop. This ole trail rider was high tailing it away from their night camp; I just couldn't wait for them. This half sick dude had to find his wife and spring her loose from that group.

Matt was kicking dirt on the camp fire as I left out of there. Looking back at Mathew he was filling his saddle with the seat of his pants. Mr. Barnard, whoever he was, was already moving out of camp. In the gray of predawn, the darkness was slowly giving way to daylight, we hot-footed it on down the trail.

As we rode it got lighter and the sun would soon be on the scene and the darkness would give up and leave. As I scanned the trail ahead the light did away with the murky darkness altogether. I wondered who was Matt's big bearded friend a following us? "I want to thank you for his help, Lord." They didn't give up like the posse did. They are putting all this time in helping me find this bad bunch.

I should have said something to him this morning. A nod wasn't really enough. To be sure this thankful friend will take time later on and thank him properly. Funny thing though the sheriff said, "He was my friend. That was a logical mistake.

I didn't know him from Adam, but if he stays on I'll count him as a friend. He is dressed way too nice for the frontier and chasing outlaws. Was he from Michigan? I don't recall ever seeing him anywhere. Of course that long face hair covered a lot. No he wasn't one darn bit familiar to me.

This was my forth day since leaving Williamsburg and the horse tracks seem to be stopping more frequently, which means they've slowing their frantic pace down a bit.

I guess they're not worried about anyone still following, after they got rid of the posse. The county lines don't mean a whole lot to me. I hope the law will head off this wild bunch and get my family back. The county is so big and they have so much territory to cover, my guess is the law won't see hide nor hair of them when they come through their county.

I'm thinking a lot of Michele and Wendell. God only knows what she is going through out there. She needed my help and I wasn't there to give it to her. I remember her face as I rode away back up there, in Michigan. Tears flowed profusely and her pretty face was cranked up, as crying distorted her exquisite face and that hurt.

The Lord knows I didn't really want to leave. This fool should have stayed. That was my mistake. Well it is long past and there is too much water under the bridge. There's no way to go back and do it over again. Who would think that anything like this would happen this far east? I should have stayed with them. I really didn't think they would travel this far west in that short a time. But they did.

Yesterday forenoon I came upon a corpse that had been shot. He was gunned in the back, at one of their campsite. I hope this is one of the gang and not some innocent man who stumbled onto their group. I'm hoping they are having internal problems for this looks like cold blooded murder to me.

Turkey buzzards were already having a feast on his body. I now had new worries for my wife. The way I figured it they were not more than a long day's ride ahead of me. I didn't like it much as those dark storm clouds were drifting in on me.

A rain would make it most miserable out here and make the tracks harder to follow once they were washed away. If they split up their tracks could be washed away and then where would I be? I really needed to catch up to these killers and the sooner the better for all concerned. Matthew Roberts and his friend Clayborn Barnard couldn't keep up with me with only three horses between them. They were slowly slipping farther and farther behind. I liked their effort to keep pace with me. These two faithful men gave me encouragement.

A light rain came and muffled the rhythmic drumming of my horses' hooves on the ground. It became a splashing, sucking sound as we traveled south in pursuit of the kidnappers. The further south we traveled the outlaws' tracks were getting fainter in the soggy soil. At dark I left the tracks and made a campfire and prayed for no more rain. About midnight Matt and this Clayborn ambled on in. It was no problem for them for they could see my deep tracks in the Iowa mud.

In the darkness of predawn, I ventured out onto the outlaws' path. The rain had stopped and soon the light would make it so I could follow. At daylight the sound of shod hooves beating the muddy ground came to my ears, as my horses carried me through the heavy timber.

Our horses were slipping and sliding and making tracks in the soggy soil as we pushed south in pursuit of the kidnappers. Michele is ever on my mind and prayer is always on my lips, while my tired eyes search for any sign of life up ahead of me.

Always scanning the trees and meadows ahead for anything out of order, I felt that one of those low down snakes in the grass was out of the picture, thanks to someone in their group. Their buckshot had found a home in that fellow's back. That left about a dozen more kidnappers to handle with murder in their hearts.

No matter what happens to me I must free my wife from what these outlaws are putting her through. The Lord knows that killing will soon begin and my heart is not in it. I don't want to kill anyone. But Michele will be free or I will die trying and dying is not in my plans.

About noon their tracks lay before me in, the mud, looking fresh and clear. The rain had stopped and they were traveling again in the mud. Each camp that I've inspected have two guards posted, one on their back trail and another on a rise near the camp where they could see their horses and the campsite and give a signal if anyone came near. It had been seven days since Michele and Wendell were abducted from the wagons up north. Their pace has slowed considerably this last day or so. The rain is one reason and I'm sure it gave them confidence that no one would follow. They had turned eastward late yesterday.

The distance from one camp to the next was noticeably shorter. They didn't seem in that much of a hurry anymore and that worried me some for Michele's safety. Would they use her or hurt her in some way? I had many thoughts go roaming around in my mind. From all the prints in the mud I can't tell if she's been molested in her travels or not. I can't understand why they took her and Wendell in the first place. They would just be extra baggage to haul along.

She is a good looking woman and I do worry some about that. These thoughts played on my mind way too much, while there's nothing I can do now but press them until I get her back. These last couple of nights I've been staring at the moon while all I could see was Michele and uneasiness crept into my mind. I've got to trust in the One that really cares for us.

With study, I can see most of what they do in their camp. Now I need to rummage around in my mind and dig out a plan for getting them both back. A plan that doesn't put them in jeopardy. With these two new Henry rifles of mine I have lots of firepower to make them hurt and I'm not above raising havoc on them at this time.

If someone hurts her they had better hang on to their hats and head for the high hills. It seems like they stay away from her, in camp, for some reason. Wendell is over thirteen months old now and must be a handful for his mommy with them always on the move.

That man that lay dead back along the trail was he friend or foe? Did this bunch kill him? He was shot in the back up close, like my Dad was back in Michigan. I remembered Bloody Bill Anderson's bunch and how they acted. That is what Anderson's gang of cutthroat bushwhackers would do. That little incident had their trademark written all over it.

I'm sure if it had been him they would of scalped Dad, Mom Stevens and Richie Parker. Bloody Bill always wanted Michele. I hope this outfit doesn't join up with his gang. More men would make my job next to impossible. These rats had seen the posse following them and waylaid them. Did they still suspect they were being followed? If not I might use that to my advantage. Think Ron, and be ready to take advantage of any circumstance offered.

I don't understand this type of people so I really don't know what they will do or have on their minds. I guess I assume too much of this bad bunch. Who are they anyway? The war spawned many such groups as these. Bad dudes bent on murder and mayhem for profit. What motivates a group like this, to rob, kill and kidnap?

From a hillside about midnight, way up ahead just off the trail, in their camp I saw the red glow of coals and flicker of a small flame. It was the dying embers of a campfire and bedrolls told me of their exact location. The camp was in a tiny wood lot. I saw no movement anywhere around the fire pit.

Off to my left, by a big tree, near the base of this hill, just off their back trail aways, a man struck a phosphorus match. Let it burn then lit a pipe giving away his location. Only a fool would smoke on guard duty. The match light could blind a person for a short while to anything that might be in the area.

What was he thinking? Apparently they didn't think anyone was out here. Well they're in for a big surprise and soon. Ah it's a good break for me. Slowly I made my way downhill on foot without my shoes on. All I heard as I moved off the hill was a slight swish in the tall grass as the breeze moved it to and fro and the occasional sound of the night birds. Like an owl that hooted and the steady chirping of insects making a racket on this dark summer's night.

The barrel of my Colt revolver made a dull thud as it flattened hair to the scalp, of the now unconscious man. I tied and gagged him before I retrieved my shoes and horses then dragged him to his mount. I loaded him on his horse and headed back up the trail. Leaving him bound and gagged in the horse's tracks for Matt and Clayborn to find. Then I returned to the guard's post under the Oak tree and waited for his relief to come.

An hour later the new guard came strolling my way and walked right up to me and said, "How is it Samuel?" Without an answer I whopped him along side of his head, his knees buckled and down he went. Later Mister Clayborn Barnard, with a big smile on his face, called me "The headache maker." I bound and gagged the prisoner and I lay him beside his buddy. Two presents, gift wrapped for Matthew Roberts and Mr. Barnard to find as they followed. They would deliver them to the law office in a small town along the back trail, somewhere.

Now my attention was focused on the camp lookout, somewhere on the hillside near their night camp. Leaving my mount out of sight and in slow motion I snuck up the hill and lay in the grass gazing down on the outlaws' camp. Where in the world was that dad blame lookout?

The tall grass stirred slightly, in the early morning breeze, and I looked for him without success. Maybe he wasn't on this hill tonight although they usually posted a man close to their camp generally on a hillside somewhere. The first two men seemed at ease in the darkness.

An hour and a half past and a man left the darkness of the campsite below and headed our way searching the hillside for the guard. As the relief came closer a man not fifty feet away stood up and to my surprise it was Jerry Howard. That slim frame and narrow brimmed hat gave him away. I thought to myself, Jerry, you're on my list for killing my family and stealing my wife. You will soon be history.

Now the man that was shot gunned in the back, made more sense. Jerry Howard was here still doing his dirty work. This outfit would never do this again. How many families has this outfit put through Hell like they did mine? If it was one family it was way too many. People didn't deserve to go through what my family went through.

As Jerry made his way downhill toward the woods the new sentry settled into his spot. The crickets' mating songs had intensified. Ever so quietly I circled in behind this young fellow and made this lawbreaker number three on my list, for Matt and Mr. Claiborne's collection.

By the time I deposited number three and returned to the camp area the alarm had gone out that the men had deserted. The low down scoundrels, in camp, were milling around wondering what had happened.

What was Jerry Howard doing here in Missouri? Donald his brother must be here somewhere. I could see Michele and it looked like Wendell was nursing. I couldn't really see him all that well. I wanted to reach out and pull her to me but first things first. What was my next move?

First I must get as many horses as I can away from them and drive them off. I couldn't steal their string but if I could stampede them, that way I might get some and that would put a few of these men afoot. Riding double would slow them some and that would help us out a lot.

I must get as close to their camp as possible and surprise them. Rifle fire could be deadly, so it must be by surprise, that way most of the shots would come from revolvers and not rifles. The safe way would be to kill their mounts, although I would rather not do it that way. That would be a last resort. If I cannot shake any horses loose then I must start killing them and that went against the grain.

Getting my family free is my ultimate goal. Everyone else in that camp must look out for themselves. Sneaking to within fifty yards of their camp I led my horse into a shallow gully. It ran the right way for me to draw even closer to the horses. At thirty-five yards I mounted my mare and came at a frantic gallop. At twenty yards I must have sounded like a bunch of wild Indians on the war path with all that howling and yelling that was going on. It probably sounded more like the Banshee from down under.

As I rode closer, horses' heads jerked up and they started moving away from me in fear of the noise I made. Pistol fire sounded and a man came up in front of me and Mr. Henry blew him away. My horse shied a bit then moved on out of their camp following their horses south.

This ole horse thief pursued about eighteen nags the rest went in other directions. The outlaws would need to round them up if they were going to travel today. Pistol fire was steady and directed at me. In a hail of bullets, a horse next to me faltered, then ran a few yards, went down and rolled head over heels in the damp soil and then struggled to get up but couldn't.

The firing slowed then stopped. I moved the horses back around their camp and back to the trail, heading north. When I reached the three pieces of bound up baggage, the outlaws were still lying on the ground. I took time to hobble the seventeen mounts and check the men's bonds to see if they were tight. These boys would like nothing better than to escape and return to warn the renegades that it was only one man out here causing all the trouble.

Seventeen horses freed and one dead. If they rounded up the rest they would have about six mounts to ride with a dozen or so adult riders, counting my wife. I had separated these ponies from the kidnappers and they needed every horse, they had, to haul men and the loot they had stolen from people along the stage route.

I must be careful. They will be watching for me. They now know I'm here. I must be one step ahead of them at all times, or I might wind up dead. What would happen to my wife and son then? No way, I just couldn't let that happen. They'd be slowed without horses. These low down greedy scum would be at a high state of alertness and looking for their horses and me.

I must not let them steal horses from local farmers in the area. They might do damage to their families.

Before noon Matthew Roberts and Clayborn Barnard rode in. Clayborn seemed a bit nervous. He seemed uneasy being around me, although I'm glad he's here. We needed his help in the worst way but could I trust him if and when the shooting started? I sure hope so!

Matt informed me there was a town two miles back. I had ridden on by it late last night and didn't see it, with all the lamps off. We hustled on back to the town and deposited our trash in their calaboose and boarded the outlaws' horses at the livery stable adding one to our string so we each had two mounts to ride. We warned the locals of the trouble we've had and that we were right now pursuing the outlaws south.

Mr. Barnard had the town Marshall telegraph the sheriff of the counties ahead about the no good trash that we were following. We would try to keep them from stealing any more mounts if we could. The town folks chained these three hard cases to a huge log for safekeeping. No way could they break free from that unmovable oak log. It must have weighted a couple of tons. With only a few men in this whole town we didn't ask for any help.

As we rode out Barnard held back, he came but stayed behind. I guess he would rather follow than lead. I wouldn't depend on him to heavily. He is probably a city slicker and didn't really understand the West and its ways. Making tracks south we must exercise extreme care in whatever we do. These outlaws are now alerted to our presence here.

What have I done to my woman? Would this reckless foolhardy play hurt her? I've got to think things through and not take so many chances. There is no need to be careless.

Whether the bushwhackers get away or not I must save Michele and that son of mine. If all else fails my family must be gotten free from these poor excuses for men.

My thoughts were of her and how she loves and needs me and people in general. This sweet lady has my admiration and my undying love. This may be my last chance to bring her out of here alive. As I thought on it I can see where we were not out of the woods yet, not by a long shot. There is still way to many outlaws for three men to deal with unless we come up with a workable plan.

This trail is way too long for me. I'm getting sick and tired of my back being a mattress and being laid out on the ground every night. What a fool I was leaving my family back in Michigan and not looking after them like a man should. What a mistake I made. Well no sense crying over spilled milk, what's done is done. A man isn't worth much if he doesn't provide for his family. "Forgive me Lord for that."

That ranch got out of line in my priorities. Money is one thing, but not the main thing. My Dad often said, 'Keep the main thing the main thing.' First God, then family, health and money is way down on the totem pole. God knows they're all important. Michele is worth more than all that stuff. Compared to her, stuff is just stuff and stuff can be replaced. "Starting right now this kid needs to get his priorities straight." Oh how foolish a man can be sometimes.

MICHELE'S THOUGHTS

My Ronnie was long gone. He had already gone west to move the livestock to market. Wendell and I left Mid-Michigan with my folks. Dad was driving one wagon and Richie Parker was driving the other. We had two good Morgan mares we'd brought along. Dad had paid a fancy price for them and they were sleek and fast and pretty as a picture. I loved to see their manes flutter in the breeze when they ran.

They had just been bred in the last month or so. Matthew Roberts and I rode them each day, keeping them in shape, plus checking out the sights of Michigan, for this might be our last chance to see what we were leaving behind us. The state of Michigan was fast slipping behind us.

Dakota Territory was now our permanent home with Dad and Mom out here. There would be no need to return to Mid-Michigan again. I was thinking of my Ronnie a lot lately. My whole life was out West and in these two wagons. My man, my life and my everything would be in Dakota Territory very soon. We had new friends that loved us out there. Each day we plodded closer.

This good land we plodded through was filling up with new arrivals. We saw many more farmhouses than when we came this way, three years ago, with the Jenkins, Ronnie and Warren Drake. The Congress bill that opened this land to settlers back in '61 would cause a mad rush after the Civil War was over and men would hurry to stake out a claim.

At Bureau Crossing, on the Illinois River, there were many more houses, but a whole lot less people standing around. These new folks were farmers working the land and making a new life for themselves and their families.

The ferry raft owner remembered our predicament. He said," he prayed for us as the bad element followed after our wagons. Yes, I ate my lunch on the west side and held them up for about forty-five minutes which wasn't much." He was happy to hear we made it without a real bad incident or loss of life. After the gang crossed the river he never saw them again and was he ever glad of that." This person was a God fearing man who was hoping we'd made it and had gotten free of Bloody Bill Anderson's bushwhackers.

We crossed the Mississippi River at Davenport, Iowa making great time moving on the trail Ronnie laid out for us. On this trip we saw houses every couple of miles or so, along the Iowa Trail. Sometimes we set up our camp in someone's yard and used their well water and their outhouses. The farther west we went the fewer houses we saw.

One Sunday, in early June, we took the day off, out in the middle of nowhere, and camped by a fast moving stream. It was a day of rest for both man and beast. I was cooking, dad was working mending harnesses, mom was in the front wagon looking for something and Mr. Parker was watering our horses at the creek. Matt was exploring upstream on horseback. Today Mathew was just kind of taking it easy and fooling around out there somewhere. The boy was a hard worker and Dad gave him the day off.

I heard the shot and then another as dad staggered and dropped to the ground. I saw a red spot on his shirt. As I ran toward him six riders came out of a patch of woods and killed Richard Parker then rushed our camp. The men all wore bandannas over their faces. One man climbed into ma's wagon and pushed her to the ground, as eight other riders rode in from behind us blocking any escape.

It looked like ma broke her leg and pa was hurt bad. The bandits ransacked both wagons taking guns, money and everything of value to them, as I tended dad's gunshot wound. It was a small caliber wound in his side. The wound could have been a whole lot worse than it was.

While working on dad's wound, I saw mom crawling our way. She showed pain on her face as she came on hands and knees. She was laboring hard to reach us. The bullet that hit dad had been fired from a long distance so it didn't blow up inside him, but went straight through. The exit wound was about the same size as the entrance hole. Dad was hurting and the blood flowed profusely from the wound.

When mom arrived, she tried to help by holding the rags tight to the wounds. There were boards and some cloth in the wagon. I grabbed a stack of blankets and two splints then returned to my parents. I took time to set mom's leg, it looked pretty bad. She didn't pass out but her pain was intense. I hoped the break would stay in place once we got it set and bound up with the splints. We needed to get her to a doctor as soon as we got to a town. In fact both my parents needed a doctor.

We had no sentry out, I should have known better than this. I've watched Ronnie enough. We were caught off guard like a bunch of greenhorn Pilgrims. Looking off to the west I saw Matthew Roberts on a hill watching us. I gave him a casual arm wave and he turned his horse and lit out heading west. I knew he was looking for help. That is just the way Matt was.

The young man who stood watching us said, "I saw him ma'am. But I won't say anything. We'll be gone in a little bit anyway. I'm sorry these men did this to your family. I hope your brother finds help up ahead."

Wendell, our baby, was a good kid and slept through it all and seemed quite content. Things were hitting the ground all around the wagons. It was outrageous what they were doing to a lifetime of living. These hoodlums were just throwing precious heirlooms on the ground. The things that were of value to us while not to them. I yelled, "You men take what you want but don't destroy keepsakes."

This is just unreasonable. They didn't care a whit if they destroyed things or not. They were looking for what would sell and any cash we might have. Even more outrageous was the shooting of my dad, the breaking of mom's leg and the killing of Mr. Parker. If Ronnie was here this wouldn't be happening.

Strolling to the wagons I picked up, from the ground, three-Mackinaw coats and a couple Mackinaw blankets. The blankets were for dad and the coats for us three. We had no way of knowing where this little episode was going and dad might go into shock at any time. I hope Matt hurries!

Soon with their dirty work done they saddled our remaining Morgan horse. Their boss mounted her and forced me onto an old bay. Now fear jumped on to me and hung on tight and I couldn't shake it. "Sir, I need to stay here with my dad and ma. They're both hurt bad and pa might die." My plea was to no avail. It fell on deaf ears.

They handed Wendell to me along with some diapers and a blanket and we were on our way out of camp at a frantic pace, heading south. Why did they take me? I was of no use to them or was I? That thought worried me.

As they came to a stop to let the horses blow they took time to tie my feet under the bay to keep me on him. The gelding was a good horse but not like the high stepping Morgans of dad's. They led my mount with a long lead rope. They removed their masks and long face hair covered most of the faces of these rough looking kidnappers. One of the men I knew, yes, it was Mr. Howard. No Ronnie killed him. It had to be his boy, Jerry. His hat along with his missing teeth and that twisted smile gave him away. Over there was Donald Howard. What are they doing out here? I thought they were in the army. Must be they didn't join up after all.

How in the world did the Howard boys get hooked up with this bunch of border trash? 'Well birds of a feather flock together they say'. They found their own kind in these treacherous border ruffians, bad men who would kill at the drop of a hat. Jerry acted whacko to me. 'I never thought he had both oars in the water anyway'. As I watched, men shied away from him.

Either he had them buffaloed or he truly is unstable in all his ways and I guess it would be the latter. He just looks unstable. He had a crazy way about him. The bad part was whenever I looked at him he was a-looking at me and he gives me the heebie-jeebies.

The heavy mackinaw I had belonged to my brother Ransom and it would come in handy when it cools off at night. Wendell could cuddle up under it with me. One of the blankets I will use at night and when I'm nursing Wendell. I was really careful I didn't want to arouse any of these men by my actions. Changing Wendell was a big setback and washing and drying diapers on the run was next to impossible.

The Howard boys fit right in with this gang of misfits, deserters from the Union Army or whoever they were. They looked like outlaws on the run. The leader gave orders and the men jumped to it. He was a strong leader and men did as he said. One man wanted to use me. I was trembling inwardly and this heart of mine beat faster. The boss said, "No, not now" and that settled it, but two nights later he came by and was pestering me.

Jerry shot-gunned him in the back. That did it for me; no one even said a bad word around me after that. Through it all I bit my lip and showed courage on the outside. As Jerry walked away, he told Donald, "she's Greg's girl and we are going to save her for him. His talk was absurd. What kind of thinking is this? Gregory doesn't want me anymore and I don't want him. I could see the good in it for me though. It will keep men away from me as long as Jerry is alive and able to scare them off.

Right now I have what I've always wanted the most wonderful man anywhere, a husband that desires me and loves me. He'll be along soon that much I know and it won't be very long either.

These men laid an ambush back there for those following us. Ronnie wasn't with them or that surprise attack would have been reversed and this outfit would have a few less men riding with them. Ronnie is a dangerous man but not to his friends. He always said, "Jared Jenkins was the fastest man he ever saw, with a revolver, and I believed it until Jared and the boys were talking about him. They agreed Ronnie was faster than anyone they'd ever saw. Ben and Jared have seen some very good men, in their life.

Benjamin said, "Without him even sighting it in, when his handgun comes loose from that leather it automatically is on the target and lead is flying. He never saw anything like it in all his born days. Ronald doesn't even seem to think about it, and that old muzzleloader 50 of his is dead on at any distance. That old rifle fits him to a tee. I'm sure glad we're on the same team."

I remembered back to what that outlaw Doc told Jeff, "a buck popped up and in two jumps he was as dead all get out. If he hadn't seen it he wouldn't have believed it." He told Jeff, "I was still in shock from the noise the deer made and the buck was dead. No way could anyone do that. I think the thing that confused me most was this boy, Ronald, has such a tender heart, he hates killing, but he knows how."

Those men back home, at the ranch, have become very capable men. If they were all here, look out bad dudes. These men I ride with have fear of pursuit for they're pushing the horses from daylight until after dark, like the devil himself was after them. They are racing for the Missouri State line; I guess they think that imaginary lines would save them from trouble.

The young man named Bill Christopher said, "Jerry and Don Howard wanted you along for some reason, something about their paw. Mrs. Holden that is why you're here. Those two are looking to kill your husband. I guess the big reason is they wanted him for some reason. But why I just don't know."

Well, once Ronnie arrives on the scene life will be a bad dream for them. My man is careful and I knew it. We would see signs of his presence long before we ever saw him. He moves like a ghost hidden in a heavy fog bank. He'll be silent and deadly as he pursues this wild bunch.

Jared Jenkins says, "Ronnie fears no one." These men will soon be scrambling to stay alive. My big worry is can Jerry Howard keep the men off me with his threats? As much as I dislike Jerry and Don, they may be my only hope until Ronnie gets here.

I'm still alive and as long as there is life there is hope." My hope is that my man will come soon. Somehow he'll spring me loose. That's my hope and everyone needs hope. Without hope what would I lean on?

These riders kept moving. I had no idea where we were or where we were going. Twice I saw small towns, east of us. We would leave the trail and circle the town. These dyed in the wood outlaws must have a plan but what it could be I had no idea. Is there a reason for what they do, other than greed? You could tell some had been at this business for quite a spell.

I hope Matthew Roberts got help for my folks. I wonder how far it was to the next town. How long it took, would determine if dad lived or died. I saw Matt flying west. It shouldn't have been too long, on that Morgan mare.

My ma knew about gunshot wounds and dad's didn't look as bad as Ronnie's did back in '60. But who knows what happened on the inside. Yes, ma would stop the blood flow while in great pain herself. Dad's ribs were not broken, nicked maybe.

The frantic pace of the outlaws had slowed a bit, the baby was sleeping well and now the drizzly rain came. It rained hard for a while washing our tracks away as we fled south. The mackinaw is all that kept the baby dry. The super tight weave held out the rain, but it weighed a ton with all the water it held.

The trip was hard on us. Six days of pounding leather made my seat end sore. They hoped to put some distance between us and whoever was following us. This would be an enjoyable trip if my man and I were taking it without this riff raff to contend with.

We've slowed considerably and made camp earlier tonight. We left camp a little bit later this morning. They must feel safe now, but I know something they don't. I will not be surprised about anything that happens in the next few days.

I sat with my legs in irons and my back against a big oh tree nursing Wendell. A gust of wind blew drops of water down on us and sparks scooted across the damp ground. It was dark, the flames were dying and very little smoke drifted skyward, as the men slept.

This prisoner in chains took note of the two new guards when they left camp to relieve those that had been on watch. One would keep an eye on our camp and the other would watch our back trail. It seemed to slip being noticed by these lawless men. It was an interesting thing that happened. Was this ole girl the only one that caught it? The rest were in their bedrolls getting some shut eye. One of the night guards didn't return. He was our rear guard.

I was so excited I had to tell someone. Wendell your daddy's here. He's come for us. Didn't I tell you he loves us and would be along shortly? From now on son we must be alert and ready to move at a moment's notice.

I cat napped sleeping lightly and was awakened as the next two guards moved out. What got me excited was another rear night guard, didn't show up either. Later on I watched Jerry Howard come off the hill none the wiser. I laid there for a spell waiting and watching and no one even paid any attention. Two men were missing and not a shot was fired.

I'm glad they're getting caught up on their long lost sleep. They need their rest. Ha! Ha! I'm really encouraged, "Ronnie, is that you out there? Have you really come for us? Who else could it be? Yes, it was Ronnie and he's come for us, Wendell."

Thinking back on all that's happened to us in just three short years of marriage, when will it ever end? Sometimes living is hard out here. Frontier life has changed me a lot. Ronnie taught me some good things to live by. He said, "Pray and then believe God will answer your prayers. Honey, that's called faith. Just trust Him in a situation like this.

Michele honey, in a situation like this talk only when spoken too, so I kept my mouth closed. 'A closed mouth catches no flies' they say. Don't try to change anyone's mind or help out in a delicate situation like this. 'Action is worry's worst enemy'. 'If you don't help yourself no one else will'. 'Where there's a will there's a way.' This is the positive thinking my man has and I've learned it from him.

'If you lie down with a dog you may rise up with fleas' and these positive thoughts are some of the fleas he has given me in the last three years. Fleas of wisdom and a faith so deep I know without a doubt he's coming to spring me free and this time he won't let bygones be bygones. He loves me and I know he will come. That's how I look at my Jesus, like a loving husband wanting to help me out of a tight situation.

In camp someone yelled and a tall man came running in from the rear guard post. The night watch had deserted his post. He left with his horse in the middle of the night. My smile was hidden by the heavy coat that covered me. The leader was upset. As it turned out three men were missing. Joy filled my soul as I listened to the comments bantered back and forth by loud angry men.

That is when I heard it. I heard it before they did for they were busy arguing with each other way to loud. It was a rhythmic drum of a horse moving fast toward the outlaws' horses. Then he yelled and waved his coat around and around. What was he up too? As his horse moved in a flat out run the outlaws' horses' heads came up, turned and in a frantic gallop they vacated the camping area.

Now I know what Ronnie had up his sleeve, and now so did they. A smile touched my lips and I quickly suppressed it. Bad news has come riding in on a fast moving horse and now he was riding away with most of their horses. Ronnie picked up dad's Morgan horse in that bunch. Dad wanted to breed excellent horseflesh like those two Morgan's when he got settled down in the Sioux Falls area.

Side arms' fire exploded as he slipped into the trees a hundred yards away. I caught my breath as a horse went down in the woods. It had no saddle so Ronnie wasn't riding him.

His getaway was clean except for that chestnut lying dead in the woods.

This morning the air was turning blue with the foul language that escaped unholy mouths. My man escaped through the trees with their horses. It would take awhile for them to round up any strays left behind, with the outlaws being on foot.

This bunch was missing quite a few horses, my guess is about eighteen of their nags are gone including the one that was dead. A slew of horseflesh plus three men were missing and insecurity spread throughout the camp. The outlaws paid a fancy price for their carelessness, even I knew you couldn't get careless out on the frontier. I'm enjoying myself in their time of trouble.

Their deal had gone sour and their prospects looked mighty bleak. They didn't know at this time, just how bleak their prospects were. But little ole Michele did! Arguments began working their way into all the conversations.

Two p.m. came and went and finally their leader Black Jack Nelson sent three men to steal some horses from farmers in this area. That left six men in camp. He was dividing his forces and I bet Ronnie was smiling if he knew. Then he divided them even more sending two men up the hill as lookouts. I'm guessing he didn't trust anyone alone, they might run off.

Ronnie must know all this; he must have anticipated that the outlaws needed extra horses. Why else would he run them off? Sure that's why he did it. A good leader would have an idea what the opposition might do next and act accordingly. Ronnie would have more than one plan of action. Like he told me, "There's more than one way to skin a pole cat."

Ronnie knew the first thing they would do was respond to the loss of horseflesh. That's why he ran their horses off in the first place. He is one who thinks things through, if he has time.

Ronnie's good friend Jared Jenkins said, "His instincts are uncanny, it's weird how he knows these things. My Ronnie is not shallow, in my man there is some real deep water, that can be as cold as ice if needs be.

We waited all the rest of the day and the three riders didn't return from their horse stealing expedition. Shortly after dark a single horseman materialized out of the darkness pushing his pony at a frantic gallop. Ha! Ha! More trouble I bet.

Coming into camp he hit the skids, leaving his leather seat in a hurry and with haste he headed for the fire and a hot cup of coffee. He had a wild look about him. He got his coffee, moved into the darkness and stood with his back against a tree.

The gang gathered around asking, "Where's Pete and Henry?"

"Dead maybe, I really don't know. We were over west aways and had liberated half a dozen mares and a couple of geldings and were leaving with them when a barrage of systematic rifle fire came from the hills around us, it rained down on us hot and heavy. I'd say about ten or twelve shots from a man or two, possibly ten men. I'm just not sure how many. If it's two men then they must have a couple of those new fan dangled repeating rifles and they can hit whatever their shooting at.

They killed Henry's dun first. Pete and I fired off several rounds with our side arms a waiting for Henry to get remounted. Then Pete's pony took a slug and went down. By this time Henry was mounted and he joined in the shootout. Then they killed his new horse, where it stood. Both men were down and my pistol was empty so I made tracks out of there and headed here before we were all down in the dirt.

As I high tailed it back here the rifle fire increased. They must have gotten more help. I glanced back at Pete and Henry as I broke clear and they were down behind their dead horses making a fight of it."

The head man said, "Get saddled up we're going to help them out."

"You are, maybe, but not me; whoever they are, those boys don't miss. This time they weren't trying to kill us. If they were we'd all be dead back there. I'm thinking if we stay in this spot here and they get above us we're all goners. Those guys didn't miss a lick." Pete and Henry were forgotten as they fought for their lives out there. I smiled for no help was forth coming from this camp. The thought of sending help was abandon in a hurry.

The two hill guards didn't know what was happening down here and were slow to return to the camp. Amid the loud talk and the pounding of hooves we moved to a higher place, on a wooded hill to the east. The guards on the nearby hill were forgotten. Once they realized something was amiss they followed at full speed as fast as their legs would carry them. They really didn't know why the gang was in such a rush to leave here.

I smiled on the inside, as this outlaw menace now looked more like a bunch of disorganized clowns. This small army has lost its purpose. Their invincibility was now in doubt their forces were shrinking. Only four horses were now left for seven men, all their booty and me. It didn't look like there was much of a chance of them picking up any horses close by either.

The leader was mad and meaner than a cornered wolf. Skepticism and doubt now ruled in this outlaw camp. I don't know how many men are out there. A posse must have joined forces with those that followed us.

Ronnie couldn't produce that much fire power with those old muzzleloaders of his so he must have lots of help out there. If that's true these bushwhackers were in real trouble. I now fear for the safety of Wendell Holden. The posse might not be as careful as Ronnie or Matthew would be in recovering us. I must stay out of the line of fire, if at all possible.

The early morning sun was quite bright and the red sky gave promise of rain later today. By ten a.m. black clouds began to hide the sun. These clouds were low and dark and carried a lot of rain. True to the promise rain came in torrents shortly after the noon day meal.

The young man, named Billy Christopher, gave me his slicker. This rain garment would keep out most of the rain. This older teen had looked out for us when he could. Wendell and I only got damp as the wind came before the storm and blew the rain horizontally to the ground. The force of it stung my face until I covered it to protect myself.

Loneliness crept in under his slicker and hung tightly to me and I couldn't shake it loose. Wendell gave me some comfort, with his baby play.

The young man, Billy Christopher, had looked out for us as we'd moved away from the trail up north, even as I waved to Matt at our campsite. Why was he mixed up in this awful mess? I think this boy has a healthy respect for women. He always refers to me as ma'am.

As I sat there in misery a shot broke the stillness. A mustang hit the dirt and men scrambled for cover. I was encouraged somewhat. I was still on someone's mind. The shot came from a hilltop about five hundred yards away. The distance was long but the shot was true to its mark. It was Ronnie; he could shoot from that distance.

Without a single doubt in my mind that was my man and by his shot I was comforted. Of all the people I know only he could make that shot, but that didn't sound like his muzzleloader. It had a crisper, sharper sound to it.

By 1:30 the rain had ceased and the wind died to nothing. About two p.m. a man came off the hill with a white flag. It was Ronnie. He came to the bottom of this hill and waited as the outlaw leader moved downhill to talk. Ronnie was mud covered with a month's growth of whiskers. I listened intently to what was said. So I could hear him he spoke loudly, "we've got you surrounded and there's no way out. Give up or die. There's no other way about it."

The outlaw chief answered, "we ain't out of this game yet and we ain't giving up so don't count your chickens until they are hatched. "

Ronnie said, "as far as we know you haven't killed anyone yet. Now is a good time to give up. You're on the path to know-where-ville and bucking impossible odds. We have you surrounded and there's no escape from this hill, so give up."

"Wendell, did you hear that? Daddy just said, grandma and grandpa are still alive. No one's dead. Oh thank you, Jesus! Mom and dad are still alive. I'm sure he knows about the man that was shot in the back, by Jerry, and without a doubt he knows poor Rich Parker is dead".

"Listen stranger, we ain't going to give up so do what you have too."

"Okay then. One last thing if anything happens to the lady or her kid, death will come to each and every one of you. That's my guarantee to you and your friends. No matter how long it takes. I'll ride you down and kill every last one of you, if you somehow break free."

"Listen Mister, tomorrow is promised to no one, not me and least of all you or that posse you brought with ya."

"Sir, if you touch her, death will come home to roost on you and your carcass will feed the turkey buzzards tomorrow."

I looked down at Wendell and said, "Sonny boy, your dad is a fighter and soon these boys will either be dead or wish they were. Little one, their reign of terror has just come to an end. You just watch how your dad takes care of this wild bunch."

When I caught Billy's eye, with my finger I said, come here. He nodded. Slowly and in a roundabout manner he made his way toward our tree. "Billy Christopher, if you protect Wendell and me when the shooting starts, I'll see to it that you make it out of here alive. That was my husband and he will kill every last one on this hill except my baby and me.

In that conversation he said so. Listen son, my Ronnie doesn't lie. So you're as good as dead unless I help you. You've been good to me and looked out for us. Bill, I don't believe you belong with this bunch. So stay close to me and listen. Please don't die out here with this bunch of cutthroats. Bill, I'm giving you this one last chance to save yourself and make it out of here alive."

His boyish face looked strained. He gave no sign of what he would do. He turned away, although he didn't go far. Finding a small depression, in the ground, he kicked dirt and leaves out of it making it a little deeper and settled onto the damp ground, about twenty feet away and stared at me. Several minutes slipped by and another horse went down into a heap. They were down to two horses and soon it would be zero.

I watched, Jerry and Don Howard edged closer to the last two mounts, and then sprang into action. Moving fast they made a run for the last two geldings. Jerry's shotgun sounded first and the gang leader and his right hand man died as both Jerry and Don opened up on them with their shotguns. Mounting up Jerry headed downhill with Don in hot pursuit, away from Ronnie's position. In a flat out run they sent lots of lead in all directions as they raced away, bent low over their horses necks and their sharp spurs found horseflesh to be imbedded in.

Billy took this all in then looked at me and slightly nodded his head, yes. The outlaw head count, on this hill, was down to three. The count changed quickly in the lasts ten minutes, except for Billy. The rest would soon be pushing up daisies.

OLD AQUAINTANCE

Matthew, Barnard and I sat watching three riders leave their camp looking for horses for the gang and their escape. The clouds had covered the moon as they pushed their nags to the east. It was pitch black out and they disappeared into the dark night. A Whipper-will sang from a tree nearby and the insects were chirping up a storm.

We worked quickly and followed those boys knowing the direction but not able to see them because of a big ole black cloud. The moon slowly got free of the cloud and let its light shine down on us. The three riders were clean out of sight but their tracks were deep in the mud and easy to see.

After traveling several miles off in the distance we saw the lights of a homesteader's cabin in a small wood. The outlaws were talking with a farmer about something when all of a sudden the three riders threw down on him and pointed their firearms in his face. One of the dirty rotten scoundrels whacked the poor man along side of his head with his long barrel revolver. The man dropped like a sack of potatoes and lay still on the ground.

The three of us settled into our chosen position a short ways back along their trail. It wasn't very long and here they come in the bright moonlight with several horses in tow. They were headed back toward their camp and their comrades in arms.

Mr. Clayborn was using one of my Henry's and we waited until they came even with us. My Henry spoke a language they understood and it spoke loud and clear on this moonlit night. In the moonlight I saw a horse go down. They acted surprised and confused and soon another one of their horses was down thrashing in the muddy dirt. They looked frantic as they tried to leave pouring revolver lead all over the place hoping to keep us from shooting at them. I watched the horses that they just picked up and they were heading back home. They were forgotten by the men that had rustled them.

Their small arms fire stabbed into the darkness sometimes close to my hiding spot. We had good cover and weren't worried all that much. Their pistol fire was from horseback and was not accurate and none came really close. By golly we were ready to carry it to them.

The first rider to go down was now remounted on another horse. He had no saddle but he was ready to leave. That's when I touched off my Henry again and down he went one more time. He stayed down behind his horse as I pumped shot after shot into his dead mount. He stayed down this time using his mount as a barricade to hide and to shoot behind.

The last remaining rider emptied his revolver in my direction then left this scene of confusion as fast as he could go. His horse's hoof beats got fainter as he rushed away from the killing field. When it quieted down I yelled down to the two men below, "do you want to give up; this is your last chance."

Their cursing came fast and furious. I waited a bit and they tried to sneak off as another dark cloud covered the moon.

Clayborn Barnard, who is on the other hill, killed one man and the second dove back behind his dead horse and was sucking sod using the horse for cover. The last outlaw yelled, "Who's out there? Who are you guys anyway? Why are you shooting at us? Are ya a posse?"

Clayborn yelled out from the hillside, "no we are not the posse; we're the ones who have come to give you a dose of lead poison. Sir, we are your worst enemy. Hang on, soon it will all be over for you and you won't have any more worries, ever. I guarantee it."

That's a voice I should know. I knew it from somewhere, but where? The posse did say he was my old friend. But who is he? I didn't need to think of that now. Other things were occupying my tired mind; mostly my thoughts were of my family.

We must end this now, before that wild bunch comes back or this dude lights out of here. "Mister, you must surrender now or we will have to shoot you out of there. Come out now with your hands up or face the consequences of your actions." As I talked to him I pushed ammo into the receiver of my rifle.

The outlaw hesitated, so I hollered down to him, "See that rock by your dead horse's head? About three inches in diameter, the light colored one?" He didn't answer. I sighted my Henry in on it, in the moonlight, and touched it off. The strike of the bullet hit it on center.

Waiting long enough for it to sink in, I yelled again. "In one minute the lead will be hitting you. So make up your mind, young man. Give up or fight. In a moment it will be like a summer hailstorm down there and it will come hot and heavy. If you want to see tomorrow stand up now."

"Don't shoot I give up. He tossed his rifle away and stood by his dead horse with both hands high. As I started down the hill, he picked up his friend's rifle that he had leaned against his dead horse. The first thing I was aware of was him pitching forward, into the short grass, and the report of my other Henry. The dying man lay shaking in the long grass. For an instant I was madder than hops for I'd given him my word, until I realized the man had a rifle in his hands. I'd been a sitting duck. Mr. Barnard, without a doubt, had saved my life. Who was this distinguished gentleman that came out of nowhere to help us? Talking to myself, I said, Ron, you had better start being more cautious if you want to see Wendell grow up or feel hugs from your wife again."

Both bushwhackers lay still where they hit the ground from a slug high up in the back. We left them where they lay. We were now pursuing the last horse thief northward, as he raced in the direction of the outlaws' camp. He was in an almighty big hurry as he rode out of sight. We took our time and made our way back to their camping area.

As we rode I slipped my mount in next to Claiborne's horse. "Sir, I want to thank you for the much needed help. Your dress says you're city, while your actions say you know the West and its wild ways. How long have you been out here? The sheriff said, 'you were an old friend of mine. At twenty-one I'm not all that old. Do I know you from somewhere? When you yelled down at the bushwhackers, the voice sounded familiar to me. Mr. Barnard, who are you? That voice of yours, I just can't get a handle on it."

"Well Ron, I knew you would catch on sooner or later. I just hoped it wouldn't be this soon."

"Doc?"

"Ya, How you been Ronald?"

"Not to good lately. I've got lots a troubles as you already know."

"Was there ever a time when you didn't have trouble a chasing you. Ronald, we'll get her back for you. We will get this little problem ironed out and it'll be real soon. The time has come to finish it once and for all."

"I know, it has gone on long enough!"

"Is that ranch of yours doing okay, I sure hope so? Looks to me like trouble is following you around wherever you go like you had a leash on it."

"Doc, why are you using the goofy name and why the long beard?"

He laughed, "Ronald, the goofy name is the name ma gave me; the beard that's a different story. I hoped it would disguise me for a while longer. After you let me escape the second time, I decided the third time I might not be so lucky. When I left you on that old nag I headed for the tall timbers of the East. I went home and finished school and was out here looking for you. I was in Williamsburg when Matthew rode in and when I heard the name Holden, Michele Holden I took notice.

I asked Matt some questions and found out you were married to her. I was sure your last name was Drake, Holden or Jenkins, so when I heard the name, Holden, I was all ears.

I joined the sheriff's posse to give a hand and I've been giving a hand ever since. No way could I just sit there and twiddle my thumbs. Ronald, you saved my backside and I really do appreciate you springing me loose from Bloody Bill Anderson's bunch.

He's still out there doing his dirty work down in Missouri and over in Kansas, killing and all that goes along with it. Thinking back on it, if your wife's family hadn't had trouble I'm not sure I could have ever found you out here. The West is a mighty big place, Ronald.

This ole boy went home to finish his education and now he wants to help you build that town of yours. I can teach school and my paw was a doctor. He taught me lots and lots and this kid took many classes in medicine. I can run a business and keep its books and do a whole lot more and I want to be a force for good and not evil anymore.

When I first met you back in sixty you were a breath of fresh air to me. But I didn't see it at first. Ron, you're a game rooster and I liked you right off. In my travels I've turned over a new leaf. I've found Jesus and I'm going to try living for Him. This is one area you might help me to live right. Maybe help me iron out some of my problems."

"I've got to admit it Doc, for once it's good to see ya. Before I couldn't take any stock in your cock and bull stories. Now it's different." I wanted to believe what he said, while I knew how slick and smooth he could be. Words came easy from his mouth. I must be extra careful, this could all be just a big line of crap he is forking out to me. I'd better not let all his earnest sounding yarns blind me to the truth. His slick tongue can sway a person real easy. But this time though his actions speak louder than his words. Ronald, my boy, you had better think straight and don't let him pull the wool over your eyes with a bunch of phony baloney.

At this stage of the game I need all the help I could get. If worst comes to worst I can handle him later. For now I must use him. If I had my druthers, I'd druther not but I can't be particular in this deadly game we are in.

When we finished Matthew asked, "How many more of the kidnappers are there?"

"Matt, I'd say seven or eight men and about four horses. I'm not for sure on the head count, but that's close." While making a hasty retreat back to the place where the bushwhackers were hold up, I searched for a plan of action where we wouldn't have to shoot anyone.

I guess I must talk first and try a bluff or lie whichever you want to call it. I pondered what I could say to get Michele and Wendell back safely. Her safety was first and foremost in my mind. We must not do anything foolhardy and put her in danger.

Later in the afternoon, this ole dude slipped down off the hill with a long white bandage tied to my rifle barrel. It was time to talk turkey with these thugs. So I made my way down the steep incline, of this hill, and headed for the hill across the small ravine. I hope they honor this flag of truce or I could be in some serious trouble.

A man that looked like the leader came most of the way down to meet me. Another man with a rifle came half way down and we talked. I laid out my terms and a warning was given.

Watching me real close he backed part way up the hill and then turned and quickly retreated all the way to the top. I returned to my hill and got ready for trouble. I then took some time and fired across the small valley killing a couple of horses. This would cause them to give my words some thought.

After waiting about fifteen minutes for something to happen, all of a sudden there was a commotion on their hill. Someone started cussing a blue streak as a shotgun sounded, then another. Then hoof beats descended the far side of the hill. Their two remaining horses left their camp in a wild scramble to get free. Bit by bit their numbers were dwindling down to an insignificant few.

Matt opened up on them with his muzzle loading rifle and then his shotgun. Then all was quiet again. I hoped Matthew's aim was true and that he had hit someone in their quick exit. Their overall number was getting down to a manageable amount.

Matt was a fair shot but running horses makes a tough target in this kind of light. He didn't have that much time to shoot at them or that much experience in killing folks. I guess I'm glad of that. I hope he never has to cut down on a man again. I guess those killers of men believed that we have a big posse out here or otherwise they would try to put us where we would be pushing up a bunch of daisies.

I studied that hill for a long while. No one moved around up there at all, all was still. Then their heads and limbs moved and I counted three men and my family. There could be more but I doubted it. Two outlaws had abandoned the hill, killing two others in their mad dash for freedom.

This game must be finished before too long. Two shots came my way spaced out about twenty seconds apart. I counted one Mississippi, two Mississippi and three Mississippi. That's when Doc and Matt opened up and the shooting started in earnest.

A man lifted his head to shoot so I took a head shot and he died where he lay. It confused me when a gang member, on the hill, shot one of the bushwhackers. Why? That didn't make much sense to me. Then I saw something that puzzled me even more. My wife walked over and sat in front of that man and it looked like he handed her his weapon. Then my wife stood up and waved to us to come on up.

As I looked over there, Michele pointed the pistol and fired at a man that had already been wounded. He was trying to get off a shot and the force of her slug moved him sideways.

I wished she didn't have to do that. But Michele always did what had to be done no matter what. Down that hill I went in a flat out run and ascended her hill with my rifle at the ready. Michele was waiting for me as I came on the run. I eyed the disarmed man she seemed to be protecting. Even as we embraced my mind wasn't completely on our reunion until Doc crested the hill and took charge of the last outlaw.

This back woods Michigander was happy to hold her and mighty glad it was over. The anxiety and the fainting, that went on at our ranch when I returned in the winter of '60, were not present today. This wife of mine has grown up a wee bit since we came west.

Now all the anguish that I had kept nailed down broke free and I smothered her with kisses and hugs. She seemed quite composed. But this ole boy was a nervous wreck. Shaking all over, but this wife of mine comforted me this time, while I was fighting for composure. What a wife I had! Wendell raised a fuss. He was between us and just had to see what was going on. He smiled as Michele opened her coat for him to see and my eyes noticed her unbuttoned dress.

"Darling, did they hurt or molest you?"

"No Dear. When the shooting started I was nursing Wendell."

Oh how I loved this dear sweet lady of mine, so I hugged her again and couldn't let go, so I pulled her closer to me.

Matthew Roberts came slowly up the hill. The wear and tear of the last couple weeks had taken it out of him and it showed. I was proud of my young friend. He stuck in there come heck or high water and I won't forget it. Not ever! You know the saying 'A friend in need is a friend indeed.' I thought on that and I had to include Doc as a friend indeed.

When we had finished our hellos she told us of "Billy Christopher and his commitment to protect her and Wendell if a showdown came. Throughout the ordeal he kind of looked out for the two of us in spite of Jerry's threats for all to stay away from me."

I gave Billy an opportunity to haul his freight out of here, without a horse, or tag along with us. He decided to stay and ride with us. He said he had nowhere else to go.

Michele got my attention, "Honey, Jerry and Donald Howard were here, they were the two that fled to the southwest on horseback."

"Mr. Holden, I got to tell you something about those Howard boys."

"OK Billy Christopher, what is it? Spill it."

"Sir, be on your guard. That Jerry Howard has sworn to kill you if he gets a chance. That's all he talked about was how he would smash you. The main reason we took Michele with us is because he knew you would follow. He will be looking for you as soon as he gets a chance to. Sir that man is nuttier than a Christmas fruit cake.

Mr. Ronald, That guy is crazy and his hate for you has filled him up with evil. He has a terrible hate for you for some reason. Something about how you killed his pa, Mr. Holden, I don't think he will ever give up until you are dead or he is."

"What Billy Christopher said is true. Honey, I can still feel the cold hate filled stare coming from those narrow squinty eyes. He has a hate for you and your family and I am part of your family now. What saved me was he was saving me for Greg. How crazy is that kind of thinking."

"Michele, Honey, those two crazy men live a charmed life but they can't run forever. Somewhere up ahead there's a necktie party a waiting for them."

I introduced my woman to Doctor Clayborn Barnard, not Doc. Clay Barns. She liked this elegant man right away. His help in undoing this outlaw gang meant a lot in her eyes.

With Michele free we decided to let the Howard boys go for now. She was so worried about her folks. Plus our food supply had near run out. We needed a new supply and soon.

Michele made sure we took back all the things the bushwhackers had taken from her folk's wagon. These things were important to her, things that were a part of her life, back in Michigan. They were some of the few ties she has with her past. These dead men had lots and lots of money and lots of neat things they had stolen from people along the frontier.

Things I'm sure people treasured before they lost them to these border ruffians.

First we slipped over to the little ranch that we were at last night to pick up some food for our trip north. Later we would pick up our already captured prisoners and some more grub.

Jerry and Donald had already visited the ranch ahead of us stealing four fresh mounts and food. They shot and wounded a man about fifty. His four boys were hot on their trail.

Their Paw said, "Them boys of mine will get them for sure! They're as good as dead, by golly! They ain't a going to rob anyone else or kill anyone else ever! My boys will get them! You just wait and see, those crooks, are as good as dead. Those boys of mine are like bloodhounds after a fox. They will run them to ground sooner or later."

His wife and two young ladies were still working on the dad. Michele gave them a hand, along with Doc Clayborn. You could see the wear and tear on Michele. Her long months on the trail had worn her to a frazzle.

The man's wound was a flesh wound and wasn't all that serious, bad enough though. The older gentleman had an ashen look about him. Michele put another blanket over him so he wouldn't go into shock. They had no antiseptic salve so my wife took warm strained honey and poured it into the wound, which is good. The pure honey kills germs and sealed off the wound.

With Mr. Johnson's sons out hunting the men, Michele, Wendell and I got to use their bedroom to sleep in. I really love this magnificent wife of mine. Oh what a night we had! True love is grand and my wife had missed me a whole bunch and it showed!

The next morning, after sleeping in, we headed north. The Johnson's said, "It was just over a hundred and thirty miles up to Williamsburg where grandma and grandpa were recuperating. It would take us longer to return then it did to come down here on the fly.

Michele asked Bill Christopher, "Who shot my pa and Mr. Parker?"

"Ma'am it was Jerry Howard who shot your paw. Willie Marsh shot the other fellow." Willy said of Jerry, "that man is sick in the head. Everyone was half afraid of him even the boss.

No one ever talked with him. He sure enough saved Miss Michele's bacon back there. The men were afraid to go anywhere near Miss Michele even if Jerry wasn't around.

"Ma'am, Jerry hates your husband's guts with a passion. Make sure Ronald doesn't forget that! Something about him killing Jerry's paw, or something, it is the one thing those two boys' talked about all the time. If they don't kill your husband here they will hunt until they find him. They want to kill Mr. Holden for what he did to him and his family. Jerry will be looking for Mr. Holden as long as he lives. Mr. Holden, make sure you watch your back. That'll be his target, it always is."

We picked up our three prisoners, the horses, and some food and headed north toward Williamsburg, Iowa. It was a long hard ride back to the stage road, then four more miles on into town. Michele couldn't hold back. She wanted to know how her folks were making out. We saddled two rather fresh horses and she and I scooted on into town ahead of the rest. Matt, Bill and Doc. would bring the prisoners and the horseflesh with them when they came.

HEADED HOME

Our long journey was a trying trip into Williamsburg. I walked our horses on over to the livery stable leaving Michele and Wendell on the hotel porch so they could see grandma and grandpa. They left me to care for the tired horses that we were riding. I didn't mind at all, this wore out ole cowman stood and watched her amble inside and disappear into the interior.

When Doc, Matthew and Billy Christopher brought the prisoners into the gray bar hotel, I eased on over to the sheriff's office to tell him about the two gang members that escaped and helped deliver the three men we had captured earlier. The lawman was glad to see us and the outlaws and hear that the gang of murdering marauders had been destroyed. The county sheriff was sick of all the crime and killing in his jurisdiction. He asked me if we could stick around and maybe help get the rest of those gang behind bars. Before I said no he already knew the answer.

"He said he was sorry he couldn't ride all the way to completion on this dastardly crime. He told me later, "Mr. Holden, I sure enough hated to give up after what that rotten slime did to your wife and family. They probably did the same thing to others up and down the Mississippi River for the last couple of years. I got back here and thought if it was my family would this ole boy ride to completion or give up at the county line?"

Communications are getting better and one of these days there would be no place for dirty rotten scum like this to hide or operate. It couldn't come too soon to suit me. I heard tell that maybe the state of Iowa would soon have a state police force and that could make it rougher on lawbreakers. Mr. Holden, things are getting better since the Indian uprising that took place last year. People were demanding it of the Government.

We heard tell that the Yankee boys on July 4th won a big victory over in Pennsylvania at a place called Gettysburg. The Yanks whipped oh Johnnie Rebs pretty bad that day. We heard tell that maybe the war would be over very soon, I sure hope so. It can't be soon enough to suit me. I got kin folks down there and Americans were dying on both sides of that war, and for what?" So the rich rebellious cotton growers could have control of the cotton trade and the enormous profits that they made from the cotton crops.

We left his office and moved along Main Street. I saw Michele in the upstairs hotel window. She was watching for me as I trudged up Main Street. I saw her wave so this kid picked up the pace a bit and climbed the steps three at a time.

By the smell of things I was ripe and needed a bath and some quiet time with my wife and boy. All the rest could wait until tomorrow. I've got to get close to Michele and that little boy of mine. I needed her loving hands on me.

This worrying and fretting about my family, on the trail, changed my whole outlook on my life. I had to keep them safe, no matter what. What would have happened if we hadn't invested time and some cattle on the hungry Santee Sioux? Would we all be dead now? Chances are we could have suffered loss and this thing with my family; I was so cocksure of myself. What a fool I was? It will not ever happen again, my family is what really matters to me, not the land, not the cows. My family and friends, then things come in a late third.

At the top of the stairs I saw Michele standing in the doorway waiting for me with the lamp light behind her. When I reached her I grabbed her, held her close, swung her around a couple of times and did a little dance. Then hugged and loved on her right there in the hallway for about five minutes.

At first she just kissed and hugged me a bit and then tried to break loose to no avail. But this kid didn't let her go and slipped in close and let her love come flowing out to me and I matched all she did. How can I love her more? My arms had my life in them and no way will I ever let go. It just goes to show ya, we aren't the boss unless they let us be.

As we entered the room together, Mr. Stevens was sitting up. He has been walking up and down Main St. for nearly a week. He had cabin fever and he was ready to hit the trail west, although the ladies in his life said," no." So I guess we won't be leaving today or tomorrow.

Mr. Stevens was insistent that the first of next week we would make wagon tracks on the trail west and pull our freight on out of here. He looked determined and eager to be on the trail and that look did demand he be listened to.

Matthew Roberts was growing up fast. He came up to talk, with us, and he told the folks of his adventure. To me it looked like the West suited him to a tee. He insisted he stay with the horses and sleep in the wagons. That boy found no arguments from us.

Doc. Barns or Clayborn Barnard, whoever he is, wants to go with us to our ranch and help us grow a town. I guess he is truly sorry for all his shenanigans in the past. Now he wants to make it right. He talks often of his mother and family back East.

Yes, he will be traveling with us too. If he wants to live right we can sure use him in Sioux Falls. A doctor and educator, he could be an asset to any community in the years to come. The West needed men like Doctor Clayborn Barnard.

He proved himself over and over again in the years to come. He started a school just as Wendell turned six. In years to come he helped start a Christian College and delivered babies and fixed up sick people along the way. Doc was a busy man in the Sioux Falls area. Oh what an asset he became in our little settlement at Sioux Falls.

That week in Williamsburg was a pleasant week for Michele and me. But I will be glad to get on down the road toward home and see our friends at the home place.

The very next day the rain came hard to Williamsburg for four long days with no let up and there was mud everywhere. The main street of Williamsburg had hub deep mud. The latter part of the second week we harnessed up the big horses and got ready to pull our fright on out of here. Those big Belgians threw their weight into their collars and mud flew as those big wheels started to roll on out of town.

Twelve smaller horses threw globs of mud as Matt and Billy Christopher pushed them big oh nags westward. My wife and I drove the first big wagon and Doc the other one. These ole hay burners were ready to have at it so we let them. We gave them their heads and made fair time, in that soft mud.

Matt rode a strawberry roan and she was a willing worker. Matt really knew horseflesh. In the years to come he raised many prize horses on a ranch near ours. The horses we had taken we gave to him. It was a start for his cattle outfit.

This padded wagon seat felt good for a change. I had set a saddle so long it felt like it was growing to my backside. Michele took a look and she said she couldn't see it.

The warm July wind was pushing white puffy clouds across God's pretty blue painted background. The ground dried up quickly and soon dust hitched a ride on the hot summer wind, drifting where the wind took it.

The prairie was devoid of human life. We saw many antelope and deer. Prairie dogs had their own cities out here. As we traveled west a warbler sang a beautiful song perched on a weed above the grass. If a man stopped to look around wild life was everywhere.

Sioux Falls lay ahead and those big teams came rip snorting up the Main Street of our burned out town. Not a dwelling was left standing higher than the foundations. Just black coals and ashes left over from the Sioux's handiwork.

Darkness was closing in as we pulled into the Jenkins' family dooryard. They greeted us with pointed guns, then hellos, howdy's and hugs. Little Jared was growing like a weed. He was a good-looking kid, one day little Jared and Wendell would be close like Jared Jenkins and I were. They would become lifelong friends and grow up together in this country. After a bit we rattled our hocks out of there and headed on home. The tired overworked horses were happy to be home as we urged them on. The bunkhouse and our home emptied out as we hailed the house and rolled into the dooryard.

Warren Drake, Benjamin, Pat and Wesley Read came out to welcome us home. After the first hellos and introductions to Mom and Dad Stevens, Doc Barnard, Matthew Roberts and Billy Christopher, all set about pulling harnesses from the horses and putting the livestock away.

We took what we needed into the house. Doc, Matt and Billy moved into the bunkhouse and got acquainted with the men that lived on this ranch. The men looked at Doctor Barnard in a whole different way after they heard the story of his help in recovering Mrs. Holden.

Home at last; thank God Almighty we're home for good! Dakota Territory truly was home for me like no other place had ever been. A warm peace settled down around me and I felt at ease with my surroundings and contented with my loving wife. The next day we left Wendell with grandma Stevens and rode out to look over our livestock. Truly life is good once again for both of us. For the next few days we just lolly-gagged around the buildings, just playing the lazy bums, getting rested and recuperating from our long ordeal. I had been on the go ever since I left Michigan and was ready to settle down for a spell.

Benjamin Simeon told me, "They'd moved the Santee Sioux farther west last spring. Most had nothing to do with the uprising, but all suffered for the actions of a few. That is the way of things. A few cause trouble and all suffer.

The Reads, Stevens, Jenkins and my family were nearly the only family groups left in the immediate area, many were murdered, and some were trickling back to this area very slowly. Others that made it out alive just wouldn't return until they were sure the Sioux wouldn't go on the warpath again and put their lives in danger.

For one reason or another the Federal Government had moved the Santee Sioux further west. But many whites just didn't trust the situation as long as the war continued in the South. Folks felt war might erupt here again at any time. Most were waiting for that war in the East to end. They figured that would free up a lot of troops to protect the farmers. At this time most weren't so sure the army could keep the Sioux on the reservation and at the same time fight the war in the East. Could it happen again with some of the other Sioux tribes further west?

Over in Nebraska the Sioux and some Cheyenne were kicking up their heels and raising a fuss. The southern sympathizers were telling them that if they helped the South by causing trouble for the Union Army they would return the land to them when they won the war. Young bucks were already out raiding and killing settlers with the hope of freedom to urge them on.

Some hardy souls had returned to their farms in Minnesota but only a few in our area so far. It was still Sioux land in their eyes. Right after the Sioux were defeated, some settlers returned to salvage what they could and moved everything that was any good to a safer place. Many that returned were wives without husbands.

Many husbands had died back East in the War of the Rebellion. Most women wouldn't return without a man. We purchased many cows and steers from those that wanted no part of this area. Their only thought was to flee to the East.

My hired man Benjamin said, any women that stayed out here, in the West, without the protection of their men folks were, what should I say, foolish. But even stupider, if I can use those words, were the men who left good women out here alone. A lot of good families died last summer because men were fighting to preserve the Union and neglected to protect their own families. In my book a man isn't worth a plug nickel if he refuses to provide for his family and that means safety also."

Doc said, "I agree. Men that would leave their wives alone on The Great Western Prairie are darn fools. I don't understand their thinking; they should know better than that. Their judgment is questionable. The Bible says, 'a man that doesn't provide for his family is worse than an infidel' and doesn't rate very high in my book either."

In a paper we read on August 21, 1863. Bill Quantrill, Bloody Bill Anderson and four hundred men rode into

Lawrence, Kansas and murdered one hundred fifty defenseless citizens and then rode out. Anderson and Quantrill got their names in the history books that day. Thank God, Bloody Bill Anderson was later killed by Federal troops. We sure didn't need men like that running wild out here after the war was over.

Warren Drake's business of rock cutting and polishing was good. He is shipping the red rock downstream by steamboat when they could get through. He hired Billy Christopher (the young outlaw) to help him. Those two worked quite a bit together. Warren Drake is looking for a man to mind his spred, so he can devote more time to the "Drake Works" business. He is planning on building a large building right on the river's edge just south of the lower falls, on the west side, so the boats can navigate right up to the plant.

I always knew the boy had it in him to be anything he wanted to be. When he needed help from time to time his friends would lend him a hand. Everyone wanted him to do well for it would help make the town grow. We pitched in and gave him a hand, when he needed one.

After the civil war was over, all his time would be devoted to the Drake Works of Sioux Falls. He would become wealthy cutting and polishing petrified wood from Arizona and shipping his works everywhere. His work was known around the world as "The Drake Polishing Works of Sioux Falls." His stone cutting and polishing works grew and grew to several buildings on the west side of the Sioux River. Later he sent for his sister, Dorothy and her husband Jay Husted, as the business started to grow and he started to really prosper.

A hundred and fifty years later you could still see the Drake's stone works buildings and his masonry stone work throughout the Sioux Falls area. Many buildings were built in the falls area using this beautiful red rock. With his money he tied up all the land in the area that had the red rock sticking up out of the ground and Warren made millions.

Later I would buy and take over Warren's ranch. He had no time to be a rancher any more. The Drake Works was more than a full time job for him and his family. After the war in the year of 1867, Sioux Falls, the city, came back to life again. That same year, Doc started a school here and taught my kids and many more in this area to read, write and do math. Doc also had a hand in establishing two colleges in this area and he was known far and wide for his work.

He was also known for his medical practice, a man with a big vision and lots of integrity. Doc. was trustworthy and honest in all his dealings all the rest of his life. Doc. turned out to be a real good man of God.

Many shady businessmen came into our area that had deceit written all over them, trying to take the rubes from back East for a big chunk of change. Most were found out and sent packing.

The one thing that came from that war that was good besides freeing the blacks and reuniting the Union, was the cattle prices stayed high until 1871. That year the bottom fell out of things and times got rough for cattlemen and farmers. We were lucky for we had made lots and lots of money in the sixties and were prepared for a time when the prices would fall through the floor. We had an inkling that it might happen as farmers back East got their herds built up and flooded the market.

My good friend Jared Jenkins who came out here on a shoe string is well off and his family is doing things besides ranching. His four young boys are a handful for Debbie. Jared's parents had moved out here and have farms close by.

Matthew Roberts and Benjamin Simeon ranched together and moved into land speculation and breeding Kentucky horses on the side. They bought and subdivided large parcels, of land into small farms, and made a fortune in land sales. Benjamin looked up his family, back East, and put the family members into businesses out this way.

Matthew Roberts who helped me get my family back, married a sweet young gal from Mid-Michigan and has two good looking kids. Doc Bernard located and married a sweet lady from this area that lost her husband in the war. She had a kid but that didn't bother Doc any.

Fred and Lilly Miller never returned to Sioux Falls. Fred wrote us and said, "He'd opened up a store down in St. Joe, Missouri and they were doing quite well. St. Joe became a jumping off place for people going further west. Fred was the Mayor of St. Joe, Missouri for one term. He never ran again. In a letter he told me he didn't like politics, plus he had a business to run and needed to mind the store.

Lilly was much happier in St. Louis where many people lived and she was looked up to as a leading citizen. They loved us and thanked us over and over for our vital help in a time of great stress and thanked us time and again for our friendship in those distressing years at Sioux Falls.

In Dakota Territory Michele's folks farmed and raised cows and horses on three hundred acres. Their spread was just east of ours. Their son Ransom came west in 1866 after the big war. He was missing a foot. He had spent six months at Andersonville Prison, a nasty hole in southern Georgia, until it was closed down by the Confederacy.

Ransom would break down and cry when he talked of that place. He was part of the Michigan twenty-third Brigade. It was one tough outfit and Ransom was one brave man. You should see all those medals he kept in a tin box on his dresser. President Johnson pinned several medals on him, at his discharge, in D. C. in 1866.

My good friend Benjamin Simeon died in 1886, and left his share of the spread and business to Matt. Matthew Roberts over time had become like a son to Benjamin. His funeral was a sight to see. People came from everywhere to pay their respects to a man's man. To tell you the truth, I missed him a whole lot.

JARED JENKINS

The prices on beef stayed high and we all made plenty of money for the next six years after Ronald and his family returned home from Michigan. In the year of 1869, rustlers were a real problem for us around eastern Dakota. We were losing way too many cows, so we took time to get organized.

Each day a half a dozen of us were on call to try to get our stock back if the rustlers hit us. The day we were hit six of us took off in hot pursuit. In our crew there was Matthew, Bill Christopher, Ronald Holden my good friends and Jeff, Kevin and I. We moved southwest on the trail of a couple of rustlers. They were moving about twenty-five head of livestock southwest away from Sioux Falls. The rustlers, in the last years or so, had become really bold in their business and our profits had diminished. Ronald Holden seemed to be the hardest hit in this area.

They didn't seem to be trying to hide their tracks in any way. This made me a little bit edgy as we crossed the Vermilion

River and stopped on a knoll. In the distance we could see the livestock grazing on a hillside. Something wasn't quite right; I could feel it so I halted the group and pulled out my binoculars to glass the livestock and any riders that might be in sight.

The first thing I heard was Ronald groan, Huh, OHOOOO, I had heard something hit Ronald hard and it drove him head first from his saddle to the ground. Oh the pain, you could see it on his face as he struggled with it!

Ronald didn't lose consciousness even for an instant. The other four guys took off like a big bird in a windstorm heading back toward the Vermillion River. The river is the direction that the shot came from. Man oh man those four men just flew across the open ground. They used spurs to get the most out of their horses as they covered a lot of ground in just a short amount of time. Rifle and revolver firing made all kinds of noise as they rushed toward pucker brush along the river banks.

They forgot about poor Ronald for just a fleeting moment as he lay on the ground where he had came to rest. Poor ole Ronald was down in the dirt. Right off the bat I realized that he had his six-gun in his hand with the hammer cocked and ready for action. I heard him fighting the pain. He looked at me and said "Ohooo, man. I hurt bad, Jared!" You could see his eyes wanted to close. It was a shotgun blast that took Ron out of the saddle and did it ever hurt him.

I heard him say. "Ohooo, God it hurts!" Very soon the guys were back from the river. He said, "did we know the guys who were stealing our beef Jared?"

Bill Christopher said, "Ronald, it was Jerry and Donald Howard. Ronald, it looks like they finally located you, after all this time. They hadn't given up looking for you and they haven't landed in jail for all their shady business."

"Did they say anything to ya?" Ohooo, man do I hurt!"

"Ron, they didn't have time to say much. These ole Henrys put several periods in their hides. They won't be getting away this time Ron. Those boys are deader than last year's beef steaks and they ain't going anywhere. Ronald, with all that lead in them they are weighted down and can't move a lick."

"Jared. Where's Kevin did he get hurt?"

"No Ronald, Kevin is heading for help. He is flying east right now to find Doc Bernard. How do you feel, my friend? I'm sorry Ron, that's a stupid question."

Ronald tried to smile. "Not so good, my friend. Jared, would you tell my wife that I've always loved her. Tell her that it is only her that I desire."

"No Ron. That's your job, you tell her yourself. I ain't a messenger boy for you or anyone else. So you tell her yourself when you see her."

We laid him out on the ground on his bedroll, stripped off his gun belt and shirt and tore his shirt up and made bandages. We worked on the wounds trying to get the blood flow stopped, and we did somewhat but there were too many holes in his back. With all the blood it made the wounds look bad, real bad. We left him where he lay, on his bed roll, and covered him with our blankets. We had no way to move him anyway.

If the truth be known I'm really surprised he was still conscious or alive. We'd covered him up and built a fire to help keep him warm, before he went into shock. I'm worried about him. He was hit pretty hard with that shotgun blast, of double 0 buckshot, from the Howard boys.

Ronald asked, "How does it look, Jared?"

"Not so good Ron but remember I'm not a doctor. Eight pellets hit you in the back. It's like being shot eight times, and no way can that be good." As we worked on those wounds Ron talked of his wife and kids. How sorry he was for leaving them. He wanted to see Michele one more time if he could. He struggled to stay alert and keep his eyes open and with effort he did pretty well. It looked like he was willing himself to live so he could see Michele one more time.

"You know Jared; she's so far away and probably doesn't even know I'm hurt. I could be dead and she wouldn't even know it." In a loud voice, Ronald yelled out, "Michele, I need you!" Then he slumped back on his bedroll and said, "Hurry, Michele, please hurry."

Somehow and I don't know why, there was no blood coming from his mouth. Somehow all those 00 buckshot seemed to have missed his lungs. A lung wound would have been fatal out here.

Then very softly he said, "Michele, Michele, where are you honey? I'm trying to stay alert and alive until you get here. Michele, please hurry." This battle for life went on with him trying to hold on, but he was losing ground. You could see it. His life was seeping out of him and soaking in the ground around him.

By mid-afternoon off in the distance we could see a crowd of people hustling our way, moving through the afternoon haze and the shimmering heat of the western prairie. Ronald's great pain was eating him up and he cried out to that loving God of his. He asked many times to live until Michele got there. "Michele, where are you, Honey?"

They made good time in their race toward us. We could see them a long ways off heading our way, pushing their horses, for all they were worth, to get here in time. Doctor Clayborn Barnard arrived first. He was way out ahead of the rest. Driving reckless he laid his whip to the horse, pushing him hard and fast.

As he pulled up, his horse was covered with a thick white lather and its four legs were spread out wide. The horse was sucking hard to get his breath back and stay upright. Doc had worked him for all he was worth to get here and save his ole friend.

Doc ran the last one hundred feet with two black bags in his hands. He stopped and waited a moment and said, "Hi, Ron, what are you up too?"

Ronald summoned up a pain filled smile for Doc Clayborn and said, "Can't you see I'm on a brake now don't bother me. Doc, is this a house call? How much do you charge now? Ooooo, I'm hurting bad doc. My good friend I'm really glad you're here."

Doc said, "I know Ron so shut up and let me see what's holding you down."

This mild bickering was how Ron and Doc always said hello.

"It's all that lead I'm saving for you Doc." He smiled but it didn't look much like a smile. "Doc I got to have some help getting them out. They're weighting me down. OHOOOO, Lord help me."

"I know, Ron." As the doctor knelt down he lifted the blankets that were covering Ronald and his face changed. It got serious and he glanced at me with a sad look on his face. As Doc Barnard fingered Ron Holden's ugly looking wounds a cry of pain took him away from his excruciating pain. Then Doc inspected his whole body and after that he looked at me and slowly shook his head. He took some kind of a gismo from his black bag and he probed each wound and extracted four small lead balls. There were four holes that still had lead down deep inside.

The Doc was working on the next wound when Michele and Debbie rode up with some of the guys from the ranches. Michele looked worried as she climbed down from their buggy. As she drew near the doctor met her, a short distance from Ronald. She whispered for our ears only, "Doc Barnard, how's my Ronnie doing?"

He took a moment and said in low tones, "not so good he's looking pretty bad Mrs. Holden. It'll take time to tell. Ma'am, Mr. Holden is a tough nut and a fighter. But I've not seen anyone with a worse wound that made it. I will do all I can for him, Mrs. Holden I think you know that."

"I know you will, Doctor Barnard." She eased away from him and moved up close and took hold of her man's hand and said, "Ronnie, I think you'll do okay. We've fought longer odds and did just fine. Honey, I love you and need you to fight this thing. Sweetie pie, the kids are coming. Darling, fight this for us. I have faith in you and so does God. Come on now Ronnie Holden, you fight this thing, you hear me? Fight hard!"

I saw Ron's hand squeeze hers and she responded by sliding her hand up and down his forearm and saying many things to him. Man-oh-man, I could feel the love in the air as I watched this transpire on this lonely hill. Her loving touch made his fingers move ever so slightly. As I took this in I saw big drops of water flow from her blue eyes as she wept silently. This lady had a lot of love for her man. I've seen it so many times.

I glanced over at Debbie, my wife, and she was taking it hard. Michele wouldn't let herself cry out loud for Ronald's sake as she held tight to his hand. A couple times it was close, but she kept control as Doctor Barnard did his thing.

Ron looked really bad to me. His breath came hard and ragged and his face was gray, the color of ashes from a dead campfire. It wasn't long and twenty-five friends stood in silence and watched this heart wrenching drama play out here on the ground before us. A drama of life and death. To my way of thinking, it was more a drama of death. Daylight had disappeared over the horizon and still they worked on him.

All the long night through, Ronald fought for his life as Doc Barnard dug for pierces of lead and Mrs. Holden worked on him cleaning and fixing his wounds, as best they could. The thing that hurt me down to the marrow of my bones was Michele, as she talked to him for hours about intimate things from their life together. It looked like she was forcing him to remember the good times in their lives and it seemed to be working.

She talked of funny things, sad things, things that only the two of them knew but today she didn't care who heard what she said. She was giving Ronald some hope, something to live for, for a remembrance of their life together. Oh how that lady loved him. I believe she would lay down her life for him. This lady wasn't going anywhere and leave him alone.

Throughout the long night in his unconscious state, he called out to her several times and she responded with love. He thinks the bushwhackers still have her and that was six years ago. He also told her how much he loved her. The pain is overwhelming him and I could feel his pain as he yelled for her several times that night. I'm pretty sure Michele could feel it too.

This man was my closest friend. "Lord, please work a miracle here." My good friend, Ronald Holden, reached out his hand to us with help way back there at the Illinois River Crossing and kept that hand extended to everyone. This man made a real difference in other people's lives.

All those times when people needed help, like the Millers, when we first arrived in Sioux Falls or Doc Barnard, Warren Drake, Ben or the Sioux when they were hungry. There are so many that he took time to help. He often poured out his life to people up and down the frontier. This area of the country was richer because of him. It's sad how the good always die young.

I looked over at Debbie, my wonderful wife, and she was looking at me. Debbie was weeping softly. Oh how lucky I am. She slowly moved over to my side and took my hand. We were remembering great moments in our lives. Ron's God blesses everyone that comes in contact with him and Michele. It's been that way with us. Ron serves a compassionate God who rewards those that love and worship Him.

A big wagon was coming. When it arrived eight year old Wendell jumped down and raced to his mother and just stared at his dad. Not a dry eye could I see anywhere. People truly loved this kind generous man.

Off in the distance a lone horseman came flying across the prairie with a string of fine Kentucky bred horseflesh. The horses looked pretty much spent. It was Ronald's rich friend Warren Drake. He came sliding to a stop and ran on up the hill. He came and stood with Michele and Debbie.

Ronald Holden really loved this young man and the feelings were mutual. Warren Drake wouldn't have been able to start his business without Ron's help. Ronald got Warren Drake's herd started that first year out here and loaned him money when he needed tools for his red rock business.

Most everyone Ron had touched, in Sioux Falls, was here or coming. People the Holden's had poured out their lives to, close friends. Everyone in this area loved and respected them both for all they had done. It truly looked like Ronald was pouring his life's blood out on the ground here today.

As Doctor Barnard would remove a chunk of lead, he would try to stop the bleeding and put antiseptic salve in the wounds, then move to the next wound and try to remove another chunk of lead. He had seven lead balls snaked out of Ron's back. Doc Barnard looked at me and said, "Jared, the one thing Ron has going for him is the pellet wounds aren't all that deep. It seems to me they should have penetrated deeper into his body. Thank God for small miracles." The heavy bleeding was down to a watery red stuff seeping from every wound.

I asked Doctor Clayborn, "Will he make it?"

"I don't think so; there are way too many wounds. They all did some damage down deep inside. How much I don't know. He could still be bleeding on the inside. Just pray hard and hope for the best."

Michele's got her face in mine and was it ever red with anger. She grabbed Doc by the shirt front and me by the arms and shoved us away from Ronald. She kept pushing and when we were a good distance from Ron she turned on us. "You two hear me good! You will not talk negatively in front of Ronnie! He will not hear a bad report from anyone do you hear me? Do you understand? You will encourage him at all times and not tear down his faith.

Come on you guys, be a friend to him. Help me out here." Michele sure enough got our attention right off the bat. I'd never saw her this riled up before. She ushered us back to Ron's side and smiled. That is the only time I ever saw her cross or maybe I should say angry, no, mad is a better word for it and I don't want to see her like that again! Not at me anyway!

She was right of course. We were careless. We had no business saying how bad he was so he could hear it. The subconscious mind remembers the things that are said. Michele set the two of us straight pretty darn fast and ole Jared won't be forgetting what she said, not very soon that's for sure.

Doctor Barnard was administering laudanum again and in a little while Ronald began to rest easier. In his fight for life he was breathing long labored breaths. He would moan as he slept. I can't imagine all the pain he's suffering. I remember hurting with a big sliver in my hand and a little toothache. How bad must he be hurting with all those wounds, pretty darn bad was my guess with eight good size holes in his back?

The large wagon that the children came out here in was covered and very slowly we worked it up the hill close to Ronald and loaded him into it. It had two cotton mattresses and on top of that a feather tick. It was a soft almost shock proof bed to lay him on.

His loving wife still had a grip on his hand and spoke kind loving words to him. Ron responded to her caring positive conversation. I really wonder what would have happened if she hadn't been here to lend a helping hand, on this dad blame hill? Doc Barns warned everyone not to ask questions, but talk positive things to Ron. Talk about the good times you all had in the past. He will respond to that.

Warren Drake had wired Sioux City, (formally Sioux Town) for an army surgeon, from the Civil War, before he left Sioux Falls, and the doctor was a coming.

You should have seen the effort Ronald's friends made on his behalf. In 1869, many hard working men from this area were building a road across the prairie back to Sioux Falls. Just for him twenty-seven teams of horses were making a roadway smooth for him to ride on.

Many men, boys and women from the area with shovels and picks worked long hours. The construction went on from daylight to dark. As a stretch of prairie became smooth they moved Ron eastward across it and in three days he was home in his own bed. The house was a whole lot better than that hilltop.

That work was not in vain, for many years it was known as the Ronald Holden Road and many folks traveled it to and from town. At home Ron awoke for a spell and talked to several people. No one dared ask him how he felt. Michele was protecting her man and all watched what they said.

Back at his ranch house, he was spiking a high fever and the battle for his life went on. They kept fighting that high fever and Michele worked many long hours to save his life. It was nip and tuck but he was responding to her love. Doc Clayborn, the doctor from Sioux City, Michele, Debbie, (my wife,) and I were the only full time visitors in his house.

Many folks just stayed away. At this point in time his kids and Michele's parents, the Stevens, usually peeked in once or twice a day to say "hi" and see how he was a doing in his battle for life. It wasn't often that they found him conscious and able to say anything.

The wounds weren't the only problem. Ronald stopped breathing, for a spell, on three different occasions. His wife would yell at him and shake him hard. She would say to him, "Ronnie, stop that and get to breathing! You will not give up on me. I need you here with me," and he'd started breathing again. I guess he didn't dare do otherwise.

The struggle went on most every day and we didn't see much progress in him. The thing that gave us a smidgen of hope is he was still alive at the end of each day. From that point in time on she wouldn't leave his bedside for any reason except to use the outhouse. When he was hot she would cool him down with cold water, from the well, laying cool rags all over his body and laid next to him when he was cold and she slept with him when she was dead tired.

As he struggled for his life she began to look haggard. We tried to give her more breaks, but no dice. People came and stayed nights to help out. Michele would let them stay and help her some. With the extra help she could now sleep nights as others came in and did the nursing for her, but she didn't stray very far from his bedside.

The surgeon doctor that came in from Sioux City told us it would be a miracle if he pulled through the gunshot wounds. But that guy didn't know these two. She held on tight to him and wouldn't let him go. This doctor from Sioux City left us, leaving directions, although he was not encouraged about Ron's chances of making it. Doc Clayborn Barnard had done much to help his chances, out there on that lonely hilltop, working diligently to save him from death. I know Ron quite well and this lovely family of his. He was the bond that held us all together back when we needed it. Michele wouldn't let him die! He just didn't dare!

My Ronnie is a fighter and he doesn't know quit. It's been over a month and he was just now sitting propped up and almost two more months before he could walk with help. Ronnie had lost so much weight he looked like a stick man walking around. That man was just a shell of the man I married. It was hard to see him this way. No matter what we did we couldn't put any meat on those bones of his.

He kidded about his chicken legs and how they looked like a wishbones a walking. His cheeks were hollow looking. That man of mine looked more like a corpse walking around the dooryard, then a man. Ronnie often referred to himself as a skinny old lizard and it broke me up. Thank God his sense of humor was still there, through all his pain and suffering. The pain was his constant companion and stayed with him wherever he went.

Our friends around Sioux Falls didn't forget him. Someone came to help and talk with him most every day. The folks around town probably had a schedule they went by. Before this Ronnie was a hard worker, like back in Michigan he worked really hard to get in shape, but this time around, it was to no avail.

He tried to make it happen but this time he just couldn't make it work. He worked hard at it but he just couldn't get in shape. No matter what he did or what he tried it just didn't work. He worked as long as he could each day but it took him over six months before he could sit a horse and only for a short spell. He needed help to just get in the saddle. He couldn't get down by himself and then he needed help to get back into the house.

The doctors were astonished that he was alive at all, if you could call this living. He should be dead and buried but here he is still moving around. When you saw him he looked like death walking. I worried that he might catch a cold or something in his run down condition and we would lose him.

Oh Lord, did that ever worry me. Ronald was my crutch that I leaned on even though he didn't know it. His soul and spirit was alive and well, but in the flesh I worry about Ronnie. He isn't getting any better. Ronnie's no fool. He knows it. What strange turns life can take sometimes. He was a man so vibrant and full of life and now the grave is laying traps for him. I try not to show it but, "oh dear Lord, I worry so much about him."

We kneeled praying one day in the parlor and we asked God for a sign of what we could do to help others. As I helped Ronnie get up, from his knees, a stranger came a knocking at the front door. A young man needed some money, to fix a broken axle on his wagon. He was out of money and needed some financial help.

We didn't know him from Adam. Although we offered to give him the money, that he needed, he wouldn't take it that way. We ended up buying ourselves a milk goat. Can you imagine that? A nanny goat on a cattle ranch! We laughed at the deal that was made. What would we do with a goat on a cattle ranch anyway. It didn't make much sense to us but the deal was made. The real laugh came when we realized the goat needed to be milked twice every day. Milk a goat twice a day and he couldn't even dress himself.

My Ronnie took the responsibility of the goat on his shoulders and worked hard milking his nanny night and morning. Many times he wanted to give up and get rid of the goat for it was way too much for him to handle. We fed the milk to the cats and our old hound dog and our cattle dog. We had so much left over that he started drinking it himself.

He didn't care much for goat's milk at first. We wondered if God truly sent us the goat or what. Within a month he started gaining weight and in three months strength came into his hands and arms and then his legs. He started filling out all over. Slowly, over the course of nine months he was born anew. He got most of his strength back and soon after that he was his old self again, riding the horses around the ranch. I often stood at the kitchen door watching him work the horses.

This is more than I will ever understand. Many times I felt like giving up on him but I hung on tight and didn't let him go. How do you figure a thing like that? I know this much I thank my Savior for his loving help in our time of need

It's funny sometimes how things work out and what strange turns life can take. Who was that guy that brought us the goat? The Bible says, "Be not forgetful to entertain strangers: For sometimes we entertain angels unawares." Hebrews 13:2.

The End

After I retire from General Motors I told my wife that I'd like to try my hand at writing books about the old west around the time of the civil war. My wife was pleasantly surprised as she began to read what I had written and now is a big help and a great fan of what I write.

In the beginning it was hard to find a publishing company that was interested in even looking at my manuscripts and I became discourage and gave up writing for a while. But I'm one of those guys that never says quit and doesn't give up easily. People that had read my manuscripts kept encouraging me to continual. A lady that was a professional reader read my first book and called me many times and kept encouraging and me to stay with it.

I now have books in print and folks seem to like what they read. Friends and relations have given me some high complements and I'm encouraged again. You may find my books on line. I'm sure you will enjoy the exciting saga that I have on paper.

BOOKS IN PRINT BY BRUCE DRAKE

Book one	Lakin
Book two	Blue River
Book three	Shorty
Book Four	English
Book Five	Sioux Falls

Printed in the United States
By Bookmasters